MERCY

JANE FLAGELLO

ZIG ZAG PRESS LLC.

ISBN-13: 978-0-9961237-7-8

Editing by Demon for Details
Cover design by WickedSmartDesigns.com
Interior formatting by Author E.M.S.

Zig Zag Press LLC
Virginia Beach, VA
2018

Published in the United States of America

OTHER BOOKS BY JANE FLAGELLO

Fiction

Gotcha!

Bamboozled

Complicity

Non-Fiction

The Change Intelligence Factor: Mastering the Promise of Extra-Ordinary

PROLOGUE

It was three in the morning when the huge semi-trailer screeched to a stop at the back door of Puppies on Parade, one of the few remaining pet store chains in the country.

"Finally," said Pete Tremble, a twentysomething crusader for whatever social cause caught his attention—or rather, the attention of the latest girl he wanted to bed. He rested the digital camera's telephoto lens on the dashboard of the black minivan to stabilize it and snapped several shots.

"What's the driver doing?" Ashley Langford asked while fumbling for her binoculars.

"Looks like he's talking on his cell."

Just then the back door of Puppies on Parade opened and two men emerged, approaching the back of the truck. A third person, a woman, went to the truck's cab and rapped on the passenger side door. The driver and his passenger jumped down from the cab and walked to the back of the truck.

"Keep shooting," said Ashley. "We need all the proof we can get to make our case." She put the binoculars to her eyes. "I know her. That's Kelly Logan, the store manager." Ashley leaned forward, resting her elbows on the dashboard. "Damn it. This is so frustrating. I wish I was in the other van so I could see better."

"Relax. We didn't know which way the truck would pull into the alley. Have a little faith, Ash. Zach and Tori will get great pictures."

"Unless they're screwing around."

"Ashley, babe." Pete's Southern drawl was low and slow. "You and Tori have been working hard to catch them in the act delivering the puppies. She won't let you down."

Ashley shot him a hopeful look, then picked up her cell. "I'm so glad we downloaded the push-to-talk app this afternoon." She pressed the talk button. "Tori, can you see what's happening at your end?"

"Just a minute." There was a long pause. "They opened the back. It's packed with cages, as usual. Here, Zach, take the camera. Zoom in and get a picture of that. Ashley, they're starting to pull out cages. Get ready on your end. They're coming around."

Pete put his eye to the viewfinder. "Thank God for telephoto lenses." He could see one man carrying a cage with what looked to be sleeping puppies. "They must have drugged the pups, because there are at least three in that first cage and none are moving."

"Oh, the poor little things." Ashley stifled her tears. "When I went into the store today and gave the manager my sob story about losing Penelope and desperately wanting a new Carin terrier puppy, she said they were getting a delivery from her two favorite local breeders later today."

"Local breeders, my ass," said Pete. "A local breeder wouldn't need to use a semi."

"Yeah, and local breeders don't drug their puppies. Having Tori get a job at the store was brilliant. We've got the manager on tape lying to customers about where they get their puppies, and tonight's photos will be the icing on the cake. We're going get these assholes good."

"Two more cages coming out." Tori's voice crackled through the phone's speaker. "Looks like two labs in one of them."

"There," pointed Ashley. "Get that shot. At least these two are awake and moving."

"Part of me wants to run out there and beat the shit out of these guys," said Pete.

"Loosen your man bun, Pete," said Ashley. "You're outnumbered, and there are more where these two came from. We have to cut puppy mills off at the source. Use laws and fines to make it too expensive to do business. That's the only way to end it."

"But legislation is slow and takes time. You've already spent a semester on this. Meanwhile how many puppies have to die? How many dogs must be neglected and abused?"

Ashley threw her arms around Pete's neck and kissed his cheek while he kept the camera's shutter clicking. "That's why I love you. You care about the puppies as much as I do."

Pete smiled and ran his eyes up and down Ashley, his boner growing. He loved how she looked, how her nipples poked out under her powder blue tank top tucked into skin-tight jeans. A surge of heat pulsed in his pants. His thoughts wandered to the after-surveillance party he had planned for himself and Ashley Langford, Miss Homecoming Queen, college student, and live-in nanny.

"Looks like they're done unloading," said Zach. "By my count, that's five cages. Couldn't tell how many actual puppies."

"Kelly told me to prepare for ten new arrivals today when I was at work," said Tori. "And yes, before you ask, I did record what she said oh my phone."

"Good job. And I'll confirm in a few hours," said Ashley. "I plan to be there at ten, when they open."

They watched while the store people retreated through the back door, the driver got behind the wheel, and his companion locked the back of the truck. With a cough, the engine came to life. The helper climbed into the cab and the gears screeched when the driver shifted into first. Slowly, the semi pulled down the alley, turned the corner, and disappeared.

"Tori, pull over here," said Ashley.

"On our way."

Within minutes the whistleblowers convened in the alley for a whispered debrief.

"The whole operation took less than fifteen minutes," said Ashley. "Wish we could have heard what they were saying."

"Next time," said Zach. "I think I know where I can get my hands on a parabolic mic."

"And you couldn't bring it this time?" asked Tori, giving him a punch in the arm.

"Lighten up," said Zach, rubbing his arm. "You just told me to bring my good camera and telephoto lens. How was I supposed to know what we were going to use it for? I'm not a mind reader."

"Okay, guys. Back to my apartment," said Tori, "so we can see what we got."

Three hours later, the pink glow of dawn's morning light peeked through a low cloud cover. Empty pizza boxes and beer bottles covered the kitchen counter in Tori's small apartment, and Zach and Pete were sound asleep, sprawled on separate ends of a gray leather sectional.

"Now what?" she asked Ashley. "Who's going to believe us? We're just a couple of community college students."

"The photos speak for themselves," said Ashley. "And we've got the manager on tape, thanks to you."

"True, but neither of us have the power to push the envelope here. To get the state government to listen to us, we need someone with... What's the word? Gravitas. Credentials. Someone who can command the attention of politicians and speak for the puppies."

"And I know exactly who. Remember, I work for a veterinarian, Dr. Darby."

"She'd be awesome." Tori's eyes brightened. "Do you think she'll do it? It took forever to get the appointment with the delegate guy we want to sponsor our bill. Wouldn't it piss him off if we bring someone else to the meeting?"

"A chance we'll have to take. And we'll be there too. We'll give her what we've collected so far, lay out the case, and provide backup. Power in numbers. I think these photos may be what we need to gain her support."

"When will you ask her?"

"When I bring Brianna home Sunday night from her Brownie troop camping trip. Darby will be so happy to see her, she'll be more receptive to helping us."

"You? Camping? I just don't see it."

"The things we do for love...and a great job."

CHAPTER 1

The wailing siren came closer and closer. Darby stopped dumping mulch into the flower bed and stood up, shading her eyes and looking down the road. Shaking away loose strands of hair fluttering across her cheeks, she saw the sheriff's car turn into her driveway, fishtail, and kick up dust. Gravel spewed out from under its tires when it came to a screeching halt feet away from her.

"Darby, get your bag," shouted Sheriff's Deputy Tommy Everett from the back seat. "You're needed."

His partner, Buddy Jenkins, shifted into reverse and turned the car around as Darby took all three porch steps in one graceful leap. She hesitated momentarily when she opened the screen door, missing its former squeak, thinking of Brody's visits and all the things he fixed around her house while he was there. Then she raced inside, grabbed her medical bag, and ran out, pausing only to lock the door.

"What's happened?" Her hand went to the passenger side door, but her eyes went to Tommy in the back seat.

Then she saw what all the fuss was about, huddled in a blanket in Tommy's arms. Big brown eyes peered out from between the folds of the yellow blanket, fearful, but pleading for help. Letting go of the door handle, Darby raced around the car, opened the door behind Buddy, and slid in next to Tommy.

"She's hurt real bad." Tommy's eyes watered. "Some guy heard whimpering when he went to the bathroom behind the 7/11 and went to look. Saw her. Said she growled when he tried to touch her. We were stopping for coffee when he flagged us down."

"Not exactly normal police duties. How'd you manage to pick her up if the other guy couldn't?" A menacing growl and bared teeth told Darby to keep her hands to herself.

"Got me." He shrugged his shoulders. "Just got down on my belly. Scooted up to her real slow, talking nice and soft and low."

"You're a natural-born dog whisperer."

"Dog whisperer, my ass. He bribed her," said Buddy from behind the wheel.

"Held out some of the Swiss cheese from my sandwich and she took it. Saw she was hurt. Buddy handed me the blanket we keep in the trunk of the car and I threw it over her head and scooped her up."

"Tried to call Dennis first," said Buddy, making a right out of the driveway, knowing his way to Darby's clinic. "He was whining at the bowling alley last night about being on call this weekend, but there was no answer at his place, so we came straight here to get you."

"Good thing you did." Darby's eyes were glued to the hurt pup. "Not sure why Dennis didn't answer. Maybe he's at church and turned his phone off. No matter. I'll take good care of her."

"Know you will, Doc." Buddy nodded when his eyes met hers in the rearview mirror.

In less than ten minutes, they pulled into the parking lot at Darby's clinic. She jumped out and unlocked the door while Buddy helped Tommy ease out of the back seat, trying hard not to jostle his precious cargo.

Darby quickly led them into the first treatment room and slid a cushy mat onto the exam table, where Tommy slowly and gently laid the dog down.

Darby took a steadying breath and whispered something.

"You say something, Doc?" asked Buddy.

"Praying. Yo-day-ah tza-deek ne-fesh b'hem-toh. Sort of like saying grace." She knew the simple prayer centered her, prepared her for whatever unknown lay ahead.

"What's it mean?"

"It's Hebrew. '*A righteous person knows the soul of his animal.*'" She took another deep breath. "Let's see what we've got." Her stomach clenched, fearing the worst, but she hummed softly as she slowly lifted the edge of the yellow blanket. A sob caught in her throat. "She's just a puppy."

She looked across the table at Tommy. Smart, strong, tough-as-nails Tommy, fighting back tears.

"A dachshund," said Buddy, who had backed up and leaned against the far wall. "Love these little hot dogs. My mom used to have one. Named him Frank."

"Frank?" asked Tommy.

"Yep. Frank, as in frankfurter, one of my favorite things to eat."

"Anything that doesn't move fast is one of your favorite things to eat."

"Don't see you skipping any meals, Tommy, old man. A few more pounds and you'll bust out of your dress blues for sure."

"Look who's talking, Buddy boy. Your shirt buttons are about ready to pop, and your gut looks like you swallowed your bowling ball rather than tossing it down the lane."

"Guys, please."

"Yes, ma'am." Tommy cleared his throat. "What do you think happened to her?"

"Too soon to tell. Best guess is she got hit by a car, run over somehow, and crawled to where you found her. Beyond that, I don't want to speculate."

"Maybe you should just put her out of her misery," said Buddy.

"Not when there's a chance I can save her. She's a puppy. Has a long life ahead of her."

"A life of medical bills. Maybe that's why whoever owns her dumped her," said Buddy. "Who's gonna want to adopt her, knowing what might lie ahead expense-wise? You're tilting at windmills, Darby. You can't save them all."

"Buddy Jenkins, hush up. Didn't you ever hear the starfish story?"

"Huh?"

"I heard it years ago at a motivational breakout session during college. It touched me deeply."

"It must have," said Tommy, "for you to remember it."

"It's part of an essay by Loren Eiseley. To make a long story short, a man walking on the beach after a storm sees it's littered with starfish. In the distance he sees a boy who he thinks is dancing, but when he gets closer, he sees the boy is really tossing starfish back into the ocean, one by one. The man tells the boy his efforts won't matter, because so many starfish had washed up, and he couldn't save them all before the heat of the sun killed them. As the boy tossed another starfish into the ocean, he responded that his actions mattered to that one."

She glanced at Buddy to check his reaction, but he quickly looked away.

"I've heard a few different versions, but the moral is always the same, and that story is part of the reason I became a vet. Because, like the little boy, I try to save as many as I possibly can. And I can save this one."

"Let's hope so." Tommy gently stroked the puppy's head. "At least she's letting me touch her."

"Stay with her while I call Tracy. I'm going to need another pair of hands for whatever surgery I decide to do."

"Take your time. The dog whisperer is here." Tommy scratched behind the pup's ears.

Several hours later, Darby sat on her front porch swing waiting for Ashley and Brianna to get back from their camping trip. It had been a difficult and painful day caring for the terribly injured puppy, who was now resting comfortably in a kennel in her bedroom. There were more surgeries to come, and it would be a while before she would know whether her hard work would be enough to save the puppy's life.

Life. Every life was precious, and the need to feel safe and secure universal. So much of her energy these days was focused on ensuring her five-year-old daughter Brianna felt safe and secure. Darby didn't want her to suffer any mommy separation anxiety as a result of the few days last fall when Darby was kidnapped, so she encouraged Brianna to go on overnight events. Camping with Ashley and her Brownie troop was a well-supervised fun time.

She stood when she saw Ashley's car turn into the driveway. Her stomach fluttered. And then Brianna flew into her arms.

"Oh, Mommy, Susie got sick all over the back seat of the bus. And Mrs. Jones had to stop and clean up the mess." Brianna giggled. "It was really stinky, so we all moved to the front."

Darby looked at Ashley.

"Well, I'm sure glad your troop leader was ready for any emergency. She lives the Brownie motto of be prepared."

"That's the Boy Scouts," whispered Ashley.

"Same thing."

"Yes, Mommy. And we sang songs all the rest of the way home."

"And you had a good time, didn't you?" Ashley smiled down at Brianna. "Why don't you tell your mom about the frog you caught?"

"You should have seen it. It was big and green and jumped out of my hands when I didn't hold it tight."

"Catching frogs is something I used to do when I was your age. Sounds like you had fun."

"Yes. Can I go again next time?"

"Of course you can." Darby felt herself relax. "Come on, let's go inside and get some dinner."

Darby took Brianna's hand. "I made meatballs for sandwiches, so there's plenty, Ashley."

"I'm going to beg off and take a long, hot shower," said Ashley. "Could we talk a bit later? I have something I want to run by you."

"Anything wrong?"

"No, nothing's wrong. Just a project I've been working on with some friends from class. I want to get your thoughts."

It was after nine when Ashley and Darby finally met in the kitchen.

"She's finally asleep," said Darby. "Took a while. She was still pretty wound up."

"She had a good time. And I think Susie got sick from bouncing around in the back of the bus," said Ashley. "No one else got sick, so I suspect it was a mix of the bouncing and all the candy her mother packed for her."

"Here, have a glass of wine." Darby handed Ashely a glass of red and gestured to the living room. "It's a bit too nippy to sit outside, so I've got the fireplace lit to take the chill off."

"I've been outside for two days with ten screaming little girls. I am more than ready for the creature comforts of a hot shower, a glass of wine, a warm living room, a cuddly blanket, and a little peace and quiet."

"I can appreciate where you're coming from. Knowing you were there did help me feel better about Brianna going. I'd worry regardless, but I worried a little less because I knew you'd watch out for her."

"She's my little angel." Ashley snuggled into the sofa and sipped her wine.

"What did you want to talk about?"

"I need your help. As you know, I've been taking a few online law classes at Regent, and I've decided to become a lawyer."

"That's great. I'm so glad you found something that excites you."

"There's one class project that helped me decide to study law. We had to pick a social issue or challenge, something we think is wrong, and delve into what policies and laws need to change to improve the situation. I chose puppy mills."

"Ugh. They should be outlawed, and everyone who runs one, strung up by his or her—"

"Exactly. And I've been doing research and field work on how to make that happen, or at least bring it closer to reality in Virginia."

"I'm impressed, Ashley. What do you need from me?"

"Your voice." She could see confusion cross Darby's face. "I've—well we, my friend Tori and I—have an appointment with Bradford Cummings on Wednesday afternoon. He's the delegate from the Eastern Shore, and we hope he'll agree to sponsor the bill we want to introduce to the General Assembly."

"What does the bill say?"

"It's simple, really. Our bill says counties can choose to control the source of puppies for sale in pet stores. Then each county can decide who is a reputable breeder and who is really a corporate breeding operation. Translation—a puppy mill."

"I can support that initiative."

"Thought you might." Ashley smiled and took a big breath. "Now the favor. Will you come with us to our appointment? You're a vet. You have the reputation and prestige we don't. Your voice would add power to our argument. We'd be there to speak also, and back you up."

"What made you pick puppy mills, if you don't mind me asking?"

"I walked into a pet store in Virginia Beach last Christmas to get a new toy for Tori's dog and saw all these puppies in cages. I started talking to the manager about them, asking questions about where they came from. And I got this awful feeling she was lying to me. Then I kept seeing the Humane Society and ASPCA ads, with such sad puppy faces, asking for sixty cents a day to save a dog. What can I say? It pissed me off that so many animals were being mistreated. When this assignment came up for my class, one thing led to another. I was hooked."

"It's a good hook, Ashley, and I'm very proud of you. Where do you need me, and what time?"

"It's this Wednesday, 11 a.m., at our delegate's local office."

"I'll have Josie rearrange my Wednesday schedule first thing in the morning."

"You're always so supportive of whatever I want to do. Can't imagine where I'd be right now if my own family was even half as supportive."

"Ancient history, Ashley. Can't change the past. Let it go. I'm glad I can be here for you."

"I'm going to call Tori and let her know you're on board. Then I think I'll hit the sheets. I'm pooped. Those little girls wore me out."

"Good night. Sleep well."

CHAPTER 2

Tommy and Buddy walked into Darby's clinic bright and early Monday morning and laid a box of donuts on the counter.

"How's the pup doing?" asked Tommy.

"Good."

Tommy read something in her facial expression and tone. "What's wrong?"

"In addition to a severely fractured leg..." She paused and took a breath. "There were bite marks, like she'd been attacked by another dog. And some appear older than others. Like it happened more than once. I'm thinking she was used as a bait dog and left for dead."

"A bait dog?" asked Buddy, grabbing a chocolate-covered donut from the box.

"You know, to bait a dog someone is training for the dog fighting ring."

"I know what it is, Darby." Buddy wiped chocolate icing off his mouth with his finger and licked it. "Just surprised you're jumping to that conclusion."

She reached into her credenza and handed Buddy a napkin. "With the marks on her body, it isn't much of a jump. What else can explain the number of bite marks, or the fact I can tell they happened over time?" Darby noticed Buddy's reluctance to make eye contact. "But she has fight inside her, wants to live, is fighting to live. I've been giving her pain meds every six hours. Even took her home with me last night. Named her Mercy."

"Cute. I like it," said Tommy. He helped himself to a glazed donut.

"There's coffee in the back, guys. Help yourselves."

"She gonna make it?" asked Tommy when he came back with a steaming mug of fresh coffee for himself, and Darby's Dogs Rule mug refilled, which he set on the counter in front of her.

"Thanks." She broke a donut in half. "Think so. Hope so. Her heart and lungs are strong, but her back leg is crushed. I sent the X-rays to a friend in Richmond who specializes in animal orthopedics. We kind of agreed that the leg is too far gone, has too many fractures to be saved. Tracy, my lab tech, is coming in to assist me with Mercy's surgery later today. She's supposed to be on vacation, but was eager to help when I told her about Mercy." Darby ate the other half donut. "Wonder who she belongs to? She didn't have a collar or tags. No chip, either."

"Maybe she's a stray?" said Buddy, gobbling his second donut and refilling his coffee from the carafe Josie brought into the room.

"Could be. But she's young. Not more than six months old. Someone had to have her for at least a little while when she left the litter. Want to see her?"

"She's here?" Tommy's voice revealed his excitement at seeing the little pup again.

"Yeah. I didn't want to leave her home alone with my brood. You know Ken Burnett, my animal sanctuary manager, right?"

"Yeah," said Buddy. "We beat the crap out of his bowling team Saturday night."

"Must have been a fluke. Ken's team is the best around." Tommy gave Buddy a friendly nudge.

"Wasn't a fluke. We were on fire Saturday night."

"Anyway, Ken has his hands full at the sanctuary training a new guy he hired, and I want Mercy constantly monitored. Wait here. I'll go get her."

Darby returned a few minutes later with a sad-looking puppy, still wrapped in the yellow blanket, cuddled in her arms. When Buddy reached out, the pup responded with a low snarl.

"Look, but I don't suggest making a move to touch her. She's jumpy."

"She's sweet." Tommy dug into his pocket and a dog treat magically appeared in his hand, which he broke in half, held out, and Mercy took.

"You come prepared," said Darby.

"Boy Scout motto. And I was a very good Boy Scout," said Tommy. "You never know when something as simple as a dog treat can save you from a bite or worse." He carefully nuzzled Mercy.

"She likes you," said Darby.

"What are you going to do with her? No tags makes it next to impossible to find the owner."

"I know. I called Ronnie at Animal Control, but she hasn't gotten any calls about a missing dachshund puppy."

"She belongs to someone." Tommy looked from Mercy to Darby, and then fed Mercy another piece of treat. "Unless she was so badly hurt whoever had her didn't want to pay the medical bills."

"Or *they* hurt her." Darby shook her head and rubbed behind Mercy's ear. The puppy snuggled closer into her arms. "Be right back."

A few minutes passed before Darby reappeared without Mercy. "Gave her another shot. She'll sleep for a while. Buddy, have you heard from Dennis?"

"No. Why?"

"When you showed up at my house yesterday, you said you tried to call him first, but couldn't reach him."

"Tried a couple of times, but then we gave up and came to find you. Figured you'd be there fussing with your garden on a nice Sunday morning. It's almost planting time."

"You know me too well." She finished her coffee and refilled their cups. "It's not like Dennis not to pick up when he's on-call. I've been trying his cell every hour since about eight last night, but it keeps going to voice mail. I tried the clinic this morning, but no one answered there, either. It's Monday. They've got to have patients."

"Strange. Last time I saw him was Saturday night at bowling," said Tommy. "I left early. Buddy, when did you leave?"

"Dennis and I closed the place."

"You'd think Luanne would pick up," said Tommy. "Someone's got to be at the clinic."

"I know." Darby bit her lower lip. "She's been his right hand for years, runs his office like a Swiss watch. It's not like her not to show up to work. Buddy, did Dennis say anything to you about going out of town?"

"Nope. Just that he had to make a quick stop at the clinic before he went home Saturday night."

Buddy put down his mug and brushed traces of powdered sugar from his third donut off the front of his navy blue uniform shirt.

"Got time to take a ride?" asked Tommy.

"Thought you'd never ask. I've got no appointments this morning. Guess all my other pooches are healthy today. And Mercy's surgery isn't until two. Let me get my purse."

Buddy held the door open for her as she spoke to her receptionist. "Josie, hold down the fort. Call me if anyone needs me. We're going to Dennis's clinic."

Twenty minutes later they pulled into the parking lot of Brightwaters Pet Hospital. The place looked deserted.

"Odd," said Darby, getting out of the car and heading for the clinic's front door. "Why no cars?"

"Locked," said Tommy, when he turned the knob.

"Back door?" asked Darby. They walked around the clinic. "Getting stranger. There's Dennis's car." Darby pointed to the car parked under the awning Dennis built to shield it from the summer sun.

Buddy peered through the glass on the back door. "Can't see anything. You don't have a key by any chance?" As he spoke, he twisted the door knob. It opened at his touch. "Never mind."

"That's not good," said Darby.

Tommy unsnapped his holster and rested his right hand on the grip of his gun. Slowly he entered the kitchen area of the clinic with Darby at his heels. She noticed Buddy staring at his phone's screen.

"Important?"

"Nothing that can't wait."

"What's that smell?" Her hands flew to cover her mouth and nose as the stench of decay accosted them.

Tommy put his finger to his lips signaling them to be quiet. Suddenly, the treatment room door crashed open and a huge ball of fur lunged for Buddy, growling and baring its teeth.

"Sheba! No, Sheba. Down, Sheba." Darby's tone was strong and sure, and the husky obeyed her commands. Sheba went down into a submissive position at Darby's feet.

"Look at her paws and muzzle. Is that blood?"

"Stay here." Tommy pushed the door open, and he and Buddy stepped into the treatment room.

Darby knelt down and petted Sheba, who lay shaking at her feet. A few minutes later Buddy reappeared.

"He's dead."

"What?"

"Dennis. He's dead."

Darby rose and started for the treatment room door as Tommy joined them. He caught her arm.

"You don't want to go in there. It's bad. Stay here with Sheba while I call it in." He headed for the back door. "I've got shoe covers and gloves in the trunk of the car. Don't want to contaminate the scene."

Darby stood at the threshold of the treatment room, held the door open, and shivered. Dennis lay in a pool of blood, his face smeared with it, paw prints all around him. Tommy came up behind her and put his arms around her.

"Not much for doing what you're told, are you? What part of you don't want to see him didn't you understand?" He hugged her tighter when he felt her shudder. "Your first dead body?"

Big, brown, tear-filled eyes turned to him. "Yes. I mean, I was with my parents when they died, but this... All the blood."

"Call it hypovolemic shock. Massive blood loss. Heart can't pump enough blood through your body. His neck looks the worst."

"I see blood all the time. But nothing like this."

"Maybe she bit him." Buddy looked at Sheba, who was now cowering in the corner next to the refrigerator.

"No way. Sheba didn't do this. She loved Dennis. Followed him everywhere. There's no way she'd hurt him, let alone kill him."

"Maybe they were playing and it got out of hand."

"No, Buddy. Not possible. There has to be another explanation."

"Be right back," said Tommy as he put on shoe covers and latex gloves. "I'll just be a minute. Stay here." He turned to Buddy, who was still staring at Sheba. "You coming?"

20

"No. I'll wait out here with Darby for backup. The fewer people contaminating the scene the better."

Tommy shrugged and walked back into the treatment room. He bent down to examine Dennis's body. In less than five minutes he came back out and ripped off his gloves and shoe covers.

"Looks like a single shot to the right side of the neck, about where the carotid artery would be. Blood pooled around the wound entry. Sheba did a number on the area."

"She was probably trying to wake Dennis up."

"Maybe. There are paw prints everywhere. Any blood splatter evidence is now mixed with dog saliva."

"I apologize, Sheba," said Buddy, bending down to rub her ears, but he backed away when she voiced a low, menacing growl.

"Pay her no mind," said Darby. "She's upset, that's all."

"Think I'll go have a look-see," said Buddy, donning gloves and shoe covers.

"Now he wants to take a look?" said Tommy when Buddy left the room. "I can see what looks like an entry point."

Buddy reappeared. "Did you see the gun on the floor? It's under the instrument table."

"Missed it. Guess finding Dennis kind of caught me off guard. Wasn't expecting to find someone I know dead."

Darby exhaled loudly. "I knew Sheba couldn't be responsible."

Sirens wailed and tires screeched to a stop outside the back door.

"I can't believe Dennis is dead," said Darby absently.

"Wonder who might have had a beef with him? I mean, if one of his patients was unhappy, it would just bite him." Buddy laughed at his attempt at humor. "Too soon?"

"Yes, Buddy, too soon." Darby walked over and put her arms around Sheba.

"Let's get you cleaned up, girl." She wet a towel. "It's okay to clean her up, isn't it?"

"One second." Tommy pulled out his cell phone and took a few photos of Sheba. Then he took a cotton swab and ran it around her nose, and cut off a few of her nose hairs while Darby held her still. After he reviewed the pictures and put both the swab and the hair clippings in a small plastic evidence bag, he gave Darby the go-ahead. "Have at it."

Buddy walked over with a wet towel. Sheba bared her teeth and growled at him, so he handed the towel to Darby and backed up.

"She's very upset," said Darby. "She never growls at anyone."

As Darby wiped the blood from around Sheba's muzzle, she said, "Buddy, you might have been the last person to see Dennis alive. How did he seem when you guys parted ways?"

"Upbeat. Like he was on top of the world. All his problems solved. Troubles vanished without a trace."

"Did he say why he had to come back here?" asked Tommy.

"Nope. And I didn't ask. Guess I should have been more curious, but it was late, and I had a bit too much to drink."

Within minutes police were everywhere. Most rushed right past Darby and joined Tommy and Buddy in the treatment room. One officer cornered her, asking her question after question. Unfortunately, she had no answers. Out of the corner of her eye she saw Buddy bolt out the back door.

"We done?" she asked the officer.

He nodded, and she followed Buddy outside. She found him leaning against the back wall of the clinic, bent over at the waist, retching horribly.

"You okay?"

"Been better. Must have been something I ate. Tried that new Chinese all-you-can-eat buffet place out on Route 13 last night."

"Right." She looked at the clinic door and then at him. "Something you ate." She could hear buzzing. "That your phone?"

"Probably." He made no move to answer it.

Darby followed him back into the clinic, guiding him to one of the wobbly plastic chairs in the kitchen. She could tell his head was pounding, because he tried to block out the fluorescent lights by covering his eyes.

"Let me help you."

"How?"

She held up her hands and wiggled her fingers. "Magic fingers."

He leaned his head back as Darby went behind him and began to massage his temples gently.

"Has to be the food. Not like this is my first dead body."

"Perhaps a little more gruesome than most. Aren't you guys more likely to get hunting accidents, bar brawls, domestic cases around here? And Dennis was your friend. Makes it personal."

When Buddy tried to stand, he swayed and grabbed her arm to keep from falling.

"Maybe you should stay seated. And there goes your phone again. Someone wants you. I'll get you some water while you answer that." Darby took a bottle from the refrigerator and handed it to him, noticing that he still had not picked up his phone.

"Thanks." He twisted the cap off and guzzled greedily, finishing over half the bottle before his phone buzzed again.

"You going to be sick again?"

"No. Just give me a minute."

"Take all the time you need, but you better get that."

23

Darby leaned against the kitchen counter and drummed her fingers impatiently. Sheba sat at her feet licking her paws, while Tommy sat at one of the tables and made notes about the incident. Buddy had gone outside to take his call. She hated waiting and soon found herself straightening up the old magazines piled on the counter. One caught her eye, *Gamedogs, USA*.

A cough drew her attention to the treatment room where Dennis's body lay. She could see Dr. Forrester, one of the local doctors certified as a ME for Accomack County, on one knee beside the body. Then he stood, ripped off his gloves, and walked out of the room towards her.

"COD is what you thought, Tommy," said Dr. Forrester. "Looks like a textbook suicide. Single GSW. Entered here," he pointed to the right side of his neck, "severed the carotid. See an exit hole but don't see a bullet." He turned to Darby. "Think the dog could have swallowed it?"

"Are you kidding?" said Darby.

"Nope."

"I'm taking Sheba home with me. I'll monitor her poop for a few days."

"That would be great, unless the Norfolk ME gets lucky when he gets Dr. Lancaster on the table. It could still be in there. Whole area is kind of a mess. I'm sure the ME will be more precise after he completes the autopsy."

"Strange place to point a gun for suicide, don't you think?" Darby touched her neck. "Most suicides aim for the temple or shove the gun into their mouths, don't they?"

"Those are the usual places, but suicide is a different animal. Just never know what drives someone to take his own life. Maybe he changed his mind and the gun discharged accidentally when he lowered his hand." Dr. Forrester put on his jacket. "He's past rigor, cold, but no longer stiff, so it's been easily over thirty-six hours. Do you know the last time anyone saw him? Any idea of when he might have done it?"

"He and Buddy bowled Saturday night," said Tommy. "Buddy said they left the bar at midnight. Closed the place down."

Just then Buddy walked back into the clinic. "He said he had to stop back here to get something before going home."

"We called him Sunday morning with an emergency, but he never picked up," added Tommy. "So we brought the injured dog to Darby."

"The back door wasn't locked when we got here," said Darby. "Buddy, what kind of security did Dennis have here?"

"Not much. He…um…he didn't want to spend the money for a fancy security system. Had a simple door alarm system. But no alarm sounded, or our guys would have responded."

CHAPTER 3

"I've got to get back. Have Mercy's surgery this afternoon."

"Buddy, drive Darby back to her clinic. I'm staying here for a bit, See what I can learn from the crime scene techs. Then swing back and pick me up."

Darby held Sheba's leash tightly by her side as they approached Buddy's patrol car. Suddenly Sheba pulled away, rose up on her hind legs, placed her paws on Buddy's back and growled.

"Whoa." He turned quickly to free himself, but Darby could see his body tense and panic in his eyes when Sheba snapped at him.

"Sheba. Down." Darby grabbed her by the collar and pulled her away from Buddy. "I don't know what's gotten into her."

"Me neither. She knows me."

The dog looked from Darby to Buddy and back again. Darby opened the back door and Sheba jumped into the back seat. She slid in the front seat alongside Buddy.

"Glad that grate's there." Buddy wiped his forehead and started the engine.

"What could be so bad that Dennis would take his own life? It doesn't make sense. You knew him, Buddy. You said he was upbeat Saturday night. What do you think happened?"

"Don't know. We talked a few weeks ago at the Island House, at Fred Warner's retirement party. Thought he was going to finish the whole pan of chocolate bread pudding by himself."

"That's their specialty."

"And it's mighty tasty. Can't say I haven't over-indulged once or twice myself."

"Haven't we all?"

"He seemed better than I'd seen him in years, like he finally stopped blaming himself for his wife's death. He planned to do an Alaska cruise in July. Had it all booked on Princess. A singles package. He was excited to get back out there. Scared, but excited."

"The position of the gunshot seems odd to me." Darby's mind shifted to full medical mode, which eased the pain of losing her friend and colleague.

"It would have had to be one well-placed shot," said Buddy. "And I can't imagine keeping your hand steady enough to actually hit something that would kill you. The neck just doesn't have enough body mass."

"When my dad taught me to shoot, he always said to aim for the chest area. Lots of body to hit." Darby stared out the window at the trees whizzing by. "Why would Dennis take his life?" A heavy sigh escaped her. "You were his best friend. Any ideas?"

"He had issues."

"That's kind of cryptic. What sort of issues?"

"Not sure I want to talk out of school. Mostly rumor. Before his wife died."

"I remember. When was it? Last year?"

"Closer to two years ago. He told me she'd been

drinking, and they had a fight. He went to the bathroom, and while he was peeing, she grabbed the car keys and raced out. Rainy night. Slippery roads. Lost control. Hit a tree. Died instantly, thank God."

"That's a lot of guilt to carry around. He must have felt terrible." Darby stuck her finger through the grate and Sheba licked it. Her heart ached. She understood loss. Her own husband's death had been sudden, but in Afghanistan, at the hands of an enemy. "Did he ever say what they were fighting about?"

Buddy looked at Darby, weighing his options. Momentary misgivings about sharing what he knew about Dennis's problems were assuaged by his awareness that Darby was one of the most trustworthy people he'd ever met. She'd lived in Wachapreague for barely three years, but fit in like a native. Everyone loved her.

He also considered the impact anything he told Darby might have down the road. Planting a few seeds about a secret life Dennis was leading couldn't hurt should events play out in unanticipated ways. Even if it was a lie, was it bad to hedge his bets, assuming she'd share whatever he told her with others?

Dennis was a different matter. He and Dennis had been best friends since high school, and they both left Wachapreague for different lives, Dennis to college and veterinary school, him to the Army. But they found themselves back home when the lives they had planned for themselves didn't pan out.

"He never said much. Let's just say Doris had image problems."

"What does that mean? I only met her a few times. I remember the Christmas dance at the VFW post in Exmore. Never really saw her around town."

"She didn't make friends easily. He met her in college, and I always thought she latched onto him thinking he was going to make oodles of money as a veterinarian. But when his dad died, he moved back here to be near his mom. Doris wasn't the small-town, Eastern Shore of Virginia type."

"Didn't know there was a type. Maybe someone should have told me that before I moved here."

"You fit right in, Doc. But Doris…" He turned into the parking lot at Darby's clinic and pulled up to the front door. "Doris wanted the high life, country club, big city kind of stuff. And there aren't many places to go here to sample the high life."

"That's why I chose Wachapreague. I like the slower pace, more friendly kind of people. It's the perfect place to raise Brianna."

"Also, they were devout Catholics. And childless."

"Didn't follow the church's dictum on that one."

"True. He once told me she had some female problems and couldn't have children. But they held to old traditions, and didn't believe in divorce. To hear Dennis tell it, she drank herself numb, and when she wasn't drinking, she was shopping online. Kept the UPS guy ringing her doorbell on a regular basis. Maybe too regular."

"Talk about stress. I've got a good practice and all, but vets don't make that kind of money. Especially here. We couldn't. The people here don't have big bucks to pay big fees."

"Doris took care of the household accounts, so Dennis didn't know the half of it until after she died. Then he cleaned out her closet. Clothes. Shoes. Purses. Most of it still had the price tags attached. There were so many bills. Hundreds of thousands of dollars on credit cards she'd taken out that he never knew about."

"Probably what they were fighting about."

"I asked him about it a few months ago. You know, just asked him how it was going. He told me he had it under control. Had taken another job, which helped clear up his finances. Didn't say doing what."

"And you didn't ask?"

"Nope. We were friends. If he wanted me to know what he was doing, he would have told me. Simple as that. But—"

"But what?"

"The last few months at the bowling alley, he was acting kind of strange. Buying rounds of drinks. Don't get me wrong, Dennis wasn't a cheapskate, but the way he was acting, like he was printing the stuff in the basement. A few weeks ago, he flashed a fat roll of bills that had my eyeballs popping out of my head."

"And you didn't ask him?"

"Don't ask. Don't tell."

It was a long afternoon, but Mercy's surgery went well. With Tracy's help, Darby amputated the puppy's right back leg and sutured the open wounds. There would be permanent scars, but nothing Mercy couldn't overcome with some tender loving care.

"What's next?" asked Tracy as she cleaned up the surgical area and put the instruments into the autoclave for sterilization. "Do you want me to stay with her? I've got some pharmacy invoices to clear up, so I can hang around a while."

"No. I've got patients yet to see, and I'm going to take her home with me tonight. Any invoices can wait until next week when you're officially back at work. Go back to enjoying your vacation time. You've earned it in more ways than I can count."

"No problem. Wasn't doing much. Just hanging out at home."

"A young, single female? Why didn't you plan some exotic trip?"

"Funds are kind of tight at the moment." She shrugged. "The new car and all."

"Saw that Mercedes. Nice ride. Did you rob a bank or something? Have a rich uncle die? Have a sugar daddy you haven't told me about?"

"I've always wanted one, and you know what they say. Life isn't a dress rehearsal. If you can't treat yourself right, then who will treat you right?"

"Good question, girl. Haven't got an answer. All my money goes to Brianna and the sanctuary."

"Let me know if you need me again. I'm a phone call away."

Tracy grabbed her handbag and headed for the back door. "And check out my new purse. Prada. Awesome, right?"

"Prada? Wow, I'm impressed. But doesn't the devil wear Prada?"

"Funny. One of my favorite movies. Loved the clothes, but don't have any place to wear them around here, so I've settled for the bags and boots." Tracy swished from side to side showing off the bag hanging on her shoulder. "I got another one in a camel color to go with these awesome boots I bought. Also Prada."

Darby pulled her scrub top over her head and threw it into the hamper, pulling on a T-shirt, and then a sweatshirt. "Maybe one of these days I'll have enough spare change to splurge on fancy cars, purses, and boots. Enjoy the rest of your time off. I'll see you next week."

"Thanks."

Darby watched Tracy get into her fire engine red Mercedes and crank up the engine. Prada? Mercedes?

Expensive items for someone living on a technician's wages. The girl must not pay a lot in rent, and scrimp in every other way. Or maybe she has another source of income, too.

CHAPTER 4

"How did your meeting with the delegate go today?" asked Brody when he called Darby around dinner time Wednesday night.

"Frustrating as hell. How was your day?"

"Same ol', same ol'. What happened at the meeting?"

"Nothing. The guy we met with, Delegate Bradford Cummings," said Darby, in a mocking, highfalutin tone, "had to be over eighty if he was a day. Too old to still be a power player in a changing world. It took him awhile to even focus on the bill Ashley and Tori want him to support."

"Sometimes it takes people time to get down to business. It's why I like working for TJ. No bullshit. He gets down to business fast."

"This guy spent an hour pontificating about the absurdity of an anti-tethering ordinance that recently passed in Cape Charles. You should have heard him! In a southern drawl as thick as molasses, he droned on and on about how wrong it was to tell people what they could and couldn't do with their dogs."

"Ah, sounds like you got yourself a good ol' boy."

"I expected him to start blaming them damn northerners for moving to the south with their liberal moral codes any minute. He did perk up a bit when Ashley hit him with the consumer protection argument, saying consumers were being lied to about where puppies in pet stores were coming from."

"Did it fly?"

"Maybe. Too soon to tell, because he proceeded to regale us with his history as a fiscal conservative, and all the bills he's supported throughout his career to save citizens money and protect taxpayers."

"How did it end?"

"He took all the documents the girls prepared for him and said he'd review them. If he actually reads them, he'll have to support them. They did a good job showing the added costs burdening Virginia taxpayers when puppies bought at a pet store are given up because they're sick, and either find their way into shelters or have to be euthanized at taxpayer expense."

"He'll probably have one of his aides read them. None of these guys do their own research."

"I hope whoever reads them loves dogs."

"Most people do, so the odds are in your favor."

"Can I call you back later? I need to go for a run to calm down."

"Sure. Have a good run."

Brianna was finishing her dinner when Darby walked into the kitchen.

"Ashley, I'm going out for a run. Could you handle Brianna's bath tonight?" Again Darby found herself grateful for Ashley, their live-in nanny, who wanted nothing but room and board in exchange for taking care of Brianna. A godsend.

"Sure thing."

"Thanks." Darby stretched, twisting and turning, warming up for her run. "Just need to work off some excess energy."

"Be careful out there. It'll be getting dark soon."

"Will do. I won't be gone long. Just feeling stressed from our meeting and worrying about Mercy. And since Dennis died, we've been so busy at the clinic. I must have over fifty new patients."

"Good for you. You're a good vet, and people know it. They trust you."

"Let's not kid ourselves. I'm the only veterinarian for twenty miles."

"There's that, too. But don't sell yourself short. It's why Tori and I are so grateful you came with us today. Cummings is a total turd, isn't he?"

"You don't have to like him. All you have to do is pray he agrees to sponsor your bill."

"I know. But we're both a little bummed that he didn't sign on immediately." Ashley took the milk out of the fridge and poured some in an Elsa mug. The *Frozen* character was Brianna's favorite. "I've been meaning to ask you, how are the self-defense classes going?"

"Good." Darby bit her lower lip. "We started something new. It's called Krav Maga."

"Sounds exotic."

"Israeli Defense Forces developed it. Incorporates boxing and other martial arts moves. I kind of like it. Makes me feel strong, and the instructor says I'm getting pretty good at it."

"Good for you." Ashley put her arms around Darby and held her tightly. "You've been through a lot. You do what you need to do. I'll take care of Brianna."

"Thanks. I don't know what I'd do without you." Darby saw a strange look cross Ashley's face as she bent down to tie her running shoes' laces.

"I'm happy to take care of Brianna. She's such a good girl. And she's a great diversion from worrying about whether Cummings will come on board and decide to be our bill's sponsor." Ashley's voice seemed distant, like she was a thousand miles away.

"Is everything okay?"

"Yeah."

"You should come to class with me one night. Ken can watch Brianna. I think we ladies need to know how to defend ourselves."

"Maybe I'll do that, but right now it's bath time for Bri, and run time for you. Scat, before it gets too dark to see where you're going."

Exhilaration. The endorphins kicked in at the five-mile mark. Heart pumping, legs aching from pounding rock-hard asphalt, until rivulets of sweat trickled down her back. Darby made the turn into her driveway and coasted the last few feet, stopping to do cooldown stretches on the steps of her front porch.

Dennis's death and the Cummings meeting were upsetting, but something else had been gnawing at her since she found Dennis's body, and at about mile two she realized what it was. The copies of *Gamedogs, USA* that she saw in Dennis's kitchen area were out of place.

What's a vet doing with magazines about dog fighting?

It made her blood boil. She couldn't believe, didn't want to believe, that Dennis had any part in dog fighting, or that it was going on locally, right under her nose. But some of the wounds on poor little Mercy only made sense if she was willing to consider that they'd been made by an overly aggressive dog.

She made a decision during her run. Somehow she was going to find out, once and for all, if her suspicions and the rumors about dog fighting were true. Of course, she had no clue how, but after five miles, she had what she labeled "run courage"—that feeling of invincibility, that she could conquer the world, that she was unstoppable. And now she'd made the decision to put herself out there, she knew how to do it would come to her.

She recalled her mother's favorite quote from Paulo Coelho, "And, when you want something, all the universe conspires in helping you achieve it." Her mother always added that you had to be sure, and want it badly, with all your heart and soul, because the universe didn't help fakers.

"Well, I'm not faking. Come hell or high water, I want to put an end to dog fighting. And the puppy mill industry has got to stop too. Whatever it takes."

She winced slightly as she stretched her right calf muscles, still weak from the fractured patella she sustained a few years ago. She wiped her face with the towel she'd left on the porch swing, switched from running shoes to slippers, and pulled her faded Virginia Tech sweatshirt on to ward off the evening's chill.

Her phone vibrated in her pocket.

"Brody." Her heart leapt, and she smiled when she saw his face on the screen. "Great timing."

"Yes!" Ashley came rushing out to meet Darby, gushing and bubbling, when Darby arrived home from work the next day. "He's in. Cummings. He agreed to sponsor our sourcing bill. Do you believe it?"

"That's great, Ashley. You and Tori put a lot of work into this project, and I'm so glad he saw the wisdom in getting on board."

"He said he found the 'follow the money' argument impressive."

"Wise man. And it is a consumer rights issue. Buyers should know where a puppy comes from. Pet stores lie.

Tori found that out when she took the job at Puppies on Parade."

"The manager there is such a sleaze. Shelters are bulging with unwanted dogs, and they can't raise funds fast enough to cover their costs."

"What's your next step?" Darby dropped her backpack on top of the washing machine and followed Ashley into the kitchen.

"We already passed the senate forty to zero, so that hurdle is covered. Now we go before the House of Delegates Agricultural Committee. We have to convince four out of seven members. If we do that, the bill goes to the full House."

"And then?"

"Then Virginia communities can pass local ordinances restricting where puppies in pet stores come from. Hopefully, it will put commercial breeders out of business, at least around here."

"And we can hope more local municipalities follow your lead."

"It's already spreading across the country. The ASPCA and Humane Society are both behind this effort. But the problem is, it takes time, time a lot of innocent puppies and breeding dogs don't have."

CHAPTER 5

"Oh, Mommy, I have to tell you. I have to tell you!" Brianna flew off the bus and into Darby's waiting arms.

"What?" Darby knelt and got eye to eye with her daughter. "Tell me. Tell me."

"My friend, Chrissy, at show-and-tell today. She said they have a lot of puppies in the barn behind her house."

"They do?"

"Puppies, Mommy. Puppies."

Darby stood up, waved to the bus driver, picked up Brianna's backpack, took her hand, and started to walk down her driveway.

"And I asked Chrissy if I could come over and play with the puppies. But she didn't think her Mommy and Daddy would let me come. Why would she say that, Mommy?"

"I don't know, sweetie. Maybe she had things to do, and it wasn't convenient for you to go over."

"When Chrissy's Mommy came to pick her up I asked her if I could come and see the puppies. But she said no I couldn't come. And she got real mad at Chrissy. She told her she wasn't supposed to talk about the puppies. Why did she do that, Mommy?"

"I'm not sure, baby, but I'm glad you told me."

"Can you call her, Mommy? Tell her you're a veterinarian and you take care of dogs and cats."

"Maybe I could do that. But right now, why don't we go have some milk? I baked fresh chocolate chip cookies for you. You can tell me what else you did at school today."

"Okay, but why can't I play with the puppies? Don't puppies like to play with kids?"

"That's a good question. Let me think about it. In the meantime, I want a chocolate chip cookie, don't you?"

"Yes!"

That night, after bath time, after story time, and with Brianna safely tucked into bed, Darby poured a glass of wine, wrapped herself in her maroon and gold Virginia Tech fleece blanket, and headed out to the front porch. She sat down on the porch swing, pushed back using her toes, letting the swing rock her gently.

Sleep had become a luxury lately. She found herself spending more nights swinging on her porch with a glass of wine in her hand than in her bed, because when she closed her eyes, her mind went wild.

Putting her life back together, with the love of her life gone, was a slow, painful process. There were no words anyone could say to extinguish the ache inside her. She knew she had to be strong for Brianna's sake. And how could she explain to a two-year-old that her daddy wasn't coming home when she didn't understand the idea of daddy? He'd been gone more than he'd been home, so Brianna didn't have a strong attachment to him, only to Snoodles, the stuffed dog he gave her before he left on his last deployment. Even now, three years later, Snoodles went everywhere with her, slept cuddled in her arms each night.

The Red Cross phone call had ripped Darby's heart out. Then she heard the gravel in her driveway crunch, and saw the car pull up and stop. Two men got out, both in uniform. They approached her, and she saw the cross on one man's lapel. She straightened. She knew. Her beloved Benjamin was gone.

She moved to Wachapreague on Virginia's Eastern Shore because she and Benjamin once vacationed here, loved it, and they planned to move here when he was done with his tour. She remembered it as a quaint seaside town, a good place to raise a child.

To ease the pain, she dove into her veterinary practice with a vengeance. It became her saving grace, gave her something to focus on. Until last fall, when human ugliness again crossed her path. A man claiming to be her biological father had her kidnapped, and planned to cut out her kidney to save himself from dying of renal failure.

The room, the huge lights above the gurney where she'd been strapped down whirled, the monitors still beeped and hummed in her subconscious. Then the "what-ifs" started. What if the people who rescued her hadn't gotten there in time? What if someone had cut out her kidney? What if she died? What would happen to Brianna?

She quivered. She'd cried all the tears she had and then some in night's silent solitude. Daylight brought responsibility. Brianna needed her, counted on her. Her little girl had lost one parent and couldn't afford to have her mother fall apart.

Darby knew it would take time to get over what happened to her. Labeling it traumatic seemed too technical. Downright gut-wrenching fit better. And the man at the center of it all? Her father? Her real father? *How could he do that? Kidnap me? Take my kidney without even trying to ask me? Who does something like that?*

I should probably talk to someone. She finished her wine. *Yeah. Talking to someone would probably be a good idea.* She mentally added finding a therapist to her to-do list.

But on the bright side, the ugly event brought Brody into her life.

Her longing for a man's touch didn't surprise her as much as it reminded her of Benjamin, their love, and her loss when the IED blew him apart. The loss of her husband was still raw, as if it happened yesterday. But the hole in her heart was slowly being stitched together with new threads named Llewelyn Brody.

And now she was embroiled in new ugliness, something her love of animals was forcing her to confront with a vengeance.

"A barn with a lot of puppies."

She softly repeated Brianna's description as she headed inside and up to bed. To a child, a lot of puppies could be five, or seven, or even ten—a normal-sized litter, depending on the breed. Considering her recent testimony supporting the effort to shut down puppy mills, to Darby, a lot of puppies and a woman who did not want a child to play with them spelled trouble.

Early the next morning, Darby unlocked the front door to Dennis's clinic with the key he'd given her two years ago, when they agreed to share resources to cut down expenses.

The police had finished their evidence collection and given her permission to enter the property. She wanted to get the records for all her new patients. When she called Luanne, Dennis's long-time receptionist, asking for her help, Luanne begged her not to make her go back into the clinic. She couldn't face the place where Dennis died, had praised the Lord that she had taken the morning off to get her yearly blood work done at the hospital. She'd left town as soon as she heard the news, headed to Savannah to visit her mother for a few weeks to recuperate from the tragedy.

Luanne gave her the computer passwords, and told her to call Tracy, since she also worked as a surgical tech for Dennis and knew where everything was in the clinic. Darby thought about Tracy's dual incomes, and how much she paid her. Maybe Dennis paid way more than she did. Maybe that's where Tracy got the money for her Mercedes and her other expensive purchases.

Darby flipped on the lights, dropped her handbag and the keys on the reception counter, wrapped her arms across her chest, and shivered. It felt weird and uncomfortable, standing alone in the deserted office, once so full of life.

How had it come to this? What possessed Dennis to take his life? So many questions, but no answers. And unless the police found something, there would be none.

Darby paced the reception area, poked her head into the two exam rooms, and then pushed open the door into the treatment area. Everything was as she remembered it, nothing out of place, although the smell of bleach permeated the room. The cleaning crew must have come in to clean up the mess after the police released the scene.

She backed out into the reception area, got the patient list from her purse, and started to pull the files she needed, but paused when a lone tear rolled down her cheek. Wiping it away, she worked quickly to pull the remaining files and get the hell out of Dodge. She put the fifty-plus files in the box she brought, lifted them...

And stared down the hall at Dennis's office, locking onto his desk.

Slowly she made her way down the hall, setting the box of patient files on the leather sofa. Definitely a man's office, all wood paneling and military memorabilia. Diplomas, his license to practice veterinary medicine, and awards hung on one wall. And medical books were everywhere, crammed into two floor to ceiling bookcases and stacked on a credenza behind his leather desk chair. The lingering scent of Dennis's aftershave surrounded her. Darby smiled.

She turned in a slow circle. Maybe she would find something the police missed, something that might explain the tragedy. She did another full-circle turn. Nothing.

"What a waste." She squeezed her eyes shut when she felt more tears burning to be released.

Sitting behind his desk, and surprised to find it unlocked, she rifled through the drawers. Everything was neat and tidy, a far cry from her office desk. She leaned back in his chair, taking her time to scan the room. When her attention returned to the desktop, she noticed a slip of white sticking out from under the desk's blotter.

"What's this?" she asked aloud. She pulled it out.

Slowly she stood and rested her butt against the desk, her full concentration on the sheet in her hands.

She never heard the door open.

"Darby?"

A soft shriek escaped as her heart leapt into her throat.

"Sorry, I didn't mean to scare you," said Tommy as he walked into the office. "You said to meet you here."

"I know. I'm a little jumpy."

"I've only got a few minutes. What do you need?"

"Something Buddy said when he drove me back to the clinic the other day. He said Dennis was rolling in cash at the bowling alley, pulled out a roll of bills that could have choked a horse, throwing money around like it was water. But I remember Dennis told me he was in a lot of debt after Doris died."

"From what I heard, the debt was humongous. It was going to take him years to pay off all his wife's bills. So glad my wife and I agree about how we spend our money. Maybe someone died and left him a bundle?"

"We would have heard about that. Life in small towns revolves around the rumor mill."

"Ah, rumors. The gift that keeps on giving."

"Buddy thought Dennis had another job, but he didn't know what it was, and he never asked him."

"And you think…what?" Tommy leaned back against the credenza and folded his arms.

"When you keep hearing the same rumor from different, disconnected people, you've got to figure there's some truth to it. There's been whispering for years about a dog fighting ring operating in these parts. And Mercy's injuries support that."

"I've heard those rumors, too. Even got a few anonymous tips, but when we got there, all we found was an empty field. I heard they moved the fights around, so it's been hard to confirm, and even harder to catch them in the act. You think Dennis was involved?"

"Sad to say, but yes."

"A vet involved in dog fighting?"

"I know. Hard to believe. We take care of animals, we don't abuse them. I know it's small potatoes, but it's why I started my animal sanctuary. One day I hope it will be able to help more animals in need, but for right now it's all I can afford. Besides, helping animals is part of the oath we take as veterinarians."

"Hard to make the leap and believe Dennis would do anything to hurt an animal. But maybe he saw it as helping."

"How?" Darby's tone broadcast her growing frustration. "The best way he could have helped was to stop any fight."

"I agree. But maybe he couldn't stop it, so he figured that if he was there, he could take care of any injured dog."

Darby barely managed to stifle the urge to give Tommy an exaggerated eye roll. "Circumstantial."

"A few weeks ago, Buddy told me Dennis was out of debt, which made him happier than a pig in shit, because Dennis was the best bowler on his team. He told Buddy he wouldn't be missing any more bowling nights. He just had a few final details to work out."

Darby stared out across the parking lot, struggling to make sense of a senseless death.

"I hear you, but it sounds like he got out of debt really fast. And carrying that much cash around. He never did that before."

"Hello? Anybody here? Darby?"

Tommy and Darby made eye contact and then watched Buddy walk down the hall to the office.

"Hey, Darby. I saw your Jeep outside. Tommy's SUV too. What are y'all doing here?"

"I came to pick up some patient files." She pointed to the box loaded with manila folders. "Luanne couldn't deal with coming here. She's visiting her mom and told me to take what I needed."

"How'd you get in?"

"Dennis and I swapped keys years ago in case we needed supplies. Sharing equipment we each use only once in a blue moon helped us both keep costs down."

"Smart move…for both of you."

"And when I saw Darby's Jeep, I thought I'd stop in to check on Mercy, but I gotta go," said Tommy, heading for the door.

"I'm almost ready to find Mercy a forever family in case you're interested, Tommy."

He gave her a crooked grim. "I'll talk to the missus. Buddy, I'll see you back at the station for our shift. Darby, let me know if you need any TLC for Mercy. For that little pooch, the dog whisperer is always available."

"Thanks, Tommy. Be safe."

Darby let out a loud sigh and looked around the room. "Not sure what's going to happen to all this stuff now."

"Got me," said Buddy. "It was just him and Doris. Since she couldn't have kids, she claimed she never wanted them. Said it would ruin her figure."

"Now that's shallow."

"That was Doris. He doesn't have any other family that I know of." Buddy wiped his face and then parked his hands on his hips, looking around the room. "Wonder if he left a will?"

"Who would know?"

"Not sure. There are a few lawyers in town. I see you went through his desk," said Buddy, pointing to the papers in her hands. "What's that?"

"Just a spreadsheet."

"Find any business cards?"

"I didn't see anything from a lawyer, but I wasn't really looking carefully."

"Well then put those papers down and I'll walk you out."

"Will you carry my books too?"

"Cute. No, I won't carry your books, but I will carry your box of files." Buddy picked up the file box, but stopped moving when he saw Darby sit down at Dennis's desk and flip on his computer. "What are you doing?" He set the box back down on the sofa and came behind her to look over her shoulder.

"Downloading some order files. We combine orders to get a better rate from some vendors. Luanne gave me the passwords."

She pulled a sheet of paper from her pocket and followed the instructions Luanne had given her. "Here they are. This will just take a minute."

Darby started to cough.

"You okay?"

Choking, her voice raspy, "could you get me a water from the fridge?"

"Sure. Be right back."

As soon as Buddy left the room, Darby inserted a flash drive and copied the purchase order folder to it. Then she switched to Dennis's email. There were two accounts, one with his clinic's dot com address and a gmail account. Without reading them, she copied his last month's gmails to the flash drive.

"Here you go," said Buddy, unscrewing the cap and handing her a bottle of Dasani.

"Thanks." She took a hearty gulp. "Just another minute." She watched the screen. "Done."

Darby powered down the computer, slipped the flash drive into her pocket, and looked at her watch. "I need to go. I've got patients waiting for me." She picked up the patient file box when Buddy walked right by it and followed him down the hall.

Shifting the files to her left arm, she shouldered her purse, but Buddy took the keys off the desk before she could grab them.

"You've got your hands full. I'll lock up."

"Thanks." *Carrying the box of files like you said you would would be more helpful.* Buddy was often clueless about social niceties.

Darby put the file box in the back of her Jeep and waited for Buddy to join her. She held her hand out for her keys. "See you later, Buddy."

"Not if I see you first," he quipped.

Darby didn't go far. She made a fast right into the Wawa parking lot next door to Dennis's clinic. Something on the spreadsheets she left on the desk had caught her eye, and she wanted another look at them without Buddy nosing around. She got out of her Jeep and headed across the parking lot back to the clinic. As she stepped through a mound of fresh mulch in the flower beds, the sight of Buddy's shirt disappearing inside the clinic shocked her.

"That bastard. He didn't lock the door. What's he doing going back inside?"

She wanted to wait, wanted to tiptoe across the parking lot and peek in the windows, wanted to know what he was doing, see how long he stayed, but Josie had just texted that there were patients waiting.

The unanswered questions haunted her all the way back to her clinic.

Chapter 6

"Chrissy!"

Brianna bolted away from Darby, raced down the frozen food aisle of the Food Mart, her arms flung wide, and embraced a little red-headed girl. Darby hurried to catch up to her.

"Mommy, Mommy, this is Chrissy."

"I gathered that." She turned to the little girl, who was slinking away from Brianna. "Hello, Chrissy. It's nice to meet you." Darby held out her hand to the little girl, who backed away even more, her eyes bulging as large as flying saucers.

"Chrissy," snapped a broad-shouldered woman with dull, brown, frizzy hair, a plain, round face, and two-inch gray roots. "What kind of trouble have you gotten yourself into now?" The woman yanked the trembling girl's arm with such force, Darby was afraid she might pull it right out of the socket.

"I'm sorry," said Darby to the woman, whose sagging jowls, baggy eyes, and ratty-looking hair broadcast a life of neglect. "I'm Darby Dratton. Our daughters are classmates at Little Horizons. Brianna talks about Chrissy all the time."

A gnarly cackle escaped the woman's mouth. "I see."

Darby flinched and could almost hear the Wicked Witch of the West's famous line, *"I'll get you, my pretty, and your little dog too."*

Brianna tugged at the woman's arm "Can I come over and play with the puppies? Chrissy says you have lots of puppies, and I love puppies."

"I don't know what you're talking about. We don't have any dogs." She took Chrissy's hand. "Come along, child. I see you've been telling stories again. Guess we'll have to wash your mouth out with soap until you learn not to go making things up."

"Mrs...." Darby made direct eye contact with the woman.

"Trent. I'm Wanda Trent. And I'm sorry to have caused you any trouble."

"No. No trouble. And I'm sure Chrissy didn't mean any harm. Maybe Brianna didn't understand what she heard. You know how the little ones can be."

"No. I don't know what you're talking about. We teach our children to always tell the truth. This one's more trouble than she's worth sometimes. Gets things in her head. I don't know what we're going to do with her."

"But Mommy," cried Brianna.

"Come along, Brianna. I'm sure Mrs. Trent and Chrissy have to finish their shopping, and we have to get going, too. It was nice meeting you, Mrs. Trent. Maybe we can arrange a play date for the girls sometime soon. I'd love to have Chrissy come over and play one afternoon."

"That won't be possible. We only have one car at the moment, and my husband and I are busy with spring planting."

"Oh, that's not a problem. I'd be happy to drive Chrissy home. Or she can sleep over and catch the bus with Brianna in the morning."

Wanda Trent's stare could have cut her in half. Her menacing voice made the hairs on Darby's arms stand on end. "That's not gonna happen." She grabbed Chrissy's hand, dragging her away. "Come along."

Darby watched them walk away, Chrissy's face a portrait of fear.

"Mommy?"

"What, baby?"

"Why won't Chrissy's mommy let her come over and play?"

Darby bent down and gently held Brianna's arms. "They're very busy on the farm where Chrissy lives. I'm sure she has to do a lot of chores to help her family. Like you have chores to help me. Do you understand that?"

"I suppose so."

"Good. Let's finish our shopping and then bring home a pizza for dinner."

"Yay. Pizza." Brianna jumped with joy, the encounter with Chrissy forgotten. "Can we? Can we?"

"You bet. Let's go."

"Here. Let me help you with those." Ashley took two bags out of Darby's arms.

"Let me help too, Mommy."

"Here, Brianna. You take the gallon of milk. Can you carry it?"

"Yes, Mommy. I'm a big girl." She ran off to the house.

"They grow up so fast," said Darby. "Pretty soon she won't want to have anything to do with me. Adolescence."

"That's years away. She's only five."

"Wish she would stay like this forever."

"Not possible. Nothing's forever."

Darby saw the same look on Ashley's face she'd seen a few nights ago. "What's up, Ashley? I can tell something is troubling you. Want to talk about it?"

"There's not a lot to talk about. I-I..." Ashley's eyes teared up. "I'm leaving at the end of the semester."

Darby stopped dead in her tracks and looked at her.

"I'm sorry. I've been trying work up the nerve to tell you for a few weeks now. I just didn't know how."

"What brought this on? Is it something I said or did?"

"Oh, no. Nothing. You've been great to me." Ashley's voice wobbled as tears rolled down her cheeks. "This is safe. Here is safe. My whole life I've played it safe. I'm twenty-two years old, and I've done nothing except play it safe."

"That's not true. What you're doing now about puppy mills is not safe. It's important."

"I know, but it will be over by the end of the semester when my class ends."

"There's more, isn't there?"

"Last fall, when you were kidnapped, this fear took over. What if that had been me? What would I have done?"

"Ashley, no one knows what they'd do if what happened to me happened to them. There's no way to plan, no way to prepare for being kidnapped and almost having your kidney cut out."

"You say it like you're ordering a fried chicken dinner. Like you weren't scared at all."

"I was petrified."

"And then Brody and all those people saved you."

"Thank God."

"No one is going to save me. I need to save myself. I've lived in Wachapreague all my life, and instead of leaving for college like all my friends, I stayed here, went to community college and took online classes. All safe." Ashley wrung her hands. "But the thing is…I'm dying here."

"Are you sick? What's wrong? I have contacts in the medical community. We'll get you the best care."

"God, I love you." She shifted the bag of groceries into the crook of her left arm and threw her right around Darby. "No, I'm not sick, not literally dying. I'm dying emotionally.

We're reading works by Joseph Campbell in my Sociology class. There's this quote. He said, 'We must be willing to get rid of the life we've planned, so as to have the life that is waiting for us.' I don't have anything planned for my life, but I want the one waiting for me. I'm afraid I won't do anything meaningful with my life. And I need to find out what I'm made of, who I am. If I don't leave now, I'm afraid I never will."

"What did your parents say when you told them?"

"Nothing. Dad was too drunk to hear me, and my mother... Let's just say you've shown me more caring than she ever did."

"I do care about you, Ashley, very much. You've been here for two years, and you're family. Brianna is going to be terribly upset."

"I know. I don't know how I'm going to tell her. I'm hoping you can help me."

"What are your plans? Where will you go? What will you do?"

"I've been accepted at the University of Miami so I can finish my bachelor's, and then I'm going to law school. My classes don't get out until May, and I've got projects, papers and exams to get through."

"What can I do to help you?"

"Let me come back if it doesn't work out."

"Absolutely. Wherever I am, you always have a home with me. Don't ever worry about that."

"Thank you."

"Come on," said Darby wrapping her free arm around Ashley's waist. "I've got a hungry little girl inside. And a pizza getting cold."

Ashley's news that she was leaving hit Darby hard. Coming so soon after Dennis's death and the kidnapping, it compounded her stress. She'd always known Ashley would leave eventually. Everyone had to spread their wings, and Wachapreague was a small town—but with everything that was going on, the timing couldn't be worse. The living arrangement had worked so well for all of them. Ashely lived rent-free in exchange for taking care of Brianna, and she and Ken Bennett, the sanctuary manager, had become more like extended family than employees.

It was after midnight, another sleepless night. Darby got out of bed and headed straight for the kitchen to get her soul-soothing food of choice out of the freezer—Haagen Dazs chocolate chocolate chip—and grabbed a spoon from the drainboard. She pried off the lid, closed her eyes, and dug in. The first spoonful was always the best, the cold, creamy confection melting on her tongue, its sweetness tickling her taste buds. Eating chocolate chocolate chip ice cream was better than talking to a shrink for working out any problem.

"Brianna's going to be devastated. Heck, I'm devastated." She scraped her spoon across the ice cream. "Change sucks."

The problem de jour robbing her of sleep was a combination of puppy mills and dog fighting. The Agricultural Committee would be voting on Tori and Ashely's puppy mill ordinance soon, but no one was even looking into dog fighting.

When she closed her eyes, she saw Mercy's face and the pain the little pup endured. Darby was convinced she'd been used as bait to train dogs for the fighting ring.

"I want them to pay for the suffering they've caused. Now I just have to figure out who's behind it and how to stop them." She picked out a chocolate bit and crunched it. "How? How do I put an end to dog fighting? If not everywhere, at least here?"

She skimmed the ice cream and put another spoonful into her mouth.

"It's already against the law, so they're not scared of getting caught."

Another spoonful.

"Why aren't they worried about getting caught?" She held the spoon upside down in her mouth, her tongue nestled in its curve.

"What *would* they be afraid of?"

CHAPTER 7

Darby saw a full load of patients the next day. It felt good to be in scrubs, in familiar surroundings, doing routine things like yearly physicals, trimming nails on Mrs. Robinson's cat, aspirating the anal glands on Mrs. Kline's poodle, JoJo, removing a nail from Mr. Knowles's German shepherd's front paw.

"You look beat," said Josie when Darby stopped in the reception area after her last patient left.

"Long day."

"They've all been long since you took on so many of Dennis's patients."

"I'm the closest vet. Can't say no. It'll settle down in a few weeks, and then we'll learn how to work at our new normal pace."

"Maybe. Can't help but wonder if Dr. Graves is seeing an uptick in his practice."

"I'm sure he is, and I'll probably see him tomorrow at the Kiwanis breakfast, so I'll ask him."

"Are you ever sorry you didn't partner with ACC? I know they came to you before they went to Dr. Graves."

"How do you know that?"

"Come on, Darby. You've been here long enough to know how fast word travels. Small towns. Love 'em or move."

Darby hung up her lab coat, pulled out her scrunchie, and scratched the back of her head. "Animal Care Clinics is a good operation—fast-growing and well-funded. Its model wasn't a good fit for how I want to deliver veterinary medicine, but Tony thought it could work for him."

"Is it?"

"What?"

"Working for him?"

"For the most part. There are a few hitches he complains about when we talk, but nothing he can't handle, especially considering the perks. His patients get good care, and that's what's important."

"In fifteen-minute increments. They only allow fifteen minutes for each appointment. Heck, it takes five minutes to settle most pups down."

"It's a good fit for him."

"But it leaves you at a disadvantage. You're the only vet for miles without a huge corporation behind you."

"Only means I have fewer resources, especially now that Dennis is gone. Our sharing arrangement really helped both of us."

"It also means each furry baby gets individualized care. You're not some machine vet with regimented fifteen-minute appointments."

"Enough. What's done is done." Darby smiled at Josie. She put on her sweater and picked up her backpack. "Anything I need to know before I go?"

"Not really. Moose is your first appointment tomorrow. He comes in at ten."

"I love Moose. He's the cutest cat."

"Very undignified name for a Siamese."

"See you in the morning," said Darby as she opened the door and ran into an almost hysterical Henrietta James, who was clutching her new puppy, Scarecrow, wrapped in a towel.

"Thank God you're still here. There's something wrong with Scarecrow. He's throwing up and gagging, and I can't get him to stop."

Darby backed into the clinic, dropped her backpack and took Scarecrow into her arms. She could feel the little guy trembling. "How long has he been like this?"

"Since this morning. I didn't want to panic too soon. You know how I get after losing Trixie so suddenly. But it's getting worse not better."

"When did it start?"

"I'm not sure. Only got him on Saturday. He slept most of yesterday, but I figured it was because it was such a rainy cold day. We have an appointment for tomorrow, but I didn't feel it was safe to wait any longer."

"Good thinking. Where did you get him?"

"Puppies on Parade in Virginia Beach. He's so cute. A little on the thin side for a Cairn, but I know I can fatten him up. Then when he wouldn't eat his puppy food I got concerned, so I made him some plain chicken. He ate some."

"Drinking water?"

"Not a lot. Dr. Darby, something's wrong."

"Come on. Let's see what we can figure out." Darby led the way into exam room one. "Josie, could you call Ashley and tell her I'm going to be late?"

"Already done." Darby shot her a grateful look.

Twenty minutes later the door to exam room one opened and a somewhat relieved Henrietta walked out with Scarecrow in her arms.

"Upper respiratory infection," said Darby to Josie who prepared the bill. "Pretty sure it's not parvovirus, so that's a good thing. We'll have to wait for the lab results to confirm."

"Whew. I was so scared I was going to lose him."
Henrietta's eyes teared up. "I can't take another death right
now."

"You've had a difficult time, I know, Henrietta. Milton
was a wonderful man."

"We'd been married fifty-two years. And then to lose
Trixie. I wasn't ready."

"Trixie had a great life."

"Who knew it would be so short? Now it's just me in that
big house. The kids have their own lives. They're close,
Virginia Beach, but I don't want to intrude too much. I
thought a puppy would be good company. And he was so
cute. Just sitting there in his kennel. The guy at the pet store
said he came from a very reputable breeder down the road in
Cape Charles. So I bought him."

"Dogs are a lot of work, and a puppy… It's like having a
baby all over again. Are you sure you're up for it?"

"Yes." Henrietta scratched Scarecrow's ears and stroked
the top of his head. "I'm totally ready. Will he be okay?"

"Let's give it some time. Here's his medication. One pill
every twelve hours. I gave him an antibiotic injection, so
wait to start the pills till tomorrow. Bring him back on
Saturday around noon. He won't be done with his meds, but
I want to check his progress."

"You're a dear, Darby. Thank you."

"And call my cell if his condition changes tonight."
Darby wrapped her arms around Henrietta and gave
Scarecrow one last scratch before escorting them to the door.

After Henrietta left, Josie said, "There's another Cairn
coming in Wednesday for his initial puppy visit. New
people. Kingsley is the name. When I asked if there was
anything going on with the pup, Mrs. Kingsley said he had
loose stool. She's bringing a sample with her."

"Okay. What's bothering you?"

"Same store. Puppies on Parade in Virginia Beach."

"Let's leave it for tomorrow. Call them when you get in and see what you can find out over the phone. Pretend you're in the market for a pup. If I have to, I can always take a ride to Virginia Beach and check the place out myself. Come on. Get your things, and let's get out of here."

A bulldog-looking man came out of the barn and headed toward Tommy and Buddy's clearly marked sheriff's car with a cocky stride, like he just got off a horse, his thumbs hooked into his belt loops. Pushing back a dingy straw hat, mopping his brow with a filthy red bandanna, he looked at the intruders and smiled.

"You folks lost? This here's private property."

"No. We're not lost," said Tommy as he got out of the car, leaving Buddy behind the wheel. "We're looking for Wilbur Trent."

"That'd be me." He took off his hat and raked beefy fingers through sweaty hair. Dull, expressionless eyes met Tommy's.

"I'm Tommy Everett, with the Accomack sheriff's office."

"That you, Buddy?" asked the man, looking right past Tommy as if he wasn't there.

"Yeah, Wilbur, it's me."

"We're looking into the death of Dr. Lancaster," said Tommy, surprised Buddy hadn't gotten out of the car. "He shows you as a client of his veterinary practice."

"That so?"

"Yeah." Tommy pulled out a notepad and pen. "We're talking to all of his clients, trying to build a picture of his practice and who might have seen him recently."

"Doc Lancaster's dead, you say?"

"Very dead," said Tommy. "And we're just making sure we have all the facts, so if you could just tell us the last time you and he met, we'll be on our way."

"Can't rightly say. Haven't had the need for a vet in a coon's age. Didn't use Doc unless there was a problem one of us couldn't handle." He wiped the back of his neck with the grimy red bandana. "And we been raising horses and farming for years, so there ain't too much one of us haven't seen."

"Who exactly are you including in your we?" Tommy looked at Buddy, hoping he'd ask a question or two, but Buddy remained silent, gazing out the windshield over the field.

Wilbur Trent stuck the handkerchief back in his pocket and walked over to the driver's side window. "Come on, Buddy. You know how it goes. We're all kin, and we work together out here. If I don't know how to handle something, I call Earl or Beau before I go dropping money for a vet. Shit, Earl'd skin me alive if he knew I'd waste money on a vet."

"I know, Wilbur, but we have to check."

"You done?"

"For now." Tommy looked Wilbur up one side and down the other.

"Let's go, Tommy," said Buddy. "We ain't gonna learn anything else out here. And it'll be dark before we get back. Mandy's making me dinner tonight, and I want to clean up."

Tommy walked around to the passenger side, got in, slammed the door and glared at Buddy. "You could have been a little more helpful. These are your people."

"And that's the reason I let you take the lead. There's kin, and then there's kin. Wouldn't want to give the impression that I might be soft on any of them because of a distant family tie."

"You weren't soft. You were nonexistent."

"Face it, Tommy. Wilbur Trent had nothing to tell us. Earl's his brother-in-law, and both are cheaper than dirt. Wouldn't spend the money for a vet, probably even if one of his prize horses was dying. I'm pretty sure if the school didn't require a health checkup before each year starts, their kids would never see a doctor either."

"You're kidding, right?"

"No, I'm not. Things are done different out here. Just how it is. They don't like outsiders. Take care of their own."

Tommy stared at Buddy for a good, long minute. He wanted to challenge him on his family ties to the Trents and the Sojacks, but he held his tongue. There would be time, he thought. And he needed something more concrete than his gut screaming at him.

"You gonna start the car?" asked Tommy. "You're the one with the hot dinner date."

CHAPTER 8

Darby had been awake for hours, her right arm flung above her head, her fingers twisting strands of her hair, her mind a flurry of activity. Brianna slept sweetly beside her. She showed up with Snoodles about an hour ago, and was now fast asleep, tucked against Darby's side, her head nestled in the crook of Darby's left arm. Casper, Tucker and Sammy Jo had claimed the foot of the bed for their own. What a sight! Daughter and three pooches snoring away, Mom keeping watch.

Sheba was on the floor next to the bed. She hadn't left Darby's side while she was home since Darby brought her home. Every day, when Darby left, Sheba lay next to the door, waiting for her to return. She only ate when Darby fed her.

Competing thoughts had Darby tossing and turning for yet another night. She couldn't get Brody out of her mind. It had been months since she'd seen him, and their calls were getting more strained. It was her fault. When he called, she was usually busy with something and begged off, telling him she'd call him back later. Sometimes she did, most times she didn't.

Darby straightened her left leg, nudging Tucker, who looked at her, yawned, and plopped his head back down. She lifted her head off the bed to check the time. Five o'clock. Another hour before everyone got moving. Her right forearm slid down to her head and she covered her eyes.

Brody's week-long visit at Thanksgiving had been heaven-sent. For once in her life, everything went right. Brianna was shy at first, but by the time he carved the turkey, she was glued to his side. And he couldn't get enough of her. He took her horseback riding, holding her snugly in the saddle in front of him, her screams of joy music to a mother's ears. They played catch, tag, and he even seemed to enjoy being a guest at her dolls' tea party.

Christmas was awesome. There had never been a man in the house at Christmas, and Darby didn't know what to expect. After what felt like an endless argument, Brody finally agreed to stay in her guest room rather than at the Wachapreague Inn. But he'd set strict ground rules to ensure Brianna didn't accidentally catch them in a compromising position. Her mind wandered to stolen kisses and quick embraces, while her imagination worked overtime imagining making love with Llewelyn Brody. Keeping her hands to herself had been challenging.

She loved that he thought enough of her daughter's emotional well-being to stipulate up front what was out-of-bounds while Brianna was around. It both surprised and delighted her. Everything he did, everything he said, confirmed her initial impression—Brody was a keeper.

Her only question. Could she keep him?

One of their more interesting conversations replayed in a loop in her head, word-for-word, like it happened a moment ago.

"About Bri. I…I'm…how can I say this without sounding like an ass?"

"You're a mom. Just say it, though I suspect I already know what you're gonna say."

"Think so?"

"Know so. You're worried that Brianna might become, you know, attached to me, since I'm visiting again so soon." He had tucked a stray strand of hair behind her ear. "Like I told you at Thanksgiving, I'm not going anywhere."

"That's exactly what Benjamin told me before we got married. Then his best friend was killed in Iraq, and he felt honor bound to join up."

"Been there done that. My war days are behind me."

"I never expected Benjamin to have any wars days since he wasn't in the military when we got married."

"Things change. Events happen, and they change us. It's about how we respond to those changes. Your husband honored his friend. You can't fault him for that."

"I don't. He was a good man. What I worry about is going through that pain again. I'm not sure I'd survive it, even with Brianna depending on me. And you still put yourself out there.

"I do. For friends and family."

"You rescued me and you didn't even know me."

"But you were important to someone on my team, someone I care about, and that was all that mattered." She remembered Brody's touch as he lifted her chin ever so gently to look into her eyes.

"I get to use my unique talents and training with people I trust like Kyle, Moss, TJ, and Brett, in an environment where we control the battle, not some stupid politicians in DC, most of whom have never laid their lives on the line."

"I hear that."

"Darby, honey, I'm in this for the long haul. If we play our cards right, take it slow, don't screw up, Brianna will come out on top, and so will you."

"You're that sure this fast?"

"This isn't my first rodeo. I'm older and wiser. Know what I want. Just waiting for you to catch up."

Then there was the bombshell Ashley dropped. She was leaving. The news couldn't have come at a worse time, but she understood Ashley's reasoning, and in many ways agreed with her decision. The Eastern Shore was a small, isolated place. Ashley needed to broaden her world, experience new things, meet new people. *There's no dress rehearsal for your life. If she doesn't do it now, when will she?* Telling Brianna was going to be hard, but she'd soften the blow by assuring the little girl that Ashley loved her and would come visit often.

Darby looked at the clock. Five forty-five. Close enough. Time to rise and shine. Work would take her mind off Ashley, off Brody. The image of Dennis lying in his own blood was going to be much harder to erase from her mind.

Unfortunately, when her mind wasn't on Brody, or Ashley, or Dennis's death, it ran a looped replay of Chrissy and Brianna at the food mart. Mrs. Trent's scowl was etched in her memory. What was bothering her so much about this woman's curt reaction to Brianna wanting to play with puppies?

She snuck out of bed so as not to awaken Brianna, pulled her hair into a ponytail and headed downstairs to get the coffee going.

Her cell vibrated in her pocket.

"Hello."

Silence.

"Not again." Answering the phone to no one, or to heavy breathing had become routine, starting right after her meeting with Delegate Cummings about the puppy sourcing bill.

"Hello?"

Silence.

"Who is this? I know you're there. I can hear you breathing."

A click. The line went dead.

"Asshole."

Darby pressed the End button and stared at the phone. Searching missed calls proved useless. Nothing showed up, like the call never happened. She noted the date and time on the sheet of paper she'd put on the counter in the kitchen.

"I see we're starting the day off with a bang. Wonder how many hang ups I'll get today."

Three hang ups yesterday, and two the day before. Someone wanted to get her attention. She assumed it related to her support of the sourcing bill. Nothing else made sense.

The phone chirped again. She let her fury off the leash. "Look, whoever you are, I'm done playing your stupid game. Call again, and I'll have the sheriff trace the call, find out who you are, and bring you up on harassment charges. Got that, asshole?"

"Darby?"

"Who is this?"

"It's Brody, honey. What's going on? You okay?"

"Oh, Brody. I'm so sorry." She bit her tongue, not wanting to lie to him, but not ready to share all the crap that had been going on in her life. So far she'd only shared her concerns about the puppy mill and the dog fighting. "I'm fine. Just been getting a few annoying hang ups lately. No biggie. Probably some local kids fooling around. How are you?"

"I'm good. We hadn't talked in a few days, so I thought I'd give you a call. Hope I didn't wake you."

"No. In fact I can't really talk now. I've got to get Brianna ready for school. Can I call you later?"

"Sure. I've got the morning shift this week. I get off at three today. How about we talk after dinner?"

"Sounds good to me. I'll call around seven."

"It's a date."

Brody's phone rang exactly at seven.

"I love a woman who's prompt. How are you?"

"I'm okay."

"Funny. You didn't sound okay this morning."

"A lot of stuff going on."

Brody's forehead knotted. "You said that this morning. What's up?"

"Just busy. Got a lot of new patients. And two new puppy patients have been sick. Looks like another pet store lied about only dealing with reputable breeders. I know these puppies came from a puppy mill, and it makes me angry."

"I hate those places. Can't understand why anyone buys a puppy from a pet store. You said Ashley was going to participate in a protest at the local pet shop. How'd it go?"

"It was good. They sold a lot of T-shirts, raised some money for the cause, but they're up against some huge corporations with a lot of money to spread around in politicians' pockets. Hell, they'd have to be out there every hour of the day in front of every pet store to stop people from buying whatever adorable little fur ball catches their eye. And don't get me started about online sales. That's a huge black hole."

"Puppies are pure emotion," said Brody. "People don't think about where the puppy comes from, only that they want it. And want it now."

"I know. Ashley and Tori shot a video of a huge tractor-trailer pulling up at the back of a local store and unloading puppies. It was after hours and a little dark—"

"Not like they'd unload in the light of day."

"Anyone seeing it would know the puppies were from a commercial breeding operation and not the loving home-raised breeders they claim. We uploaded it to YouTube."

"Don't most places like PetSmart do adoption days?"

"Yes. They're great, and all the rescue groups and local humane societies push adoption. There are so many wonderful people working tirelessly to help dogs and cats who are unwanted for any number of reasons. Unfortunately, it doesn't stop enough people from buying at pet stores or online. Supply and demand. Follow the money. You name the cliche. It fits."

"You sound so down."

"I am. And then there's Ashley leaving—"

"What? Ashley's leaving?" Brody knew that had to hit her hard.

"Yeah. She told me the other day. She's going to finish her degree in Miami and then go to law school. The puppy mill project she started and roped me into gave her a much-needed focus. I'm proud of her, but stressed. She's leaving at the end of the semester. That means May. I don't know what I'm going to do without her."

"Have you told Brianna yet?"

"No. I keep hoping she'll change her mind, or something will pop up for her here, but I know it's not going to happen. And for her sake, it can't. She needs to leave here, make her way in the world, find something she loves to do."

"Do you ever think about leaving there?"

A long silence filled the air.

"This is my home."

She heard him take a deep breath. "Home is anywhere you make it. With people you love and who love you." Another breath. "I have an idea. Before you say anything, hear me out. It's wild. It's crazy."

"Your ideas usually are."

"But I promise you, it will be fun, and I'm confident you won't be sorry. Think of it as the ultimate adventure."

"Mothers don't do adventures. Especially not when we have a five-year-old daughter to take care of. We do logical. We do safe. We do predictable."

"You can't tell me what's been happening in your life these last six months has been predictable."

Darby stared at the phone. "Point taken. Okay, I'm listening. What's your idea?"

"Move here. I've been talking to Marco, TJ's boss, and he knows some people who know some people who can make you a really good offer on some land down here."

"You're right. That's a crazy idea." Her smile belied her words. "Moving would only add to the craziness. What I want is calm. Normal."

"Normal is highly overrated."

"But right now, calm and normal are highly desirable."

"What is highly desirable for me is you, here."

Darby didn't answer. She didn't trust her voice, wasn't sure what would come out.

"I'm sorry, Darby. With all that's going on up there, I was just throwing out an idea in my sloppy guy way." He waited but she said nothing.

Tears pooled in Darby's eyes and her throat ached. What was that saying? *The truth hurts.* And, truth be told, she had thought about, had daydreamed about a new place, a different place, with a more complete family, and acres and acres of land for all her furry family.

"Want me to come up?"

"No. It's okay. I'm just tired." She ran her fingers through her hair. "I gotta go. Brianna needs her bath."

"You rest well, love. I'll talk to you tomorrow."

"'Night, Brody."

She clicked off, held the phone to her chest and whispered, "I love you."

What the hell am I so afraid of?

CHAPTER 9

They gathered at dusk. Hardy, hardworking men. Flannel shirts covering wife-beaters. Jeans and overalls riddled with dirt and sweat. They were there for one reason and one reason only. A night of drinking and carousing. A night to lose themselves, forget about the mortgage, the kids, paying for their braces, the nagging wife. To hang with the guys, throw back some beers, and cut loose.

Tonight's match was being held in a back pasture, as far from the main Sojack farm as you could get and still be on Sojack land. The roads leading to the clearing were unmarked, so only invited guests would be able to successfully navigate them. And tonight's code word, the sign on the main road marking the first turn, was "honey," chosen because there were several unbeaten champions fighting. The email flyer announcing the match promised everyone a "honey" of an evening.

Buddy tensed as the crowd grew. He had a lot to lose if someone saw him, but saying no to Earl was akin to signing your own death certificate. He'd volunteered to work security along the outer rim of the parking field. That way he could stay in the shadows, out of sight, unless some of the guests got too rowdy. Good thing the spectators were mostly from out of town, and they knew the code, the secret handshake, and to keep their mouths shut.

"What do you know?" Wilbur asked Earl lightheartedly as he came up behind him.

"I know we're creating a stir among certain local folks. That's what I know."

"What do you mean?"

Earl gave him an evil-eyed stare, his thin lips taut. "You got shit for brains, boy? Your kid? Chrissy?" Smoke wafted through his nose and mouth, spent ash hanging precariously from the business end of the hand-rolled cigarette pressed between his tobacco-stained lips.

"Wanda told me Chrissy talked about the puppies at school. Ran into some kid and her mother at the store, wanting to see the puppies. Shit, Wilbur. Don't we have enough to worry about without your little rug rat shooting her mouth off?"

"She never said anything to me, but I don't think Chrissy was shooting her mouth off. You know how kids are."

"I know how they should be. Seen, but not heard," Earl snarled.

"Those days are long gone, I'm afraid. But my kid talking in school can't be what's got a stick up your ass."

"A dead vet ring any bells? Who ordered the hit?"

"What hit? Word around town is that Doc committed suicide."

"Believe that and I've got some swamp land in Florida ripe for development."

"That's what they're saying. You know something they don't know?"

"No. Too many coincidences for comfort, is all."

"Not on my end. Think someone took matters into his own hands?"

"No one does nothing around here without me giving the go-ahead. And I sure as hell didn't authorize removing Doc from this world." Earl flicked his cigarette butt down and ground it into the dirt with his heel. "Suicide, my ass. What do you know about the lady vet?"

"Not much. Been here 'bout three years, give or take. Her kid's in school with Chrissy. Was it her in the store?"

"Ya think?!"

"I hear she's a good vet. Up on the latest procedures. Talk around town is she saved that runt pup Thor almost killed."

"You're kidding. Thought it was a goner for sure when I had Rory toss it. Shoulda just killed it and buried it out back like the rest."

"She set up a Go-Fund-Me page to help with its medical bills. I hear it's got over six thousand dollars in it already."

"Wish people would mind their own business." Earl lit up another cigarette. "Think I may have to meet this lady vet."

Wilbur's eyes swept the growing crowd. "Gonna be a good night."

"Better be. Need to hook 'em into coming back for the big match next week between Thor and Bullet."

Darby plugged in the flash drive and spent the evening at her computer, digging through Dennis's emails. An invitation to dinner he turned down saddened the woman who sent it. Another email confirmed Dennis's speaking engagement at the Virginia Beach Rotary. A third confirmed his attendance at a veterinary conference in DC next month. All routine. All boring. None giving her a hint of why he might decide to take his own life.

She found several purchase orders attached to emails reordering various supplies and drugs. One discussed a mix-up in an order for Tramadol, which surprised her. According to the email, dated two weeks ago, the supplier informed Dennis that four bottles would be shipped the following day. She noted the email's date and realized the shipment should have arrived the day after they found Dennis's body. She didn't remember seeing a package either time she was in Dennis's office. And his receptionist, Luanne, had not been back to the office, having left town the day after Dennis's body was found. Other than herself, only Tracy had a key, but she would have no reason to go into the clinic either. The government was cracking down on veterinarians, requiring mounds of paperwork accounting for everything they ordered. So where were the drugs?

She looked up when she heard the back door slam.

"Why the sad faces?" she asked when Ashley and Tori came into the kitchen. They looked like they'd lost their best friend.

"They killed it. The bastards killed it," said Ashley, plopping down on a chair across from Darby. "A semester's worth of work down the tubes."

"We only got two of seven votes on the agricultural subcommittee." Tori's pretty face twisted into a cross between anger and grief. "So our bill won't get to the House of Delegates for a full vote. We have to wait until next January and start all over again."

Darby shot a quick look at Ashley, wondering if she'd told Tori she was leaving. "There's beer in the fridge if you want to drown your sorrows."

"Thanks." Ashley got up and pulled two beers out, giving one to Tori and returning to her seat.

"Hopefully we'll get the unanimous Senate vote again," sighed Tori, after taking a seat and guzzling her beer, "unless someone loses the election and we have to start sucking up to a new senator and convince him of the merits of the bill."

"I'm so sorry. You both worked really hard, and you should be proud of yourselves."

"Would have been prouder if the assholes on the agricultural committee weren't close-minded jerks." Tori finished off her beer and started picking at the label with her fingernail.

"Did they tell you why?"

"Slippery slope crap," said Ashley. "If we make restrictions on puppies, what about horses or pigs?"

"It's not fair. All that work for nothing." Tori got up and tossed her empty bottle into the recycle bin.

"Tori, it wasn't for nothing. You and Ashley got a good education in how the system works."

"Yeah, it sucks."

"Sometimes it does. But you know your opposition now, and have the summer to plan your arguments to counter their resistance."

"But we don't," said Ashley. "I'm leaving, remember?"

"Then Tori, you'll have to find another partner. What about the guys who helped you film the video?"

"Their commitment was about getting in our pants, not saving puppies."

"Okay, then. Maybe someone in your class? Ask around. I'll bet you can find someone to take Ashley's place. And I'm still here to help, too."

"Thanks, Doc."

Chapter 10

A lightning bolt of panic tore through Darby when she came home for lunch the next day, opened the back door, and saw red paw prints leading from the mud room into the kitchen.

Blood?

"Casper? Sammy Jo? Tucker? Sheba?"

All four dogs came running, almost knocking her down, licking her, wagging their tails, so happy to see her. She quickly checked each dog's paws. Nothing cut or hurt, but red streaks dotted Casper's white hair.

She bent down and touched one of the paw prints with her index finger. *Sticky.* She sniffed her fingers and rubbed them together.

"Paint?"

Someone had been in her home, violated her privacy.

Brianna!

Seething like a crazed velociraptor protecting her young, Darby raced to the stairs, but stopped short when she remembered Brianna was at school.

Thank God!

Anguish gripped her, and she slumped down on the bottom step, her head falling into her hands, tears flowing.

Her fur babies surrounded her, nuzzling her, wagging, and making soothing doggy noises.

What if Brianna'd been home?

Darby felt the need to check on her, pulled out her cell, and punched in the school's phone number. She spoke to the principal and demanded that she go look personally and make sure Brianna was in her classroom. "I'll wait," she said adamantly.

Barely five minutes passed before she heard Brianna's sweet voice on the phone. Relief swept over her when she said goodbye.

And then strength took hold.

"No. I will not be a victim. And they will not *touch* Brianna."

Standing, she wiped her tears away and strode back into the kitchen.

"Too precise to be real. These are stencils."

The tracks ended at the cabinet under the sink. Slowly, she opened the cabinet door. Red smears painted stripes on the white garbage can. Slowly, she tipped the can towards her and gasped. Inside was one of Brianna's stuffed teddy bears, its insides ripped out and coated in red paint.

Rage swelled until Darby thought she'd explode. They were threatening Brianna, her precious child. They had no idea who they were up against, or what she was willing to do to protect her daughter.

But they'd soon find out.

Deputy Buddy Jenkins arrived within ten minutes of her call.

"Where's Tommy?"

"Said he had an errand to run, and I told him I could handle this on my own."

His visit was short and to the point. Nothing showed on the security cameras, so whoever broke into her home knew how to avoid being seen. Ken Bennett had been running errands, and Ashley was in class, so neither could shed any light on the intruder, and there were none of the usual signs of a break-in. He called for a tech team to come out and dust for prints, but short of finding any, which he doubted they would, there was little he could do.

She stared after Buddy as he drove away. The prank phone calls were one thing, but a home invasion crossed the line. Far, far beyond the line.

Without thinking, she pulled out her cell and speed-dialed the one man she knew could help her. Brody.

She didn't know how he'd respond. Every time they spoke, the distance between them grew wider and wider. His idea about moving to Florida and her silence exacerbated the situation, and confirmed again that long distance relationships carried more baggage than a tourist-laden 747 during spring break.

But she knew he had what she needed.

"Brody."

His voice sent chills down her spine. She wanted and needed this man, but fought her desires with logic and a fear of being hurt again.

"It's me."

"Is everything okay? You sound funny. What's going on?"

"I…I…it's…"

Dread fueled his voice. "Are you and Brianna okay?"

"Yes, we're fine. But…"

"You're making me worry about you, and it seems that's all I do lately is worry about you. Is there something to be worried about?"

She heard the sharpness in his words and instantly regretted calling.

"Well, the thing is…there's been some trouble up here. I told you one of the local vets died a few weeks ago. What I didn't say was it was ruled a suicide. At first they tried to blame Sheba, his dog, for mauling him. She was covered in blood when we found them. But she's the sweetest thing. Wouldn't hurt a fly. And they found a gun."

"We found him? Who's we?"

"Me and two local cops.

"I remember you telling me one of your colleagues died, but you didn't say you found the body."

"I know. I didn't want you to worry about me, so I left that part out."

"What else did you leave out?"

"Tommy, one of the detectives who was with me when we found him, thinks it might not be a suicide. Thinks Dennis was murdered."

"Murdered? Does he have anything to back that up?"

"Not yet. More of a gut call, mostly because the wound was to his neck."

"Shooting yourself in the neck is a very hard shot for a suicide, so I agree with your detective friend. But how does this affect you, besides being sad about losing a colleague so tragically and getting some new patients?"

She took a deep breath. "Someone's been in my house."

"What?" She knew Brody was pacing around the room. She'd seen him take business calls when they were together, and pacing was his modus operandi.

"Whoever it was destroyed one of Brianna's stuffed animals. Used red paint and made paw prints on my floor."

"Darby, honey, that's very personal."

"But why?"

"The why is easy. To scare you. Somebody wants to scare you big time. Threatened the person most dear to you. The teddy bear was a warning. What we don't know is who. Who broke into your house? Did you call the police?"

"Yes. Buddy, the other detective who was with me when we found Dennis, came. Said there's little they could do. No sign of forced entry. Techs found no prints."

"What about the security cameras? Anything show up there?"

"Nothing. Buddy and I reviewed the tape."

Brody remembered the extra cameras he had installed unbeknownst to Darby. If nothing showed up on the tape replay, the only assumption he could make was that the intruder scoped the place out somehow, saw where the security cameras were, and avoided them. The mark of a professional.

"Both Ashley and Ken were out and..." She took a deep breath. "And Brianna was in school."

He could hear her struggling to hold it together.

"I didn't know who else to call."

"I'm glad you called me. Can you think of anyone you've pissed off lately?

"N-no. Maybe some folks who don't like me supporting the puppy mill bill, but this seems like overkill. The bill's already dead for this year, and there are easier ways to kill a bill, like paying off a politician. No one would be the wiser."

Then the dam broke and she sobbed.

"Please don't cry," he said. "I can be there in about two hours."

"How?" She pulled the phone away from her ear for a second. "Where are you?"

"Williamsburg. I was going to tell you the other night when we talked, but I didn't want you to feel I was intruding on your space. Rachel invited us up for Passover dinner. I came this morning so I could help cook."

"Oh!" Her mouth started to water as memories of other things he'd cooked swamped her senses. "Bet she's making brisket."

"There's brisket, chicken fricassee, and gefilte fish. At least the thought of food got you to stop crying."

"Chopped liver?"

"Would a Jewish holiday be a Jewish holiday without it?"

"No." Food is memory, she thought, her mind drifting to a time years ago when holiday dinners had special meaning. "How do you know so much about Jewish holiday foods?"

"Had a Jewish mom. If I say so myself, my brisket is to die for."

"I've had your cooking, so I don't doubt it. My mom was Jewish, too."

"Another thing we have in common."

"Love brisket. Can't remember the last time I had chopped liver." She sniffled into the phone. "I'm sorry. I don't mean to be such a wimp. It's all just too much."

"You're not a wimp. You're a concerned mom. I can only imagine how scared you are after all you've been through. Why do you think I've been trying so hard to get you to visit me in Florida? You need a change of scenery."

"I suppose you're right."

"You know I am." And then, without missing a beat, "And I'll make it easy. Come here. To Rachel's. Pack some clothes for you and Brianna, go pick her up from school, and hit the road."

"I wouldn't want to intrude."

"You kidding? I know Rachel won't mind. She's a more-the-merrier lady and she'd love to meet you after all she's heard. You've got plenty of time to get here. Seder dinner isn't until tomorrow night."

"She wants to meet me, huh? Who's been talking out of school?"

"I might have said a few things while I was chopping onions."

"Great."

"Hey, look on the bright side. You'll get a great meal."

"If I remember Passover dinner right, we're talking a four-hour meal with lots of wine."

"We're doing seder lite. Kind of like a CliffsNotes version. I promise."

While she was blowing her nose, she heard him say, "Come on up. You can tell me what's going on. The gang's all here."

"The gang?"

"Moss is here, and so are Carolyn, Kyle, Marco, and his fiancée, Marissa."

Brody was right. After confirming with Rachel that two more mouths to feed wouldn't be an imposition, and hearing Rachel's assurances that she had a bedroom waiting for them, Darby packed a bag for herself and Brianna, asked Ken Bennett to take care of the dogs, and hit the road.

It was after seven when she pulled into Rachel's driveway. The front door opened and a mob of people rushed out to greet them. Her heart raced and her stomach clutched when she saw Brody, but she clamped down the urge to run into his arms.

Too needy.

But she did need him, needed to feel his strong arms around her, his breath in her ear as he whispered sweet nothings, and promised her everything would be okay.

She peeked in the rearview mirror and saw that Brianna was slowly waking up. Then she looked back to Brody and her heart kicked. She put the car in park, stopped the engine, popped her seat belt, opened the door, and ran into his outstretched arms.

Brody made the rest of the introductions, and watched Darby hug everyone. *God, she's beautiful! What a smile. A man could get lost in that smile. I sure am.*

Darby ignited sensations in him he'd worked hard to ignore for years. He was a man of strength—a man of action, not feelings. Let your emotions get even the slightest foothold in your psyche, and your life went to shit. That had been his experience—his past experience.

Why he dared to tempt the emotion monster with Darby didn't make sense. Then again, nothing about his reaction to Darby made sense. *The heart wants what the heart wants.* From the moment he saw her, so helpless and tied to the gurney, every waking thought had been about her. He was acting like a goofy schoolboy. The more he tried to stop, the worse it got. The only people enjoying his plight were his coworkers, who teased him mercilessly every chance they got.

Thanksgiving was the best he could remember. But Christmas…Christmas was exceptional. He finally understood Christmas after watching the unabashed joy in Brianna's eyes as she opened her presents. Seeing Christmas through the eyes of a child was priceless, and he found himself wanting more.

The love bug had bitten him, hard, and it was an itch he planned to enjoy scratching. For a long, long time. And, as much as he never pictured himself being a father, he was head-over-heels gaga over Brianna.

He'd made his decision. Darby and Brianna were the family he had convinced himself he didn't deserve. But he planned to do everything in his power to convince Darby their relationship could work. He'd only told TJ of his plans. Surprise her. Arrive unexpectedly. Spend a few normal days together without the holiday crazies to offer distractions. And at the end of the week, pop the question.

Now this. A stranger in her house. Painted paws on the floor to make it look like blood. Scaring her with a slashed teddy bear, dripping red paint. Whoever it was, was sending a message, and he planned to send one back, loud and clear. *Don't mess with my woman, my family.*

"Brody!" The moment Brianna saw him, she unlatched her seat belt and bolted out of the car, her arms outstretched. "Mommy just said she had a surprise for me. I didn't know we were coming to see you."

"It's so good to see you."

He looked down into the glistening eyes of an innocent child, lifted her into his arms and gave her a big hug. When he put her down, he took her hand and one of their bags and led the way into the house.

Darby walked over to Moss, put her arms around him, and gave him a warm kiss on the cheek.

"It's good to see you."

"You too."

"I never got to thank you."

"Not necessary."

"Yes, very necessary." She hugged him again. "Maybe we could spend some time talking. I'd like to hear about my mother. I think you have a unique perspective."

"We can do that."

"Good. I'll look forward to it."

Moss grabbed the bag in Darby's hand and took up the rear.

Moss excused himself after he heard Darby's story and went out to the back deck. He dialed Ken Bennett, who had remained his man on the scene. Ken loved working for Darby, managing the animal sanctuary.

"I hear there's been some more trouble."

"Nothing like last time. Think it was more an attempt to scare her. She's been working on closing down puppy mills and the pet stores that sell puppies from them, and I'm thinking some owners don't appreciate her meddling. Could also be something connected to the vet who died. I just don't know at this point."

"A stuffed bear ripped to shreds? Sounded mighty personal to hear her tell it."

"I suppose it does."

"How'd someone get into her house?"

"Good question. Not sure about that. Your guy, Brody, got her to upgrade the security system when he was here at Christmas. Then we got the guy to add a few more bells and whistles on the sly. Didn't bother to tell her, so I'd appreciate it if you don't either. She still thinks nothing bad happens out in the country."

"We've got to break her of that thinking."

"I agree. But after what she's been through, now is not the time. I convinced her I needed a helper and got her to hire an Army buddy of mine, so I've increased coverage."

"Sounds like you're on top of things. Keep me posted."

"Will do."

CHAPTER 11

Brody finally got Darby alone by pulling her into the powder room. He touched her face, the back of his hand barely grazing her cheek.

"I've missed you."

And then she was in his arms. He kissed the top of her head and held her tight. His fingers deftly pulled out the ponytail scrunchie, freeing her wavy tresses, which now fully framed her face. He slid his hand behind her neck, cradling her head, sought her lips with his own.

"I've wanted to kiss you since you got here." Gently caressing her lips with his, a flame ignited within him, burning to be quenched with more kisses.

"Thanks for waiting. PDAs aren't my thing."

"Mine either."

He gazed into sparkling eyes, noticed flushed cheeks, and ruby-red lips yearning for more.

He pressed her tighter against him, feeling her heat, the pillows of her breasts against his chest. They clung to each other, warm bodies pressing closer and closer together. Vanilla and jasmine scents teased him as he nibbled her neck. Then he slid his lips back onto hers, plunging with his tongue.

"I've missed you, too," she gasped as he again found the soft spot below her ear and her arms encircled his waist.

Darby loved being in Brody's arms, the touch of his hands on her skin, the smell of him, the heat of him. She loved snuggling against him, fitting perfectly into his side.

"Good, because if missing was one-sided, only me missing you, I'd be in a heap of trouble." He found her breasts, his thumbs rubbing her nipples taut. "Only I sense there's a 'but' coming."

She hesitated. "About this 'we' thing." Her fingers made air quotes. "During dinner, the way you referred to us. You keep using we. Like there's a we...an us." Darby looked away. "There is no we...no us."

"Sure there is." His strong hands touched her shoulders, and he turned her to face him squarely. "You just don't know it yet—or haven't accepted it."

"Get real, Brody. I'm here, in Virginia. And you're over a thousand miles away. It's not like Florida and Virginia are neighboring states. Our lives don't intersect."

Soulful eyes, puppy-dog eyes, peered at him through the same long lashes he first fell in love with that horrible day, as she lay helpless on the gurney. He cupped her face gently and smiled. "I'm a patient man. I can wait for you to catch up."

"Thanks. I think I need a little more time. With all that's going on, I'm not..."

Not sure how it would be received, and not wanting to break the magic of the moment, he didn't repeat his idea about her moving to Florida. His thumb gently stroked her cheek.

"You okay?"

"I'm fine." Darby averted her eyes and pulled away from him.

"Are you?" He touched her arm. "Fine?"

"Yes. Why are you asking?"

"The look…on your face. Everything you've been telling us about what's going on at home. It's all trouble. What's got you upset is way more than me using the 'we' word."

She said nothing for what felt like an eternity to Brody, finally sitting down on the toilet seat.

"Awkward silence. Come on. Spit it out."

"Sorry. I'm a little out of practice confiding in anyone."

"It's okay. You're safe with me."

The woman has guts, he thought. She'd gone from victim to woman-in-charge within the six months he'd known her. Her natural confidence punctuated a newfound sense of self, marked by a budding independent streak. There was intention in her actions. He hadn't known her before her ordeal, but what he saw now, he wanted for himself in more ways than he could count.

Darby put her head in her hands. "You're getting to know me too well. Can't hide anything from you."

"I don't want you hiding stuff from me. From all you've told me about what's going on, I want you to know I'm here for you."

"I know… But your 'here' is hundreds of miles away. You've got a job and a life in Florida. All this is happening here, and I can't call you to rescue me every time the big, bad wolf comes calling."

"Sure you can."

Brody knelt beside her and took her hands in his.

"I don't know why anyone would be in my house, let alone rip apart a stuffed bear and paint bloody-looking fake paw prints on my floor."

"What do you think is going on?"

"I don't know."

"Other than the death of the vet you mentioned, is anything else out of the ordinary happening around you?

Anything going on at the sanctuary? Or with Ken or Ashley, that could bleed over onto you?"

"There's the ordinance I'm helping Ashley and her friend get through Virginia's version of Congress, which is now on hold until the next legislative year. Other than that, there's nothing I can think of that would warrant trying to scare me so blatantly."

"What about the hang ups you mentioned?"

"No idea. Tommy, my other cop friend, gave me a number to call the next time it happens. It's supposed to tell me where the call is coming from."

"What about your connection to the dead vet? What's his name?"

"Dennis. Dennis Lancaster." Darby hesitated. "Other than both of us being vets, and two of the three vets who rotate an emergency on-call service on our part of the Eastern Shore, I can't think of anything that would make someone want to rip apart a teddy bear."

A gentle knock at the bathroom door stopped their conversation.

"Shit. So much for a little privacy."

"Be right out," called Brody, sheepishly. "To be continued?" He watched Darby gather strands of her hair and retie her ponytail. He loved her neck, its length, its softness.

"Most definitely. The sooner the better."

"Guess we have to face the music." He unlocked the door and twisted the doorknob. "After you."

The alcove and hall were empty. Whoever had knocked had moved on.

Darby rested her palm over his heart, gazing at him with a peaceful, half-smiling expression.

"I'm glad you decided to come. Just so you know, now that I've heard your story, my plan is to go back to your house with you, spend a few days, and check things out. I think Moss plans to come too. And we've already cleared missing work with TJ."

"The more the merrier. Brianna will be thrilled."

The next twenty-four hours were full of friends, family, food, and fun. The seder and its four required glasses of wine had been so much fun. Everyone doted on Brianna, while she reveled in this new, exciting experience and the friendly attention of so many grownups.

Brody helped her hide the *afikoman*, and coached her to hold out for five dollars before relinquishing it to end the seder. She was now tucked safely in bed, off to dreamland, with Snoodles at her side.

A half-moon cast a shimmering sliver of light along the James River. Beyond that, darkness. Darby sat on the deck wrapped in a blanket to ward off the evening chill. She turned when she heard the door open, and smiled at Carolyn, who held out a wine bottle.

"Thanks," said Darby, when Carolyn topped off her glass. "There were so many people trying to help Rachel clean up, I figured I'd be more help to her by getting out of the way, so I came out here."

"Smart move. Her friend Sara just called, so she's not even supervising," Carolyn laughed, looking through the windows. "Watching the men in the kitchen, military men at that, always tickles me. They move with precision even when all they're doing is loading the dishwasher and putting away leftovers."

"I'm surprised they aren't tripping over each other."

"Nope. Marco divided up the work. He's telling everyone what to do. That's Marco for you. He likes to be in charge."

"Do you know him well?"

"Not really. Met him last year when he helped me find my daughter, Amelia. She got herself in a mess, and I was trying to get her out of it when Kyle literally tripped over me in the woods, hogtied me and carried me off."

"Sounds like there's an interesting story there."

"Hairy for a while, but everything worked out, and now Kyle and I are talking marriage."

"From the conversation at dinner it sounds like the marriage bug has been rather active in your little group. I guess Marco and Marissa are going to head down the aisle soon."

"Yes. I don't know a lot about their history, but Kyle said they've been together for years—decades. They're just going to make it official. And if their wedding is half the affair Marco threw for Rachel and Daniel last year when they got married, it will be the social event of the season. You'll come down for it, won't you?"

"If I'm invited, I'll think about it."

"Oh, you're invited. Brody looked like a lost puppy until you showed up yesterday. The man is smitten."

"Could we not go there?"

"Sure. I'm sorry. I don't mean to touch a sore spot."

"You're not. It's just that…well…when I lost my husband so suddenly three years ago. That pain… I swore I'd never allow myself to get that close to another man—to open myself to that kind of pain—ever again."

"I can understand that. My creep of a husband didn't die, though there were times when I did want to kill him. Divorce is gut-wrenching too."

"I'll drink to that." They clinked glasses. "So, what's the story behind Kyle carrying you off?"

"I almost lost my daughter, Amelia. Just when I was at my wits' end searching for her, Kyle and his band of merry men came into my life and helped save the day." Carolyn stopped talking and stared out into the darkness, across the James River.

"Sounds like you've been through the wringer, too."

"We all have war stories, our histories, our baggage." Carolyn sipped her wine. "I learned a long time ago that my past is just that, past. What's the famous quote? Your past has a vote, not a veto. It can't define me unless I want it to, or let it. When Kyle asked me to stay, I decided to roll the dice and see if we could make it work. These last few months with him have been more wonderful than I ever imagined was possible for me."

"I'm happy for you."

"Thanks."

"Can I borrow your dice?

"With pleasure. Brody's one of the good ones."

"My past is all about moving." Bitterness tinged Darby's voice. "My dad was military, and we moved a lot. Lasting relationships, good friendships, never happened. Just when I'd get close to someone, it was on to the next base. We'd stay in touch for a while, but then life got in the way."

"It's a lonely way to grow up."

"Yes. Although it wasn't all bad. I got to see a lot of the world."

"And look at all you've accomplished." Carolyn took a sip of her wine. "Your parents supported you as you worked to achieve your goals, didn't they?"

"Very much. They were awesome. I am so lucky, and I know it."

"Well, to hear Brody tell it, they raised one fine daughter."

"Thanks." Darby finished her wine and waved Carolyn's hand away when she tried to refill her glass. "I knew I was adopted. They asked me once if I wanted help tracking my birth parents down, but I figured they must have had a good reason for giving me up, so I didn't bother."

"Do you regret it?"

"After meeting the monster who was my biological father, no way. He was the personification of evil. I thank my lucky stars my birth mother gave me up for adoption. But—"

"But?" Carolyn could feel the heaviness of Darby's heart, her pain.

"Having my own daughter changed my thinking. I think I would have liked to know a little about my birth mother. I understand it's too late to meet her. Moss said she died in a boating accident. Something about a faulty gas line."

Carolyn felt the weight of the lie, and the weight of the trinket in her pocket.

"She and Moss were lifelong friends. I asked him about her this afternoon while he was helping me set the table."

"What did he tell you?"

"She was…she was fun. A thousand laughs, he said. And he said she was kind. He told me a story about when she found a wasp trapped between the screen and the window. And how she went into the shed and got out a weed puller and worked it under the screen to lift it enough so she could get her fingers under it. Then she lifted it all the way and used a broom to sweep the wasp to freedom."

"All that for a wasp?" Carolyn tried to reconcile the story with her own memories of Desiree. What could she add that would bring Darby closure?

"Yep. That's what he said." Darby pulled the blanket tighter. "And he said she was beautiful, like me, but I wouldn't go that far. He said he sees her face when he looks at me. I asked him if he had any photos, but he said he didn't."

"She would have been very proud of all you've accomplished. Very proud."

"What makes you say that?"

Carolyn took a deep breath. "I knew your mother, too. Not for as long as Moss, but we spent some time together over the course of several years."

"How did you know her?"

"We met a few years ago. I played in mah jongg tournaments with her." Carolyn's inner voice was working overtime. *Do I go into the ugly details? No. I can choose my words carefully. Darby doesn't need to know anything about her mother's role in kidnapping Amelia. Or how she made her money, imprisoning girls in a hellhole of despair. Let her have positive thoughts about a woman who loved her so much, she gave her up so she could have a better life.*

"Sometimes Brianna asks about her grandparents. I don't think she really understands what grandparents are, exactly. One of her dear friends lives with her mom, grams and poppa."

"Explaining family to children can be challenging."

"I know it's a long shot, but you don't happen to have a picture of my mother? Of Desiree? I love her name. So cosmopolitan. Intriguing. Almost mysterious."

Carolyn didn't think the photos she had uncovered of Desiree would help, so another lie got heaped on the pile. "I'm sorry. I'm pretty sure I don't. I'm not big on taking pictures." Her hand slipped into her pocket and fondled her secret stash. *Was it time?*

"I...I—." Carolyn stopped and looked at Darby.

"What? What's wrong?"

Carolyn took a deep breath, then reached across the space between them, taking Darby's hands in hers. "I have something for you. Before your mother died, she met with a lawyer and wrote out a will, entrusting me with the job of finding you."

"I don't understand. You've been looking for me?"

"It's a long story. And you know parts of it because of Brody's involvement in rescuing you. I work with Brody at Marco's. They were part of the group who helped me rescue Amelia."

"Rescue?"

"Yes. Rescue. I just met Moss, so I can't fill in any blanks about his role, but I'm sure when he's ready he'll share more."

Carolyn pulled the white jade dragon pendant from her pocket and held it in the palm of her hand. It glistened in the moonlight.

"That's beautiful."

"It was Desiree's, your mother's. She wore it everywhere. I never saw her without it, so it must have been very special to her. She left it to me along with her antique mah jongg set, asking me to accept both as gifts in return for finding you."

Darby gently took the pendant.

"I've given the law firm she used your name and contact information. You should be hearing from them soon about anything else she might have left you. But I want you to have this. I think she would be pleased, and maybe secretly knew I'd give it to you."

Tears rolled down Darby's cheeks. Carolyn could see how much her gift meant, and she felt her cheeks flush with delight.

CHAPTER 12

Brianna was beside herself with excitement on the ride home. She kept looking behind her at Brody's car, making sure he was still there.

"I can't wait for him to meet Mercy, Mommy."

"We'll see. Mercy is still very weak. Too much excitement could hurt her."

"I'll be careful." Brianna had Snoodles hugged to her chest. "How long can Brody stay?"

"As long as he wants to. But he probably has to go back home for work, so it may only be for a day or two."

"I like Moss, Mommy. He's the biggest man I ever saw."

"He is rather big."

The three-car caravan turned into her driveway, and Ashley and Ken stopped what they were doing and hurried over to meet them, helping carry the few suitcases and bags of groceries into the house.

When Brody entered Darby's home, Sheba raced to him and shoved her nose into his crotch.

"Whoa. A new addition?"

"Sheba. She was Dennis's dog. Don't worry. She's harmless. Just wants to get to know you."

"Lucky me." Sheba cocked her head to the right, then left, when he spoke to her.

"Pretty, isn't she?"

He grabbed both her ears and rubbed and scratched. Her head went back and her eyes narrowed.

"She likes that. Think you've made a friend."

"I can tell." He bent down and gave ear scratches to the rest of Darby's four-pawed brood. "You've got your hands full."

"Tell me about it."

Brody did a causal walk-through of Darby's home while she was busy putting away groceries, so it took her a while to realize he wasn't in the kitchen helping.

As she watched him move down the hall she could see his military training. He stood straight and tall, and moved with purpose, triggering a flashback to her father that hit her like a ton of bricks He did the exact same thing every time they entered their home when she was a child. You can take the man out of the military, but you can rarely take the military out of the man. Her dad was always doing that—scanning his surroundings, noticing details most people didn't see, looking for things out of place, people who didn't fit.

Brody finally made it back to the kitchen.

"Everything okay?"

"Looks good to me." He pulled a beer from the fridge. "Looks like we're in for a chilly night. I can start a fire after we eat, and I'm doing the cooking."

"You won't get an argument from me. Have at it."

He popped the cork on a bottle of Pinot Noir and poured her a glass. "Moss and Brianna are outside playing on her trampoline. Sit. Relax."

They were alone.

Darby watched him work. The man was a whiz in the kitchen, with impeccable knife skills. She knew his culinary talents would create a meal worthy of a fine restaurant, but damn, who needed food when what she really wanted to feast on was him. He was over-the-top good-looking, a handsome hunk of man, a manly delicacy if ever she'd seen one.

Brody felt his throat tighten when he caught her watching him. Whenever they were together, he knew his feelings were real, and she was the right woman for him. He wanted to wash away her fear of being hurt again, an impossible feat. Her commitment fear was human. Trusting that he would be there for her and not run off to play soldier would take time to establish, time he was very willing to invest. Any fears associated with whoever was trying to scare her now were more easily handled. He vowed to catch and remove the instigator.

By all outward appearances, she was on her way to a full recovery from her kidnapping last fall, but it was too soon to tell how the memory of her experience would impact her life. Emotional scars ran deeper and lingered longer. Some never left.

Hours later, after another fantastic Brody-prepared meal and the kitchen cleaned up, Moss said his goodbyes.

"Where are you going? I made up one of the bedrooms for you."

"Can't stay here. Need to be loose so I can learn things we might not already know about what's going on and who's doing what to whom around here."

"No point objecting," said Brody, signaling Darby to be quiet. "I'll walk you out."

"Cryptic?" said Darby when Brody came back inside.

"That's Moss. He thinks he'll be more helpful if he's on the outside, not connected to you. If he stays here, someone might see him."

"Makes sense, but even one night?"

"We don't know whose eyes are on this place. Hopefully him being here these past few hours hasn't already messed up his plans."

The phone rang and she answered it. A click then the dial tone hummed in her ear. She stared at the phone in her hand. "The little shit."

"Next time it rings, I'll answer it. Hearing a man's voice might change things. Hang ups and a bloody teddy bear in your garbage are not routine events."

An hour later Brianna lay sprawled across Darby's lap, sound asleep, her small feet resting on Brody's knees. It was family movie night. Popcorn and the latest Disney video.

"I saw that."

"What?"

"Potato chips are not on Casper's eating plan."

"It was one chip." He picked up the fluffy Westie and cuddled her. "What could it hurt?"

"You're kidding. I don't want her getting used to human food."

"One chip? How can you deny this face?" Casper wiggled all over, so Brody put her down. She tilted her head from side to side, a bouncing ball of white fluff, cuter than any puppy needed to be to get another salty treat.

"Easy. She certainly has you wrapped around her paw."

"Oh, yeah."

"Unfortunately, the more you indulge her, the more difficult it becomes to keep her from driving us nuts whenever we eat anything."

"Okay. Okay. Sorry, Casper." He stroked her head. "Please don't bite the hand that can no longer feed you yummies. Your mommy has ruled."

Patience, thought Brody. *Don't push. Just enjoy.*

"Penny for your thoughts," whispered Darby when the movie ended and she got up to pull it out of the DVD player.

"Only a penny?" He gave her a smile. "Just enjoying."

"This can't be the type of evening entertainment you're used to."

"True. But I'm enjoying it. Peaceful. Canine bliss." He pointed to the four dogs sprawled out, feet splayed in the air, bellies exposed. "Tell me about the puppy mill campaign you're helping Ashley with."

Darby took a deep breath.

"Did you know the Humane Society estimates there are close to ten thousand puppy mills across the country? It's a shadow industry, hidden from view of people who only want a loving fur baby. And it is very profitable for companies who run commercial breeding operations."

"I never knew that. I see the commercials around Christmas asking for donations and showing horrendous pictures, but in thirty seconds they're gone."

"It gets worse." Darby went to her desk and brought back a folder of photos which she laid out in front of him. "Some unscrupulous breeders are importing puppies from God only knows where. Many die in transit, but those who live are sold in pet stores and online. Foreign countries have fewer breeding restrictions, so genetic lines mean nothing in the money game they're playing."

"And of course no one wants consumers to know any of this."

"The more I learn, the sicker I get, but more than that, it makes me angry. Makes me want to fight these bastards with every ounce of my being."

There was fire in Darby's eyes. Brody could tell she'd crossed the Rubicon on the puppy mill issue.

"There's so little oversight. Most kennels aren't licensed by the Feds or the states where they do business. And if a breeder sells direct to consumers, like on the internet, or through Craigslist, then no license is even required. Caveat emptor. Let the buyer beware."

"Do you really think people make the connection between the cruelty they see on the screen and the adorable face in the pet shop?"

"No. That's part of the problem. Puppies are an impulse buy. There's an old Patti Page song, *How Much is that Doggie in the Window?* The purchase is made, and unaware consumers take home sick puppies. It's why increased legislation, new laws, and higher fines for abusers are critically important. And more inspectors."

"There are inspectors?"

"Yep. Part of the USDA. But only thirty-five states have any standards at all. And there are thousands and thousands of breeding facilities and nowhere near enough inspectors. I also learned the USDA recently removed public access to breeder inspection reports, so even if consumers wanted to investigate, they'd be hard-pressed to find reliable information."

"You're giving me an education I'm not enjoying."

"Want more?"

"Not really, but go ahead."

"Breeding dogs in puppy mills live in cages their entire lives, their paws never touching ground, and many never see the light of day. Conditions are deplorable, feces-ridden, and some dogs are barely given enough food and water to live. A breeder can have fifty, sixty, hundreds of breeding females. They are bred and bred, have litter after litter, until they're unable to reproduce." Tears filled Darby's eyes. "And then they're thrown out, like so much trash. Killed. When law enforcement finally got enough complaints about one operation, they did a raid. Rescued hundreds of dogs, but found a mass grave with hundreds of carcasses."

"How do we stop it?"

"Damned if I know. It's a horrible life for man's best friend. Why do you think I started my sanctuary? I'm small potatoes compared to the money a commercial breeding operation makes. Then you've got a few companies acting as brokers and distributors for breeders. They collect the puppies and ship them all over the country in huge semis."

"Like these photos Ashley took."

"Exactly."

"Follow the money." Brody rubbed his chin. "I hate that phrase, because it always leads to trouble and tragedy. Money drives behavior for most people."

"Not all."

"I didn't say all. I said most. Present company excluded, of course."

"Thanks. But you're right. Chasing money. Money. Money. Money. Imagine what I could do with my sanctuary if I had that kind of money or won the lottery."

"Like what?"

"I'd expand. Of course, none of the adjacent land is for sale. And even if it was, I don't have the kind of money it will take to buy it. But eventually it will be for sale, and hopefully by then I'll have the money. Then I'll move my clinic here so I can be onsite all the time."

"Big plans."

"Big problems call for big plans."

CHAPTER 13

The next morning, after Brianna left for school, Darby told Brody she had a few errands to run and then would be at the clinic all afternoon if he needed her. He planned to scope out the town and then meet Brianna's bus after school and take her for ice cream.

Darby headed out, a bit concerned since she hadn't been completely forthcoming with Brody about where she was going. But Mrs. Trent had called, and sounded truly concerned about a whelping bitch. The call gave Darby an excellent excuse for being out at the Trents' place, one she planned to parlay into some first-class snooping if she got the chance.

Ten miles into the country, she turned into a driveway and stopped her car. She put the car in park and stared through the windshield. A sad-looking, dingy white house, its faded green shutters crying for fresh paint, sagged in front of her, with a tool shed and a dilapidated red barn about one hundred yards back to the right.

Darby climbed the four porch steps. No bell. She knocked on the screen door frame.

"Mrs. Trent?"

She knocked again. Louder. Nothing.

"Mrs. Trent?"

"And who might you be?" The gravely voice at her back startled her.

A stork-thin man with a hawk-like nose, sunken cheeks, and long, gray-speckled beard that reached to his chest appeared from nowhere. He was wearing torn blue jeans, a denim shirt, high-top work boots encrusted with dried gunk, and a weathered straw cowboy hat. Years of hard work were etched into lines and furrows on his face. His stern countenance announced to the world he was not someone to trifle with.

At his side, a brindled pit bull terrier stood knee-high. The dog's chest was marred with scars, and its low, throaty growl resonated in the air.

"Tyson, sit." The dog complied with the stern command.

"I'm looking for Wanda Trent." Darby eyed him warily, because she hadn't heard him approach. She walked to the top of the porch steps and looked down at him, extending her hand. "I'm Darby Dratton. I own Saints Animal Wellness on Church Street. Are you Mr. Trent?"

He wagged his head and pulled the toothpick out of his mouth. "What makes you think that?"

She dropped her outstretched hand when it was clear he had no intention of shaking it. "Mrs. Trent called me. She said a bitch was starting to whelp and having trouble. I know I'm not your regular vet. Dr. Lancaster is, but they found him dead at his clinic last week. May he rest in peace."

"Didn't hear anything about that."

"Everyone's talking about it in town. Not too often we get a suicide here. Though there is some talk he was murdered."

"Don't get to town much." He kicked at the dirt. "Suicide? Murder? That why you're out here?"

"No. I'm here because your wife called me. I'm a veterinarian."

His eyes flashed. "Wanda's my sister."

"Oh?"

"I'm Earl Sojack. Don't think your skills are exactly what we'd be looking for."

"You don't have a bitch ready to whelp?"

"We do, but—"

"So, do you need a vet?"

"Always in the market for the right type of talent."

"I'm very good at what I do. With dogs, cats, and horses, too."

"Them ain't all the talents I might be needing."

"Not sure what other talents I can claim, Mr. Sojack. Helping a bitch whelp is important, especially if she's suffering. We wouldn't want any of the puppies to die because the mom struggled birthing them, would we?"

No response.

Darby shot Tyson a look and took a step closer to the edge of the porch. Then she took another and came down one porch step, her eyes moving from Sojack to the dog and back again, her creep meter registering off the charts.

"I don't want to see a dog suffer. Since I'm out here, do you want me to take a look at the bitch or not? If not, I'll be on my way. I have other patients who need me."

She went down one more step. Tyson didn't budge. But he didn't take his eyes off her, either. When she reached the ground, she stood practically nose-to-nose with Sojack, so close his stench invaded her senses. She put him at over six feet tall, and had to look up into his beady, close-set eyes, dark as coal. She walked past him towards her Jeep.

Playing a hunch, she turned to face him, walking backwards, not missing a step. "I don't talk out of school. Was raised in a military family. My dad did a lot of traveling he couldn't rightly talk about, and he taught me the importance of silence."

Even as the words left her mouth her inner voice started screaming. *Stupid. Stupid. Stupid. What am I doing? Who will take care of Brianna if something happens to me?* But the other part of her psyche, the pissed-off Mama Bear part, took over, and she couldn't take it back. He was surely the devil's handiwork, and she'd just offered him her services. What was she thinking?

"That so?"

"Yep. If you're needing a vet, you might want to consider visiting my practice. As I said, it's over on Church Street." She held out her business card, the gesture causing Tyson to jump to his feet with a menacing growl. "Or—" She stopped talking and stepped back.

"Or what?" He reached down and scratched behind Tyson's ear. "Don't worry about Tyson. He's my prize stud. Harmless most times."

"Most times?"

"Harmless unless provoked. He kind of thinks like I do. You don't bother me, and I don't bother you."

"I see."

"You left off at or. Or what?"

"Right. Some of my clients like me to make house calls, like I'm doing now." She let her words hang in the air. "At no extra charge, of course."

"Of course."

She could feel his eyes taking her measure, and hated his smug, shit-eating grin.

"Well, Dr. Dratton, I appreciate your kind offer and visit. You came a long way." Earl eyed her with amused interest. "And so soon. Doc Lancaster is barely cold in the ground."

Guess he knows more than he's letting on, thought Darby. Dennis's funeral was yesterday morning.

"Follow me." With Tyson glued to his side, Earl Sojack walked up the porch steps and opened the screen door.

Getting weirder and weirder. She followed him into the house. Depressing was the mildest of the words that popped into Darby's mind as she noted the shabby furnishings and tired, dirty curtains, and the smell of mildew permeating the space. *This place could definitely use a good cleaning and some fresh air.*

Fluorescent lights flickered when he flipped the switch in the kitchen, revealing a collection of dead bugs under the plastic casing. The sink overflowed with dirty dishes, and the black and white linoleum floor tiles looked like they hadn't been washed in years.

She almost ran into him when he stopped at a worn wooden door tucked into an alcove behind the refrigerator. He pulled out an old fashioned skeleton key and inserted it in the lock, which scraped slightly, metal on metal, when he turned it. She heard a plunk when the lock released.

"Stay, Tyson. Down." He held up his hand in front of the dog's face, then pointed to the floor. Tyson sat and then laid down.

When he opened the door, the smell of damp earth accosted her. A simple chain hung from the ceiling connected to a light fixture, and when Earl jerked the chain, a lone incandescent bulb cast a yellowish glow into the darkened hole, revealing a set of wooden steps.

He looked at her, grinned, then ducked through the door so he wouldn't hit his head.

Darby hesitated at the top of the stairs.

"Ya comin'?"

"Yeah… Sure…"

"Watch yer step."

Too late to retreat, Darby forced herself to take a calming breath and then another. *Why am I doing this? For Brianna's safety. For the puppies.*

She flattened her hand against the stone wall for balance and followed him down the rickety steps, placing each foot carefully on the next step and leaning on the wall for support.

"Ouch." She snatched her hand back when it brushed too close to a nail jutting out of the wall. A tetanus shot just got added to her mental to-do list.

She counted fifteen steps to her descent before her shoes touched the hard-packed dirt floor.

There were no sounds, no signs of life, just cold, damp, and the pungent smell of sweat, mud, and something metallic lingering in the stale air.

"What is this place?"

He flicked an unseen switch, and a row of lightbulbs illuminated an underground tunnel with support beams every ten feet or so. It reminded her of the Mexican drug cartel tunnels she'd seen on the news. Ahead, Darby could see a sliver of light arcing down like a spotlight from heaven, piercing the darkness. But this place was not heaven; it was a hell no living creature should have to endure.

She followed Earl in silence. The passageway suddenly opened to a large cavern, a plastic dome skylight illuminating a fifty-foot square space, like a spotlight on a stage. In the center of the space someone had dug a shallow pit, about twenty feet square. Outside the square were wooden bleachers three rows high. Four oscillating fans stood like sentinels, one in each corner of the room. In one corner, she saw a makeshift bar, complete with a refrigerator and microwave. Several beer taps broadcast the names of popular brews.

"I call it the playroom. Can get pretty hot down here."

A shiver ran down her spine. She tilted her head up, peering through the plexiglass, the sunshine brightening an otherwise sad prison. She knew only too well what she was looking at—a dog fighting pit. The rumors were true.

Darby's hands went to her hips and she harnessed her courage, willing her voice to project strength. "I guess there's no bitch about to whelp, is there?" She chewed at her lower lip, waiting for his answer.

None came.

"What now?"

"Now? Now we head back upstairs, and you go on your merry way. Just wanted to show you the playroom."

"I hear you went out to the Trent's." Buddy grinned at Darby as he slid into the booth at the Island House across from her. "And ran smack into Earl Sojack. Gotta say, Doc, you've got one big set, if you know what I mean."

"I'll second that," said Tommy, taking the seat next to her.

"News travels fast. How'd you hear about my trip?"

"We got our ways," said Buddy. He held up two fingers to the server, who knew he meant two coffees. "Look at those guys." Tommy and Darby twisted in their seats to see two burly-looking guys sporting tattooed arm sleeves enter the restaurant. "A lot of ink on those two."

"Bet that hurt," said Darby as the two passed their table.

"Real men don't feel pain," laughed Buddy.

"The hell with the pain. Do you know how much those things cost? Knew a guy who spent over five thousand dollars, and that was for one arm," said Tommy.

"I can think of lots of better ways to spend that kind of money," said Darby, "and they usually have soulful eyes and a tail."

Buddy shrugged and thanked Mille, the server, who set two mugs of steaming hot coffee on the table. "So, you were saying. What made you go out to the Trent's?"

"Got a call from someone claiming to be Mrs. Trent saying a bitch was having trouble whelping." Darby smiled, took a bite of her hamburger. "Turns out there was no bitch about to deliver a litter." She sipped her club soda. "How'd you know where to find me?"

"Stopped by your place to check on Mercy." said Tommy. "Josie said you were at the Island House having lunch."

"Mercy's doing fine. Well enough that I need to find a forever home for her."

"You mean you ain't gonna keep her?" asked Buddy.

"Would prefer not to. She needs a lot of TLC, and I've already got a full house."

"I'd take her," said Tommy, "but the missus says if I bring home one more stray, she'll... Well, let's just say she told me not to. And I'm already in the doghouse."

"What'd you do?" asked Buddy.

"Bought a clunker at the auto auction last week. Needed the parts. Paid three hundred dollars. She was P-I-S-S-E-D."

"Don't worry, Tommy. If I can't find a good home for her, she has one with me." Darby turned her attention to Buddy. "Got to ask. You've been around these parts a long time."

"All my life and then some."

"What can you tell me about Earl Sojack?"

"Earl's an odd duck. Sort of a recluse," said Buddy. "Doesn't play well with others. His family's been in these parts since before the Civil War. Always claim they're descendants of the original settlers."

"Aren't you related?" asked Tommy, before thanking the waitress who came by with fresh donuts and told them they were on the house.

"Sort of by marriage. Some distant cousin or some such thing. The Sojacks own most of the land just west of town. You know, the stretch out beyond Frogstool Road."

"Love that name." Darby wiped her mouth. "Frogstool Road. Got a certain ring to it."

"Earl's the patriarch." Buddy shifted in his seat. "He parcels the land out to kin as it suits him. Like when one gets married or needs someplace to live. Got a couple of trailers back in the woods, two or three houses spread around, and a few hunting shacks." He took a sip of his coffee and cupped the mug with both hands. "And he's very protective of his privacy."

"He can be an ornery SOB when he gets his back up," laughed Tommy. "I once saw him knife a guy in a bar fight because the guy accidentally bumped into him. Tussle lasted about ten minutes. Wrecked the bar pretty bad. But even after the guy had given up, he sliced his cheek almost to bone. Left a nasty scar. Said it was something to remember him by."

Darby found herself wondering if he was sick enough to break into her house and destroy Brianna's teddy bear. *What have I gotten myself into?*

Buddy's phone chirped just as he finished his second donut. He looked at the caller ID and frowned. "Gotta take this. Be right back."

Tommy got up and took Buddy's seat across from Darby. "Don't pay me no mind. The two of us sitting side by side could get misinterpreted in these parts. Wouldn't want to start any rumors flying."

"Rumors about what?" asked a familiar voice behind Darby. "Josie said I'd find you here." He slid into the booth next to her. "I'm Llewelyn Brody."

"Tommy Everett."

"Brody is up from Florida. Visiting for a few days."

"You're the guy...Brody...the one who saved little miss Darby here a few months back."

"Not my only claim to fame, but the one I'm most proud of." He rested his arm across the back of the booth seat.

"Good job, man. Good job."

"Speaking of rumors, Tommy, were you able to learn anything more about a local puppy mill or dog fighting?"

"No. Plan to go see old man Stokes tomorrow morning before my shift starts. He's lived in these parts since before dirt. A walking, talking, breathing, local history book. If anyone knows anything, it's old man Stokes."

"Interesting." Darby sighed, slowly dredging a French fry through the ketchup. "Earl... He showed me the pit today."

"You're kidding?"

"Nope."

"Who's Earl and what pit?" asked Brody.

"It's the errand I told you about this morning." She gently touched Brody's arm, hoping to calm him down. "Dog about to whelp."

Brody got the message and leaned back in the booth, helping himself to a French fry from Darby's plate.

"Took me down there. It's underground, which is probably why you can't find it when you go looking."

"Hear any dogs barking?"

"I did hear some barking when Earl and I were talking out in front of the house. Couldn't place what direction it was coming from. Felt like it was all around me." She pushed her plate over to Brody, who continued to munch on the fries.

"I don't get it." She threw up her hands. "What does Earl get out of watching one dog maim, and usually kill, another?" She fiddled with the straw in her club soda, swirling it around, clinking the ice cubes, stabbing the innocent slice of lime trapped under the ice at the bottom of the glass.

"A sick thrill," said Tommy. "Earl lives in a parallel universe where animal cruelty is acceptable. Depraved indifference to life. As I said before, he can be meaner than a hornet to people, so being cruel to animals doesn't surprise me."

"It's barbaric. There's got to be more to it. What does he want? And how does dog fighting get it for him?"

"Male ego. Status. Honor. Respect." Tommy raised a finger with each word. "Guys like him, it validates their masculinity in ways their work, and most likely their family life, doesn't."

"But Darby," said Brody, "you said last night that dog fighting's a felony in all fifty states. We're talking jail time if he gets caught."

"So far that ain't happening." Tommy sipped his coffee. "Our raids come up empty. If you ask me, we've got a mole. Someone's tipping him off."

"Any idea who?"

Tommy looked around and then gave Darby and Brody a hard stare. "I'd rather not say."

Darby looked out the window and saw Buddy shifting from one foot to the other, gesturing wildly on his call.

"Follow the money," said Tommy, bringing her attention back to their conversation. "And there's beaucoup bucks involved."

"What are we talking?"

"Thousands and thousands of dollars. Both in the betting and then the stud fees you can demand for pups from winning dogs."

"You've got to be kidding," said Brody.

"Nope."

"And you think Dennis was involved?" asked Darby.

"Don't know for sure, but Buddy said Dennis had been throwing money around at the bowling alley the last few Saturday nights like a guy without a care in the world."

"I met one of Earl's dogs," said Darby. "Tyson. Sojack said he was a champion stud."

Tommy finished his coffee, held up and wiggled his mug, signaling for a refill. "Don't suspect that championship came from the AKC. More likely a champion game dog. That's what they call 'em. Game dogs."

"Some game." Darby sighed. "A very sad game, if you ask me."

"Winning gives a big income boost for a lot of these people. Could make more at a dog fight than from robbing your local convenience store. Remember the Michael Vick case?"

"How could I forget it? In my opinion, the bastard didn't get enough time."

"He did his time per the law."

"Spoken like the good cop you are, Tommy. He plea-bargained away the animal cruelty charges. I read the transcripts and testimony from witnesses who saw what he did to innocent dogs."

"That's how our judicial system works. It isn't always about justice," said Brody. "That's why sometimes other methods need to be employed."

"I'm going to pretend I didn't hear that, if it's okay with you," said Tommy.

Brody nodded at him. It was clear from the signals passing between them that they had already arrived at a comfortable understanding.

"Pardon me, but it sucks. I think they should have sent him to prison and thrown away the key. Let him rot in a cell for the rest of his life. I was furious when Roger Goodell reinstated him in the NFL. I stopped watching football because of it."

"Whoa. Went cold turkey, huh?" Tommy poured sugar into his refilled cup.

"He got a slap on the wrist and a few years. Not enough by a long shot. Caused horrific suffering to animals beyond description from the accounts I've read. And according to some of the news reports, the interest in dogfighting increased after his case, because he didn't get a stiffer punishment. People thought he was some sort of folk hero. Then Goodell lets him go back to playing football like nothing ever happened."

"Here comes Buddy." Seeing Buddy waving him to come, Tommy slid out of the booth. "Before he gets here, and for what it's worth, you may want to keep this conversation between us."

Darby glanced at Buddy and back to Tommy. "Gotcha."

When Buddy reached the table, he picked up his mug, finished his coffee, and grabbed the last donut. Looking at Brody, he said, "Hi, whoever you are. We gotta go, Tommy. See you later, Doc."

CHAPTER 14

Early the next morning Tommy drove up the coast to visit old man Stokes.

"Can't hurt to try," he muttered to himself as he pulled up to the rickety house on the far north side of town. "He knows where the bodies are buried. The only question is whether he chooses to tell."

Stokes was in his usual position, sitting on a rocking chair on the porch, his old hound dog, Blue, curled up next to him. He couldn't have weighed more than ninety pounds soaking wet, his tanned, leathery skin hanging on frail bones. His left foot controlled his motion, and he didn't stop rocking when he saw Tommy's car approach. Blue lifted his head, but put it right back down.

"Morning, Mr. Stokes."

"Might be." Stokes turned his head to the side and spat, then stuck another wad of chaw between his yellowed teeth and his lower lip.

"Ugly habit," he said, wiping his sleeve across his mouth. "Got hooked young and can't quit. Doc says if I don't quit soon, the cancer's gonna eat my insides.

Doing that already, apparently. "Mind if I join you?"

Stokes barely nodded, and Tommy scratched Blue behind the ears before he parked himself in the other rocker.

There they sat, two men and Blue, resting and rocking.

"How's the family?" asked Tommy. "I hear Betty's gone and had herself another kid. What's this? Your fourth great-great grandchild? Mighty amazing."

"Not amazing. What happens when ya ain't watchin' what yer doing."

Stokes leaned back and reached into a beat-up red Coleman cooler tucked behind his rocker. He pulled out two beers, handed one to Tommy, and twisted the cap off his bottle.

"Wanna tell me what ya want?" Stokes took a big pull of beer. "Folks don't come out here much just to chew the fat."

Tommy twisted the cap off his beer. He took a small sip, not wanting a beer this early in the morning, but not accepting the beer would have defeated the purpose of the visit.

"We've been having some trouble with people coming in from out of state, making a ruckus. One fool stopped Fred Winston to ask directions to a dog fight. Can you believe that?"

"Imagine that." Stokes stopped rocking for a brief second and eyed Tommy. "What's this got to do with me?"

"Nothing. We decided to talk to some of you old-timers, see if we can get a handle on the rumors about dog fighting." Tommy pretended to take a sip of his beer. "You know how upset Fred can get. And he was spitting mad at the idea that dog fighting is going on out here." Tommy thought Stokes' rocking had picked up a bit more energy. "He asked me about it, but heck, I didn't know squat." He took another pretend sip and looked out toward the road. "Was heading up this way to pick up one of Helen's tomato pies for dinner tonight and thought you might be able to shed some light on the matter."

"You thought about me, huh? Why's that?"

"Come on, Leonard. You're a legend in these parts. You know that."

"Might be. I'm old enough to be a legend." Stokes finished off his beer and aimed the bottle toward a metal can about ten yards away. He hoisted it high and it landed with a crash of breaking glass. "Don't make 'em like they used to."

"They don't make much of anything like they used to."

Tommy stole a glance at his watch. He'd been rocking for about twenty minutes. He brushed his hands against his jeans and stood up. "Mind if I take this with me?"

"No problem. Don't want you wasting good beer."

"That's a fact."

Another ear scratch for Blue and Tommy started down the porch steps.

"Ya might want to ask your partner, Buddy, about the dog fightin' thing. I hear tell his cousin Earl's been chasing squirrels up that tree."

"You don't say?"

"I didn't." Stokes leaned over and spit into the bucket at his side. "Y'all have a nice day."

Tommy texted Darby that he was on his way to her clinic. She texted back, asking him to pick up a pizza. He walked in carrying a large, loaded pie.

"Thanks for stopping for lunch, Tommy. I'm starving, but this thing is huge. Who do you think you're feeding?"

"There's always room for pizza." He put the pie on the credenza. "And I ran into Brody at the pizza place, so I asked him to join us."

"Interesting. Mind telling me why?"

"Because he looks like the type of guy who knows what's going on and can take care of himself."

"How long were you two together?"

"Just a Coke while I waited for the pizza. You look upset. Anything happen?"

"No. Not really. This thing with Dennis. I want to know why. I need to make sense of the senseless. His death, totally senseless."

"And you don't think we want that? That I want that?"

"Of...of course you want to find out why Dennis killed himself. You're the police. It's your job. But..." Darby got up and pulled some paper plates from a drawer as Brody walked in.

"Good timing."

"I always know when food's ready."

Darby handed out plates and napkins, took a slice of pizza, and went back to her desk. Tommy and Brody each took a slice and grabbed chairs opposite her.

"Dennis was a colleague. He was also my friend. Lately there were times when I felt like he wanted to tell me something. He'd start and then just stop. Like he had a secret he wanted to share."

"Everyone has secrets. You do. I do. Everyone does."

"Do they?"

"Don't they? Don't you?" Tommy looked across the desk at her. "Brody, care to chime in on this?"

"I'm not touching this topic with a ten-foot pole. I'll just sit here, eat my pizza, and mind my own business."

"Call it my cop side, but I don't think we ever really know another person."

"You know your wife, don't you?"

"I know what she wants me to know. But there's a part of her I don't think I'll ever know. And there's a part of me I hope she never knows."

"Really? Come on, Tommy. You're the nicest guy I've ever met." She look at Brody. "Present company excluded, of course."

"Of course." Brody smiled and kept eating.

"Wasn't always. When I was seventeen I kind of got caught up in some shit. Judge gave me a choice. Jail or the Army. Chose the Army and got an education for a lifetime. I saw things in Kuwait that no human being needs to ever see. It changed me."

"Sounds like you got a wake-up call just in the nick of time," said Brody.

"You could say that." He took a bite of his pizza and wiped dripping oil off his chin. He laid the rest of the slice back on his plate.

"Being in a war zone changes people," said Brody, reaching for another slice.

"My dad paid a heavy price every time he was in country," said Darby. "I could see it on his face, in his eyes when he came home. Each tour took a little bit of his humanity. And he'd fight it when he was home. Worked hard to be the kind of man my mother and I would be proud of. But it took a toll."

"It does. Even now, as a cop. Some of the things I see. What people do to each other, to people they vowed before God to love until death parted them. It takes my breath away."

"Yet you stay," said Darby.

"For now." Tommy got up, walked to the door, and closed it, handing her a blue folder.

"I did some snooping last night and managed to get into Dennis's bank records."

She opened the folder and started leafing through the documents.

"Could we keep this between us? Wouldn't want my nosing around to get out—to anyone." Tommy's emphasis made Darby shudder.

"Of course. And by anyone, can I assume you mean Buddy?" She could feel a tension knot forming between her eyes. "You didn't waste any time. We only talked about this at lunch yesterday."

He held her eyes and nodded. "See anything odd?"

"Large cash deposits followed by checks to any number of online outfits. JTV is a huge one, whatever the heck that is."

"Jewelry TV. Also QVC. It's my wife's favorite." Tommy bit into his slice, swallowed quickly. "What got my attention are the recent purchases. Like within the last year."

"Talking about recent purchases, have you seen Tracy's new car?"

"Yeah." Tommy took another bit of pizza. "Must admit I drooled when she drove by the Stop and Shop and waved."

"I asked her if she had a sugar daddy. Hard to fathom how she paid for it when she was only working part-time for me and Dennis."

"Does she have something on the side that you don't know about?" asked Brody.

"If she does, I still don't know about it."

"Me neither," said Tommy. He glanced at Brody. "Tracy's one of the local party girls."

"She's good at what she does as a vet assistant, and that's all I care about," said Darby. "What she does on her own time is her business."

"She may be a good vet assistant, but we're constantly busting her for her evening escapades." Tommy pulled some more sheets out of the folder and pointed to several dates on the printouts. "Doris has been dead going on two years. Wonder what Dennis was buying, especially from JTV, and for whom?"

"He was a good-looking guy," said Darby, "and there's only so long a man can go before... Well... Maybe he found someone new."

"Didn't say anything to me."

"Would he? Were you two close?"

"We went target shooting weekly. And he and Buddy hung around together."

Darby thought back for a minute. "I never saw Doris wear any flashy jewelry the few times I met her, but here I go repeating another rumor, the one about how she sank them into a heap of debt with her spending."

Darby closed the file folder and finished her pizza slice, then opened the lid and pulled another slice onto her plate. "Speaking of spending money, did you see that brand-new boat Buddy just bought for himself?"

"Yeah. Been thinking about that. Half a million-dollar boat on a cop's salary. Wish I could afford that."

"Where do you think he got the money?"

"Don't know. He didn't mention anyone dying and leaving him a small fortune when I asked him about it. Said he saved all his overtime pay."

"If you don't mind me asking," said Brody, "how well do you know Buddy outside of work? You been partners long?"

"Feels like forever, but it's only been the last six years."

"Just before I moved here," added Darby.

"Sounds about right. His previous partner retired early."

"That common?" asked Brody.

"Not really. Jack never said why he put in his papers. But he retired one day and moved away the next. Don't think anyone's heard from him since. Just up and left. Whoosh. Here today, gone tomorrow."

Brody leaned forward, his elbows resting on his knees. "Don't mean to interfere, but I have a friend who may be able to help with your research. Want me to give him a call?"

Tommy looked at Darby, then nodded his okay. "That would be great. What does your friend need?"

"Whatever info and numbers you have will be all he needs to get started."

Tommy scribbled some numbers on a piece of paper and handed it to Brody, who pulled out his cell phone and left the room.

"Speaking of unknown things," said Darby, "I'm wondering why I was called out to the Trents' the other day."

"What do you mean?"

"Wanda Trent wasn't there. No dog was giving birth. It was just me and Earl Sojack. But it was a woman's voice on the phone. I'm sure of it."

"Maybe Sojack had his sister make the call."

"Possible. And, like I told you, he had me follow him into the house, into the basement, and showed me a dog fighting pit."

Tommy grimaced. "I'm surprised you went."

"Me too." Darby put another slice of pizza on her plate.

"You're a hungry little thing, aren't you?"

"I eat when I'm stressed." She took a bite and chewed slowly. "He was taking my measure. I'm sure of it. Wanted to see if I'd flinch. How I'd handle seeing a dog fighting pit." Darby handed the folder back to Tommy. "Back to what you found. Any chance there's a connection between Dennis's ability to pay off his wife's credit card debts, these new purchases, and your suspicions about Buddy and his shiny new boat?"

"Could be. Maybe Brody's friend can find out. I gave him Buddy's social security number in addition to Dennis's." Tommy ran his fingers through his hair. "Saw old man Stokes this morning.

"Bet that was a one-sided conversation."

"Not sure I'd even call it a conversation."

"He's a man of few words. The few dealings I've had with him have been challenging. Did you learn anything you didn't already know?"

"He said I should ask my partner about dog fighting."

"That's not good."

"Tell me about it." Tommy filled her in on their conversation. "You know, Buddy used to complain about money all the time, but then he stopped."

"I know," said Darby. "He whined to me that two ex-wives were bleeding him dry. I told him not to marry again. Just fool around."

"Darby Dratton. Just fool around? That could get you excommunicated from the female gender." He laughed and got up to go. "I asked him about it a few weeks ago, and he struggled to look me in the eye, which told me he wasn't telling me the whole truth. There's something Buddy wasn't saying." Tommy threw his empty plate and napkin in the trash. "The more I think about it, the more I'm sure he hasn't said a word about money in over a year."

"That's interesting. Wonder what changed in his life? Did he get a second job?"

"Not that I know of." Tommy finished off his Coke and threw the can in the recycle bin.

"Must admit, I am curious."

"Curiosity killed the cat."

"Cute."

"I gave him the benefit of the doubt because we're... we're partners."

"Partners screw each other all the time. You only need look at the divorce rate to know that."

"Partners and married are different. But I see your point."

"Hard to imagine you're suspicious of Buddy."

"What can I say? I'm a cop. I get paid to be suspicious."

"Even of colleagues?"

"Especially of colleagues who might think they're above the law because they're part of a chosen group."

"What chosen group?"

"The born and bred locals club."

"Oh."

"Buddy gets away with lots. He's a local. Part of the in crowd. I've been here close to twenty years, but they look at me and see an outsider."

"I don't."

"Thanks, but you're an outsider too," he chuckled.

"Good point. And if it's any consolation, you're a much better cop than Buddy can ever hope to be, even on his best day."

"Hate the thought that Dennis died alone."

"He didn't. Sheba was with him, and she was his best friend."

"What's going to happen to her?"

"I've got her at my house."

"I see what you mean about having a full house. How many does that make?"

"Only four dogs at the moment."

"Cats?"

"Three. And the horses. There are two of them. So as I said, I've got a full house. But there will be room for Mercy if I can't find her a safe, loving home." Darby picked up the pizza box and tossed it in the trash. She followed him to the door. "Thanks for lunch."

"Nice friend. You two serious?"

CHAPTER 15

Darby looked away. "Not to change the subject or anything, but is the final autopsy report back yet?"

"No. I called the lab this morning. They said it was done and they'd fax it over later today." Tommy reached out for the doorknob, stopped in his tracks, and turned to face Darby. "But here's the thing that's been bothering me the most since it happened."

"What's that?"

"Dennis shot left-handed. We went to the range together, and I always kidded him about being a southpaw shooter. He did most everything else right-handed. Actually he was ambidextrous. But he always shot lefty."

"And?"

"The crime scene photos show the gun on his right side. And don't forget, the entry wound is also on the right side of his neck. But he shot left-handed, and I'd wager if he was going to kill himself, he'd have held the gun in his left hand, or with both hands, to make sure he didn't botch it and miss. And he'd choose a larger target than his neck. Mustering the courage to shoot yourself on purpose seems hard enough, but doing it with your non-dominant hand adds to the difficulty. What if you missed?"

"Maybe Buddy's suicide pronouncement was a bit premature?"

"What I'm thinking. Until the ME's final report comes in and says otherwise, we are assuming suicide." This time Tommy turned the doorknob and opened the door, but didn't step through. "I think it was staged to look like Dennis killed himself, staged like a suicide, but the gun and the bullet hole are both on the wrong side of the body.

"Who else knew he shot lefty?"

"Other than me, I can't think of anyone else he went shooting with. He didn't want people to know he enjoyed shooting as a sport. And I used our time at the range for my required weekly practice time."

"Why would someone go to all that trouble to stage the scene?"

"Got me. But whatever Dennis was doing made someone very nervous."

"Makes more sense. Dennis wasn't the suicide type."

"There's a type?"

"I'm just thinking out loud." She threw up her hands and shrugged. "He was getting his act together, starting to think about dating. He had everything going for him…good-looking, smart, funny, a great vet. Everything a woman could want."

"Well something wasn't working for him." Tommy took a step into the hall, but turned back to her. "Motive, method and opportunity, the golden trinity for murder. Method, the how, we know, a very lucky, once-in-a-lifetime shot to the neck that hit his carotid. Opportunity, the when, we also know, because he was alone at the clinic. My guess is whoever killed him followed him from the bowling alley. Motive… The why… Unfortunately, I've got no clue. Everyone loved Dennis."

"Clearly not everyone," said Darby. "He pissed someone off, big time. Did the techs find a suicide note? Did he leave anything behind to give us a clue as to why he did it?"

"No."

"Don't most suicides leave a note?"

"Not sure there is a formal protocol for pre-suicide communication. Dennis didn't have family. Except for Sheba."

"She can't read. But you'd think he would want to make sure she'd be taken care of, not euthanized."

"I suspect he was counting on you, Darby. He knew your heart."

"Maybe so." Her stomach flip-flopped. "What's wrong with this picture? What motive could someone have for killing him?"

"That's what the police investigation will uncover. It may take a while, but we usually get our man."

"Maybe the person didn't mean to kill him. Just scare him."

"Like he or she is trying to scare you with hang ups and breaking into your house? Which was no accident. Intentional all the way. Darby, you need to step away from this and let us do our job."

"I know you're right. I feel like I'm being swallowed up by forces I can't control. And I want to do something to help find Dennis's killer."

"I think there was someone else there. Someone killed him and tried to make it look like suicide. Someone trusted, because there were no signs of forced entry. Whoever it was, Dennis let him in, or he knew the alarm code. And if he let them in, dead wasn't the outcome he was anticipating. Bet he never saw it coming."

"Someone who didn't know he shot lefty." said Darby. "Now I'm even sadder than I was before. Dennis was a good man, a colleague and a friend. I'm sure he didn't expect his life to end this way. What happens now?"

"Once I see the ME's report later today, I'll let you know."

"I need to know for sure." Darby looked off into nothingness. "I need to know what really happened. Something's not right. If you find proof positive that it was a suicide, I'll let it go. But I won't stop trying to end dog fights around here."

"Works for me. As long as you're careful. Or have your friend serving as your sidekick. Say good-bye for me. I'm sure I'll be seeing him again real soon."

Two hours later, Darby answered her cell on the second ring. "Yes, Tommy."

"Dang. Hate caller ID. Can't surprise anyone anymore."

"Tell me you have good news."

"Not really. The coroner's report came in. Stippling around the entry place points to suicide.

"And that's what we've been thinking."

"Only problem is according to the ME's report, his hands were clean when he checked for gunshot residue. There was only a small trace of blowback."

"Blowback?"

"You aren't watching enough TV. Yes, blowback. The residue from shooting a gun that blows back onto your hand. Up close and personal in a suicide leaves blood, body matter and residue from the gunpowder.

"But there's no gunpowder residue on either hand. The ME found bullet entry and exit holes. It went in on the right and came out on the left. Nothing indicates a struggle. And there were no prints on the gun. It was wiped clean."

"That's odd. Shouldn't Dennis's prints have been on the gun?"

"You would think."

"If there's an exit hole, where's the bullet? You said the techs searched the place twice and didn't find a bullet. Did the ME find anything unusual?"

"They found ketamine in his system."

"That's a horse tranquilizer."

"Right. On the streets it's called K or Special K. Cheaper than cocaine. The ME surmises he was out cold, which allowed someone to get up close and shoot him."

"Haven't there been some drug cases recently over at the high school involving Special K?"

"You do keep up on things, don't you, Doc?"

"Yes. Especially news like that, because vets use ketamine, and high school kids shouldn't be able to get it."

"You can buy anything on the streets today if you know where to go."

"Someone's dealing locally, aren't they?"

"We think so, but it's another one of those incidents we can't seem to prove. Our suspects disappear just when we think we're getting close."

"The work of your friendly mole?"

"That's my guess."

There was a long silence.

"Darby? What are you thinking?"

"We're dealing with a very smart killer. Sets up a murder scene to look like a suicide. Smart enough to leave no sign of his presence. But all good TV detectives agree, even smart killers screw up."

"And this one did too, because he didn't know Dennis shot left-handed. And if it was suicide the bullet would be there."

"Exactly. Of course, with no prints, it's going to be next to impossible to figure out who did it."

"Maybe we'll get lucky."

"One can hope."

Darby turned out the reception room light and stepped out into the late afternoon sun. It had been a busy day at the clinic, and she was looking forward to Brianna's bright smile. So many things were troubling her, not the least of which was her last patient, another sick puppy.

She turned the key to lock the door, lost in thought. What did she really know? Fact, not conjecture? Her answer, not much.

Fact, Dennis was dead. The ME called it murder, not suicide. Someone went to a lot of trouble to make it look like suicide. Fact, her patient load had doubled since Dennis's death. Nice fact, that one. There was light at the end of her paycheck-to-paycheck existence, in those few times where she took an actual paycheck and not just enough to buy food and pay her bills. Fact, she treated two sick puppies in the past few days who were bought at the same store in Virginia Beach. Conjecture, they were puppy mill puppies. Truth, she was livid that these places existed. Fact, there was little she could do to stop puppy mills.

The heart-wrenching truth—she'd taken care of too many sick puppies recently. The ASPCA had shut down a small local puppy mill about two years ago, but the puppies and the dogs producing them had no place to go. That's when she started the sanctuary. She had the land, so she put it to good use. Some of the puppies and older dogs were eventually adopted. Sadly, a few were too sick to heal and had to be euthanized. Her heart wept over each one.

She needed to see for herself if the store in Virginia Beach was selling sick puppies. She'd go tomorrow, invite Brody to take the hour ride to Virginia Beach, visit Puppies on Parade, and see for herself. If she saw any of the same symptoms the two puppies had, she'd take pictures with her phone for evidence and call the police.

Darby's beaming smile showed how much she appreciated Brody when he lifted Brianna off her feet at the bus stop.

"Brodeeeeeee." Brianna whooped, extending the e sound, flinging her arms around his neck. "You're still here."

"Told you I would be."

"Yes, you did."

He put her down, and she gave her mom a hug and kiss.

"How was school today?" asked Darby.

"Fine." Her voice didn't match the word.

"You sound sad, honey. Did something happen?"

"Chrissy wasn't there. We were supposed to finger paint together, but her mommy showed up and told Miss Stephanie she wouldn't be there anymore." Brianna sniffled. "She's my best friend."

"You have lots of other friends, Brianna."

"Not like Chrissy. No one has puppies like Chrissy."

"But Brianna, you've never seen the puppies."

Brody felt his heart aching as he watched the interaction. *How do you cheer up a five-year-old?*

"Brianna," said Brody, putting one knee on the sidewalk to be at eye-level with her. "Do you want to help me make the dough for our pizza dinner?"

Pizza? Again? Darby's questioning expression was short-lived as Brianna's mood flipped instantly.

"Pizza! It's my favorite."

"I know," said Brody. "That's why I want you to help me make it. So it will be just the way you like it."

"With cheese and meatballs?"

"Sure. Meatballs it is." He caught Darby's eye and mouthed *meatballs?*

Darby shrugged. "I guess I better go to the store for some hamburger."

"Come on, Brianna, let's check out the pantry and see what other fixings Mommy needs to buy for dinner."

Brianna raised her arms to Brody, who lifted her over his head and onto his shoulders. Darby picked up her backpack.

"Duck. Watch your head," he said as they approached the front porch.

Watching Brody with Brianna, doing things fathers do, scared her to death. Yes, he was a keeper, but his life was in Florida and hers was here. She had so much money invested in her house and the animal sanctuary, there was no way she could leave. She'd lose her shirt trying to sell in a slow economy. And starting over held no appeal, even if her six-foot tall, six-pack abs reason for doing so had tons.

Brianna was already more attached to Brody than Darby should have allowed. She hadn't stopped it in time. Hell, she never should have let it start. What words would make sense to a five-year-old when he stopped coming around and she asked why?

Huge obstacles, like climbing Kilimanjaro in flip-flops.

"Where's Moss been these last few days?" asked Darby as she unpacked the groceries. "He didn't leave without saying goodbye, did he?"

"No." Brody hesitated a bit.

"What?"

"He got himself a job as a deck hand on one of the charter fishing boats."

"Why would he do that?"

"Because he's worried about you, and he figured he could find out more being one of the guys. He needs to blend in, not look like the outsider he is."

"That's going to be kind of hard, don't you think, given his size and how he carries himself?"

"If anyone can do it, Moss can. He's slippery as an eel. The ultimate chameleon. Fits in wherever he goes. Knows how to get the guys to open up in front of him, get a feel for the place. The best way to do that is to get a grunt job and booze it up with the boys after work. Guys talk. They like to think they don't, claim that it's the women who talk, but the truth is, get a couple of beers in them and some guys can't shut up about the shit they're into."

"Can't believe he worked for that horrible man, Hayden, all those years."

"He had a job to do. Moss is one bad-ass dude, a formidable adversary. Intimidating. Even standing around drinking beers with his new buddies, he exudes a serious 'don't fuck with me' vibe. And that's the imagine he wants to project with these guys, so if you see him around town, pretend you don't know him."

CHAPTER 16

Moss slowly took in the scene, sharp eyes absorbing details. Quonset hut to his right about one hundred yards out.

A run-down silver food truck was dead ahead, its service window loaded with bags of snacks. Two men worked a grill loaded with brats and burgers. About a hundred people milling around, mostly men looking for action, some young boys playing in a sand pit to his left, and what looked to be a few families sitting at picnic tables eating.

A motley crew, representative of everything that is both good and bad about America.

In the center was the pit, the arena where the fights took place. The crowd was subdued, so he suspected the show hadn't started yet. Time for the guys to get liquored up. Two men who were clearly over-served in the alcohol department were getting in each other's faces outside the lone porta potty. *Maybe one of them forgot to put the seat down,* thought Moss.

The husky-looking guy pulled a maneuver which forced the smaller guy to collapse facefirst into the mud. Stunned, it took him a few minutes to even raise his head, but he wasn't getting back on his feet fast. His assailant struck a fighting pose, ready for any sudden move, but then threw back his head in adolescent glee, joined by his cronies, who rapidly exchanged money. They'd bet on the fight, and the losers were paying up. Finally the husky man reached out his hand and helped the muddy loser up.

Moss snickered to himself and elbowed one of the guys who brought him. "Nothing zaps your energy and fighting skills like alcohol."

They both laughed. But now that the fight was over, the victor established, they could go back to being laughing and drinking buddies.

"Brody, I don't know who this Earl Sojack is, but I gotta tell you, he's as far off the grid as anyone I've ever seen," said Brett, when he called.

"But you found him?"

"Yep." Brett rubbed his hands together and interlaced his fingers, rotated his hands inward, then stretched them out, cracking his knuckles.

"I heard that," laughed Brody. "Sounds like you just did your warm-up routine."

"Ready to go. Gotta say, it took a while to get a bead on him. The guy's almost nonexistent."

"Almost?"

"Anyone who goes to this much trouble to appear disconnected tells me he's very connected. I just needed to find the way in."

"What's he into?"

"That's still a bit murky. Definitely illegal, whatever it is."

"What's your best guess?"

"Drugs. The rest, the dog fights and puppy mill, are ruses. Distractions. Gets the cops looking one way, scurrying around chasing their tails, while over here he's doing something totally different. Guy lives near water, right?"

"Yeah. Why?"

"Convenient to have your own dock. I'm guessing the stuff, whatever he's dealing, is smuggled in by fishing boats. I can see he runs all-day charters for tourists. Looks innocent enough, should the Coast Guard come calling."

"How's that even possible?"

"Easy. The US has thousands of miles of coastline. The good guys can't be everywhere. Small coves, harbors, deserted shorelines, are all easy entry points. And the open ocean makes it even easier to transfer goods from one ship to another. A small boat meets a big one, the goods get off-loaded, and both sail on their merry way."

"But there'd be people on a charter. Wouldn't they see what's going on?"

"Not necessarily. They're out for a good time. Put dead fish or chum on top of a bucket and no one's going to look too deep into it to see what else might be in there."

"Clever. Stuff comes in with the day's catch."

"That's what one of my Coast Guard buddies told me."

"I'll find a way to let Moss know."

"Tell him to watch his six. These guys play for keeps."

"Copy that."

"What do you think?" asked Brody bright and early the next morning, when he stood several feet away from Moss, each man pretending to be alone, fishing off the municipal pier.

"About Buddy? Okay guy. Likes to hear himself talk."

"And drink. What'd he down? Six in under an hour?"

"I lost count. But there were a lot of empty bottles on your table when you two left. It was fun watching you nurse your lone beer. And he couldn't bowl worth a damn."

"Not sure it was the best use of our time. Bowling? Really?"

"Harmless." Moss rebaited his hook and tossed his line back into the water. "I enjoyed yucking it up with my fishing buddies, but I'll admit you didn't look like you were enjoying the game or the company."

"Got me thinking there was some reason Darby pushed so hard to get us to go."

"You thinking that too?" Moss's line pulled and he reeled in his catch. "A little small." He threw the fish back.

"Yep. There was something off about Buddy. Not sure what. Seemed evasive when I asked him about the dead vet. He wasn't real forthcoming."

"I couldn't hear all of your conversation. Too much other noise. Darby said Buddy and the dead vet were friends, so maybe he was being a good friend and didn't want to talk out of school."

"Could be. But the guy's dead. And someone broke into Darby's house. And he's the cop who showed up to investigate the break-in. Without his partner, I might add."

"Do you think the dead vet and the break-in at Darby's are related?"

"Don't know. No proof, but my gut is telling me they are."

"Mine too. We're thinking the same things. We've got to stop hanging around together."

"We're not hanging around together. Just two guys out for a morning of fishing. And last night we each wound up at the bowling alley with our respective friends, tossing balls down adjacent alleys."

"Right. We don't know each other. Just happened to be at the same places at the same time."

"And we're right. There is something there that Darby felt too. Just don't know what it is yet. And she wanted us to spend some time around Buddy to see if we felt it too."

"And now that we do, what are we going to do about it?"

"Got me, but no fish are biting on my line. It's eleven o'clock and Brianna's bus should be dropping her off soon. The kids have half a day."

"Playing daddy? Getting pretty serious with this kid."

Brody smiled at Moss. "I'm outta here." He reeled in his line, started to put away his tackle. "One more thing. I talked to Brett yesterday. Says he thinks drugs are coming in on those fancy charter boats you're working."

"Tell me something I don't know," said Moss. "Hiding drugs in fish guts? Okay, good hiding place. But tourists talk. Get a few beers in them and they'll tell you about the big fish they caught or the even bigger one that got away. Or the ship they saw unloading what the crew claimed were supplies in the middle of the ocean."

"Transferring drugs in international waters with a boat filled with tourists out for a fun day fishing strikes me as the epitome of brazen, shove-it-in-your-face. Hard to believe someone in the law enforcement community doesn't know something about something."

"You think they know and are ignoring it?"

"You tell me."

"Someone is getting paid to look the other way." Moss reeled in some slack in his line. "Yankov's no dummy. He's a crazy Russian, crazy as a fox. Plays our immigration system for all he can get. Welfare, food stamps, housing. Get him drunk, and he'll tell you how much he loves America. Back home, with the shit he's into, he'd be up to his ass in ice in Siberia and he knows it. But he wouldn't risk years in a federal prison unless the payoff made taking the risk worth his while."

"Or unless he knew he wouldn't...couldn't...get caught." Brody finished packing up his fishing gear and put on his jacket. "A Coast Guard friend told Brett about some recent busts. Said to keep your eyes open and watch your back."

"Always do. Got a taste of Earl's dog fighting action last night. This boy has got to be stopped."

"That's the plan."

"Good. Thanks for the info. I've got a plan ready to go to flush this sucker out."

Moss made no move to watch Brody go or to leave the pier. Better to stay put, should any curious eyes be cast in his direction.

Earl Sojack lived in a world of his own making. Two worlds, really. His time as the country bumpkin on the Eastern Shore of Virginia was punctuated with boredom. Farming tomatoes and milking cows didn't exactly make a man rich. Fishing and running charters for well-off tourists paid well, but was hard work and unreliable. When the weather turned, the tourists disappeared. Didn't want to get their fancy duds wet.

Then there was the other Earl Sojack, who disappeared a few times each year for a week of high-rolling pleasure with some of the world's most beautiful women hanging on his arm, laughing at his jokes, and fulfilling every sexual fantasy a fifty-plus man could conjure up. He loved trading his Wranglers and flannel for Armani, Beluga caviar and Veuve Clicquot.

He didn't talk about how he made his real money, and in the circles he traveled in, no one dared to ask. He was a small fish in a big pond, envious of the larger operations, desperately working to expand his empire beyond the

Eastern Shore. To Virginia Beach. To Hampton. To Chesapeake. To Newport News. So many potential customers waiting for his unique treats.

He made sure his two worlds never crossed, though lately his time away was increasing exponentially, because things at home were spiraling out of his control. He urgently needed a way out, only the world he wanted out of refused to let him go.

Tonight's dinner aboard a private chartered yacht anchored in Norfolk could turn out to be the answer to his prayers. His host, who claimed to be the head of one of the more powerful Eastern European drug cartels, had contacted him by phone. Earl's network, while small in comparison, was just what his host was looking for—a way in to hook the backwater kids who wanted to be like the big city teens they interacted with on social media sites.

The progression was always the same, marijuana to cocaine to opioids to heroin to any and every mix of the above. You know you've got 'em when their high goes from wanting the stuff to feel good, to needing the stuff to function. Every dealer's dream client. Needy. Once hooked, they bought more and more, feeding their growing addiction with the next popular drug. Right now it was fentanyl-laced heroin.

Earl was anxious. Eager. Clean-shaven and smelling good, he arrived early, and was tipping back his second martini when his host made his appearance.

"Mr. Sojack?" The voice came from behind him.

"My friends call me Earl," he said twisting in his seat to see who was addressing him.

"I'm not your friend, Mr. Sojack. This is business, pure and simple. Friendship has nothing to do with it."

Moss slid into the plush leather chair opposite his invited guest. Neither spoke, their eyes doing the talking, appraising each other, making assessments and possibly dangerous assumptions about their respective fitness and skill.

"You? I know you. From the fight the other night. You work for Yankov, on one of the boats. I remember when we met, you stank of fish."

"Appearances can be deceiving."

"So they can." Earl glanced around the lavish chartered yacht.

"Expecting company?"

Earl didn't respond.

Moss smiled and looked around the room. "I expected you to be alone. That was our agreement."

"Your agreement. I don't remember agreeing."

"Then we're done here. Enjoy your evening." Moss rose, tapped his cell phone lightly on the table and started to leave.

"Wait." Earl looked at him and then fumbled with the toothpick holding olives in his martini.

Moss stopped, cooly staring at Earl.

The most subtle nod from Earl had two men who had been leaning against the dock railing walk back to the parking lot.

Moss watched each man depart.

"Feel better?"

"Ecstatic." Smiling inside, Moss felt alive for the first time in years. He relished the thrill of the chase, the subterfuge. The adrenaline rush. It had been a long time between assignments.

His life catering to his previous boss Hayden's every need had been boring. Maybe when this was over he'd call a friend or two at the DEA, and ask about the possibility of them throwing him the odd undercover job.

"You said you had something I might be interested in? Have we done enough foreplay? Are you ready to get down to business?"

Moss chuckled. "Dennis said you get right to the point."

"Dennis?"

"The dead vet. You remember Dennis." Moss played his hunch. "To hear him tell it, he was your ace distributor up and down the coast."

"He talked too much."

"Maybe that's what got him dead."

"I wouldn't know."

"What do you know, exactly, that would keep me interested in having this conversation with you? Or do you want to just enjoy a pleasant evening on Chesapeake Bay?"

"Who are you, and how'd you wind up on one of Yankov's boats?"

"I'm outta here. You ask too many questions about what's none of your business." Moss stood as the steward came into the salon.

"We're about to get underway, sir. Is that okay?"

"Give us a few moments before you cast off please," said Moss.

"Yes, sir."

"Relax, friend," said Earl. "I'm just the cautious type. I like to get to know the people I'm doing business with."

"You don't have to get to know me. You'll never see me again. Unless you screw up."

"Are you threatening me?"

"No." Moss chuckled. "I wouldn't dream of it. Not my style. But I'm also the cleanup crew, if you catch my drift."

"Double duty? Odd. Not too many folks handle both ends."

"Keeps expenses down. And I'm exceptionally good at what I do, unlike whoever you got to whack Dennis."

"I told you I don't know anything about that."

"Right. And I'm the tooth fairy." Moss chuckled, but made sure his eyes didn't laugh. His expression remained blank with a tinge of menace. "So, what's it going to be? You want in, or what?"

"Yeah. When? Where?" Earl paused slightly. "And how?"

"That's one more question than you need to know. You'll be contacted when your shipment is ready. Be ready with payment on your end. Non-consecutive hundreds, old bills preferred, please."

"I'll want to sample the product."

A wide grin spread across Moss's face. "It's good stuff. Top shelf. Don't you trust me?"

"Trust? A valued concept in our line of work."

"This isn't my primary line of work."

"Right. You're a hired hand on a fishing charter. I forgot." Shrewdness veiled Earl's expression. "Or is it something else?"

"There you go with twenty questions again. That's my business, not yours."

"If we decide to do business together, your business will be my business."

"Dream on. Keep your phone close." Moss tapped his index finger on the table. "Remember, should our paths cross, you don't know me. Enjoy your evening." He turned and made his way out of the salon and onto the deck as a lovely young woman appeared from the opposite hall. Her tight silver dress caressed every curve.

Earl wasn't sure where to look. He watched Moss go, but quickly turned his attention to the delectable woman now approaching him. When he looked down at the table, he saw a small plastic bag with three pills inside, one blue, one yellow and one white.

"Slick." He pocketed the sample bag.

The scent of roses and honeysuckle reached him as he felt two arms encircle his waist.

"A dangerous move, my sweet," he said, twisting to face the new arrival.

"I thought you saw me." Ruby-red lips touched his. "Hello. I'm Miss Kim, your hostess for the evening. Shall we go?"

"By all means."

CHAPTER 17

Dusk settled over Wachapreague, and it promised to be a clear night. Already Darby could see a few stars making their presence known.

Earl's call had shocked her. But she accepted his invitation to a dog fight, first because she was convinced Earl was behind the threat to Brianna, and second because her daddy had always said you had to know your enemy to defeat your enemy. His favorite quote was from Sun Tzu. *'If you know the enemy and know yourself, you need not fear the result of a hundred battles.'*

And Earl was her enemy.

Darby checked her watch. Seven o'clock. She'd followed Earl's directions carefully, turned off Route 13 onto Piggin Road, and then made the next left. As soon as she made the turn, the asphalt disappeared, replaced by a dirt road covered with stones, cutting through thick trees, which quickly fell off to marshy, muddy shoulders. Darby gripped the steering wheel. The road, nothing more than a well-beaten path, ran along the lone solid ground through the swamp. *Don't want to swerve off and get stuck in the swamp muck. Too many snakes living in there.*

A tight hairpin turn had her back tires kicking up gravel. She searched the trees close to the road, looking for a small, hand-lettered sign nailed to a tree saying *eggs*. Earl had said to turn into the driveway next to the tree with the sign and continue along until she saw a second *eggs* sign on the right. Follow that road and take the left fork by the fallen live oak until it ends.

Part of her wished she had told Brody where she was going.

Another part knew he would have never let her go alone.

And she would never have risked it if he hadn't been there with Brianna.

While she was glad Brody and Moss had followed her home after Passover dinner at Rachel's, having to explain where she was going and why irked her no end. So she lied, a little white lie.

Okay, maybe a whopper of a lie. She told him she'd been called out to take care of a horse about to give birth and struggling. She'd probably be back late, and he shouldn't wait up.

A final sharp right turn revealed a clearing ahead of her packed with a slew of macho-male SUVs and trucks. Darby parked her Jeep next to a royal blue and black Silverado, its shiny chrome exhaust pipes rising high above the interior cab. Oversized, chunky spoke tires with chrome accents raised the truck's carriage high off the ground. Decals filled the rearview window glass announcing the owner's support of the NRA, game dogs, and his membership in various American Staffordshire Terrier clubs.

The other trucks parked on the grassy field were equally tricked out, several with gun racks, others sporting the Confederate battle flag, and with license plates from places as far away as Ohio, Tennessee, and Kentucky. One truck owner displayed his patriotism with the stars and stripes emblazoned on the truck's side panels. She couldn't help but wonder whether some of the men she saw were overcompensating for deficiencies in their anatomy with these over-the-top, macho machines.

Tamping down her fear, she took a deep breath, got out of her Jeep, and walked towards the John Deere tractor. She found the footpath where Earl said it would be, to the right of the green machine. Off in the distance she thought she heard cheering. When she emerged through the copse of trees, she saw the source of the cheers.

She took a deep breath when she saw that most of the participants were armed. She figured anyone not sporting a gun in a holster on his belt carried concealed. What surprised her the most was the presence of women and children. Some of the kids looked as young as ten.

Controversy surrounded dog fighting. But bringing children to the event was so wrong. *What must witnessing the violence of a dog fight do to their fragile psyches?* Watching this level of depraved indifference towards animals had to twist their minds and psyches. For some the scars would never heal, for others it was an invitation to indulge in their own acts of cruelty. She'd read articles which documented the road to sociopathic, predatory behavior started by hurting animals when they were children.

Who am I kidding? What could I possibly do to stop this violence?

She hooked her thumbs into the unused two front belt loops of her jeans and shifted her stance slightly to release some pent-up energy. Earl emerged from the crowd and came up to her.

"Looks like you found us."

"Looks like you shaved." His clean-cut appearance surprised her. "Where do you want me?"

"Right here with me will do just fine. You're here to watch tonight, see if you've got the stomach for our little games. If something happens and we need ya, I'll be sure to let you know. For now, enjoy yourself. Place a bet with a guy named Wilbur over there. Who knows? You might win some money."

Darby stayed put, shifting from foot to foot, biting the inside of her cheek, enjoying a momentary gust of wind that blew across the field. For April, it was unseasonably warm, and the cool air felt refreshing. Too bad it couldn't cleanse the testosterone stench of the scene she was witnessing.

A gong sounded, and the gathered men grew quiet. Earl stepped into the center of the circle.

"Dogmen."

"Here," the crowd screamed together.

Darby remembered the dinner scene from the movie *The Good Shepherd*, when members of the Skull and Bones society gathered on Deer Island.

"Thank you for coming. I hope tonight's event will bring the fighters victory, the owners honor, and all of my invited guests a good time. The proceeds from your entrance fees will go to support our goal of preserving the breed. At tonight's event we'll follow Cajun Rules. You know where the refreshments are and how our proceedings unfold. Without further adieu, let the games begin."

A rowdy, deep-voiced cheer rose from the crowd.

The referee called for the first competitors. Two pit bulls, one brindle named Thor, and one black with a white bullseye circle around its left eye named Bullet, appeared in the pit, their owners holding them at the scratch line using a thick chain. Each dog had been weighed, and washed by the opponent's owner before the fight to ensure no poisons were on its skin.

The sickly sweet smell of weed infested the air. Men with joints clenched in their lips held fistfuls of money, some screaming at the top of their lungs as the two dogs lunged at each other.

I could get high just walking through this crowd. She inhaled some smoke-filled courage.

The rabid crowd, hungry for a kill, or at the very least spilled blood, whooped and hollered. Dog fighting was a blood sport. Stir in the nauseating stench of body odor, beer, alcohol, and tobacco and you've got the makings of a fun night, hidden from everyone except the privileged, invited few.

A deafening cheer from the crowd had Darby turn her head in time to see Thor's neck caught in Bullet's jaws. Grimacing, bile rising in her throat, Darby stifled the urge to puke, and a greater urge to run away from the dog fight into the darkness.

But she couldn't run. She'd put herself here, accepted Earl's invitation, and she had to stick with it. A feverish urgency boiled her blood. She had to save these dogs, these puppies. People—dogs—puppies—all counting on her.

She blinked rapidly, then forced herself to focus by studying the crowd. It took all her concentration not to wipe her sweaty palms across her pants. Her father's admonition, "never let them see you sweat" blared in the back of her mind. Right, Dad.

Fifteen minutes into the fight, the referee called a turn when Thor turned his head and shoulders away from Bullet. The wounded pit bull struggled and managed to jump out of the pit, whipping the crowd into a frenzy. Both dogs were returned to their handlers, and the referee called for the fight to continue, but Thor had lost his fighting edge and was quickly defeated. He lay, barely breathing, in the center of the pit. Darby's attention landed on a horrified face, a brawny man looking like he just lost his best friend.

Darby started to move, but felt someone grab her arm. She turned to see Earl staring at her.

"Where do you think you're going?"

"To help. He's in pain."

"Chet, his owner, will take care of him. I'll let you know when your help is needed. Until then, just relax and enjoy the show."

Fear's iron grip held her tight, her stomach roiled, her jaw clenched, the tension in her neck straining her ability to hold her head up straight. Her chest ached, constricting her breathing.

Several spectators chanted *cur-cur-cur*, the word used to label a dog who had lost its gameness. Then a man stepped up to the dog who lay in pain at the center of the pit. He pulled out a revolver and shot the dog dead. Darby gasped as her hand flew to cover her mouth.

Then the owner knelt down, his long, thinning gray hair pulled back in a ponytail, an impressive handlebar mustache, and sad-looking powder blue eyes, picked Thor up, and headed her way accompanied by the hoots and jeers of the crowd.

Her eyes brimmed with tears. She turned away from the savagery, hoping to pull her tears inside with a deep breath. As he pushed past her, they locked eyes.

Barely above a whisper, so only she could hear, he said "Couldn't let him suffer."

"Oh!" Darby's breath caught in her throat, and she turned away, tears welling up again.

"See? What did I tell you," said Earl. "We didn't need your help. The dog was doomed when he quit."

Darby had no response.

"You did good. Better than most, Doc." Earl's sickening grin made her stomach twist. "Far as I'm concerned, you're in. I'll call when I need you. And when I call, you better come running."

CHAPTER 18

"Who else might have known about Dennis's extracurricular activities?" asked Darby, taking a bite of her hamburger after begging Tommy not to bring another pizza and to instead get take-out from the Island House when they met for lunch.

"You tell me. You were colleagues." Tommy sat in Darby's office, Mercy curled up on his lap while he scratched under her chin.

"Right, but it's not like we were best friends or anything. We rotated coverage so people would always have emergency care for their pets. There's no 24-hour emergency animal hospital for miles. Kept the costs down, and our patients got the care they needed."

Mercy did a slow stretch and yawn. "Bet that felt good." Tommy steadied her while the pup turned around once and got comfortable. "She seems to be doing pretty well on three legs."

"I hated to amputate her back leg, but there was no way to save it. She's young, and already finding new ways to balance herself." Darby eyed Tommy with a curious grin. "Sure you don't want her? She's taken to you, you know, since you visit her every day. Mopes around when you leave."

"I'm working on the missus. Need a little more time."

"Gotcha." Darby popped a French fry into her mouth. "You said you have more information."

"Yeah. Now that the case is an official homicide, we can do more digging. I checked into Dennis's financials. Right after Doris died, there was an influx of cash deposits to his local bank account that went out almost as quickly, matching amounts on credit cards, but nothing matches receipts from his veterinary practice."

"He was getting money from somewhere. Did you ever ask Buddy about whether Dennis had a second job?"

"I did. He said he didn't know of one." Tommy scratched his head and frowned. "But here's the more troubling part. I pulled phone records and GPS records from his car. Looks like he spent a lot of nights driving out in the middle of nowhere, out by Frogstool and Piggin Roads. But there's nothing out where the coordinates show him going, so I Googled it."

"I've got a bad feeling I'm not going to like what you found."

"You're not. Pulled up the satellite view. Darby, it's an open field with what looks like a pit. On Sojack land. I checked the records. Consistent with the rumors of dog fighting back there.

"Shit." Darby bit her tongue. She'd decided to keep her recent foray into the world of dog fighting her own little secret. Earl had accepted her, so she didn't feel any immediate danger. When things changed, she'd scream for help.

"That's an understatement if ever I heard one. But it gets worse."

"How could it get any worse?"

"What I'm thinking makes it worse. I think Sojack, his sister Wanda, and her husband Wilbur, are augmenting their legitimate farming and horse-rearing business by sponsoring dog fights and running a puppy mill selling game dogs' offspring. Stud fees and selling puppies sired by champion game dogs is where a lot of the money gets made."

"Do you have any proof?"

"Since I was already in the database, I expanded my research into their records. I found orders for large quantities of dog food and medicines for puppy shots."

"You're saying they're hiding in plain sight. Seem like common country folk, selling tomatoes, honey, eggs, corn, and whatever else they grow, at their farm stand, but then their evil twins invade their bodies and force them to hold dog fights and run a puppy mill?"

"Yep. That's what I'm saying. Sojack owns lots of land off the main roads. Would be easy to put a pit out in the middle of nowhere. You said you saw one under the house. Maybe that's for winter fights. And the one for fights during nice weather is in some back pasture."

"Makes me so mad I've lost my appetite." Darby crumpled up her napkin, tossed it on top of her half-eaten hamburger, her appetite gone. She took a sip of her Coke. "I hate this. Hate knowing dogs are being hurt by the people who were supposed to protect them and love them."

"To Sojack, animals are livestock—all animals. Dogs included. Just not sure how Dennis fit into all of this."

"I might be able to help there." Darby moved her Coke can out of the way and turned her laptop so they both could see the screen.

"Whatcha got?"

"Remember I told you Dennis and I did some shared ordering? Well Tracy, the tech who worked for both of us, took care of the drug orders and processed the deliveries. The other day, when I stopped by Dennis's office to get some patient files, I copied some of his inventory records, because there were some orders I couldn't make heads or tails of."

"How'd you get into his computer?"

"Luanne gave me his password, and I had his social security and business tax number because of our shared ordering."

"Convenient."

"And Brody's cyber wizard friend, Brett, worked his magic online after you gave him information the other day."

"Oh, I can tell this is going to be good."

"Yes, it is. He made his way into Dennis's bank records—"

"By 'made his way,' I assume you mean hacked?"

"I know nothing about the how. I only know the what. What he found were cash deposits at a bank in Virginia Beach. Deposits into an account in guess whose name?"

"Dare I say it out loud?" He looked at her quizzically. "Buddy?"

She nodded. "Deposits he was able to match to withdrawals from Dennis's account. I think Buddy was blackmailing Dennis."

"How do you blackmail your friend?"

"Who better? Your friends know your secrets. And Buddy somehow knew Dennis worked with Earl's dog fighting business. When Dennis wanted out, Buddy saw his gravy train drying up."

"Are you saying Buddy is involved in Dennis's death?"

"He might not have pulled the trigger, but I think Dennis felt cornered. He needed money. Sold out to Earl. Got paid in cash, and used the money to pay off his dead wife's debts. Then he kind of got used to the money, liked what it got him."

Tommy stirred in his seat. "I hate where your line of thinking is going."

"You said it yourself, Every time you planned a raid on a dog fight, you found nothing. Kind of confirms your suspicions that Buddy's your mole."

"I knew I wouldn't like where you were going."

"And Brody's friend found a huge withdrawal from Buddy's account a few weeks ago. Just enough for that fancy new boat."

Tommy shook his head, staring at the floor. "Hard to believe Buddy would be on the take. Toss away his career for what? A few bucks."

"Depends on how few of those few bucks there were."

"He's a cop. We're supposed to be the good guys."

"Even good guys have needs."

"True. Having some extra cash lying around would sure be nice. Would get the missus off my back and get Mercy a new home." He finished his soda and tossed the can into the recycle bin. "Bills mount up. Wants and needs outweigh resources. And before you know it, you're bribe bait. Only a matter of price. And everyone's got a price."

"Not me."

"Really, Miss-Pure-as-the-Driven-Snow? Think so?"

"I know so."

"What if I could offer you the ten acres of land adjacent to your current property, free of charge and tax-free too, and all you'd have to do is a little favor for me?"

"Would depend on the favor."

"Gotcha. See how easy that was?"

"I—I didn't mean I'd do the favor."

"Whether you would or wouldn't is immaterial. You didn't give me an absolute no. So the wrong kind of person would just keep sweetening the pot until he saw your eyes twinkle. Until he met your price."

"But then why kill Dennis?"

"Maybe he'd had enough. Wanted out. Probably swore to keep their secret, but some secrets are hard to keep."

"And the dead tell no tales—or secrets."

The information Tommy shared weighed heavy on Darby's mind.

Guilt over not telling him about her trip to one of Earl's dog fights didn't help. Finally telling Brody last night helped after his initial anger fuse burned out and he could communicate more sanely. She loved having him here, though his presence in her home for the past few days did have her mind wandering into "what if" territory.

It was a beautiful Saturday. Brianna was at a birthday party, and Brody suggested some sightseeing. Darby welcomed his idea to take a drive into the country to, as he put it, see what they could see.

"We've got company." His eyes flashed to the rearview mirror. "Been with us for the last few miles, through my last two turns onto these side roads."

Her breathing kicked up a beat, and she felt the hairs at the back of her neck shiver when she caught sight of the tricked-out truck several yards back in the passenger side mirror. It had dual chrome exhausts rising above the cab, and so much chrome on the front grill it looked like it was wearing braces. She'd seen several trucks just like this one in the field at the dog fight.

"So much for a leisurely drive in the country on a Saturday afternoon. Why don't you slow down? Maybe they just want to pass us."

Brody slowed down, slid his window down, and motioned for the pickup truck to pass him. Instead, the truck also slowed down, then pulled off to the side of the road.

"Curious," said Brody.

"What's he doing?"

"Stopping," said Brody, who stopped in the middle of the road.

Darby twisted in her seat to look back.

"Think something's wrong with his truck?"

"Don't see any smoke. But maybe." He kept watching in the rearview mirror.

She looked at Brody, who was cool and calm behind the wheel, and let out a breath, thankful she was not alone.

"Does the truck look familiar to you?"

"Not sure. There were so many trucks there." But she was having trouble breathing. "It's a Mexican standoff," she said after a few minutes. "We just going to sit here while they sit there?"

"Guess the neighborly thing to do is to back up and see if they need help."

"That would certainly be the neighborly thing to do, but something doesn't feel right about this. Glad Brianna's not with us."

"You saying you'd prefer me not to be neighborly?"

She looked at him and let out a long sigh. "No. I'm not saying that."

"Yeah." His indecision passed. "Let's go see if they need help."

Brody put the car in reverse and twisted in his seat as he stepped on the gas and started to back up.

Suddenly the truck roared to life, belching an exhaust cloud of black smoke, and kicking up a swirl of road dust when the driver did a fast one-eighty and sped off the way it came.

"I'll be damned. Hold on." Brody shifted into drive, angled onto the side of the road, executed a perfect turn, then gunned the accelerator, chasing the truck. Suddenly, he slammed on the brakes and stopped.

"What was that all about? Why'd you stop?"

"My saner instincts just overrode macho me."

"Because I'm in the car?"

He reached out and touched her cheek. "Yep. No sense going off half-cocked."

"Well, nothing was wrong with their truck, and they clearly didn't want us seeing who they were. Too bad we couldn't see the license plate. I can give Tommy a description of the truck. Maybe he'll know who owns it."

"Maybe. I wouldn't hold your breath."

"So where does this leave us?"

"Out in the country, on a back road leading nowhere."

"Think it's time we head back, pick up Brianna, go home, and cook up an early dinner."

CHAPTER 19

Timing is everything, Darby thought. After their little adventure yesterday, during what was supposed to be a pleasant ride in the country, all she could say was bless Ashley's heart for showing up when she did and offering to take Brianna to the Sunday kids' matinee at the local movie theater.

Darby mouthed a silent thank-you to Ashely as she and Brianna walked out the door.

When she saw them make the turn out of the driveway, she excused herself. In her bedroom she set the scene with candles, changed into a delicate white teddy, walked out to the top of the stairs, and called Brody's name.

It took two tries before Brody could pry himself away from the NBA game he was watching. He finally appeared at the bottom of the stairs, his expression broadcasting his annoyance that she'd called him. But then he saw what she was wearing, cleared his throat, and slowly started up the stairs, his smile widening with each step. She backed up into her bedroom. He followed and closed the door.

"Nice room," he said, looking at the candles and the turned-down bed. "I like how you decorate."

"Thought you might."

He brushed a hair away from her eyes.

"Are you sure?"

"Yes. We've waited long enough."

Carefully, he lifted her in his arms and carried her to the bed, laying her gently on white sheets.

"You are beautiful, so beautiful."

Darby patted the sheet beside her and reached out for him.

"We've got about two hours. Think it's enough time?"

"For starters," he grinned. And then he kissed her, gently at first, like all the kisses they'd shared before. And then more deeply.

"Think I've got too many clothes on for this."

Standing up, he shucked his shirt and jeans. A wave of heat swept over her watching him. His body was a shrine to physical fitness—lean muscles, sculpted abs, a bronze tan with a sliver of white skin showing above his briefs. He sat back down on the bed, rolled on top of her, and nestled himself between her legs, their lips meshing as one.

He tasted good, manly. And he smelled good, like an ocean breeze.

She wanted him inside her, wanted to consummate their relationship.

Could this thing with Brody become the lasting love she used to believe in? She had no answer, but she wanted this one time, this first time, to be special. No matter what, though, she and Brody had waited long enough, teased and toyed with each other through Thanksgiving and Christmas, never getting the chance before today. And she wanted to experience what those teasing kisses and nuzzles and cuddles and strokes promised, right here, right now— whatever the outcome.

His lips went exploring, nibbling down her neck, his fingers gently stroking her rock-hard nipples. She kissed his shoulder and felt heat surging through him. Fiery spasms shot through her when he began to suckle at her breast.

And while he nuzzled her neck and stroked down her arm, raising goose bumps, a usually silent part of her mind whispered, *what if?* There was no doubt in her mind that Brody was a good man, and already fully committed to her...and, perhaps more important, to Brianna. Was she ready?

She nearly died herself when Benjamin died. But did her one loss truly mean more heartbreak was inevitable? And if she allowed her fears to rule, was she about to make a mistake that could break all their hearts?

Her breath caught on a throaty moan.

He pulled back slightly, and, seeming satisfied with what he saw, returned to kissing her, his tongue plunging into her receptive mouth. Hungry kisses, dueling tongues.

"You are so lovely."

His hands roamed her body, stopping at her hips. He pressed his palms to the bed and lifted himself up off her, moving back so his kisses could travel downward. He kissed and nibbled, nibbled and kissed, his tongue making circles around her belly button before it continued its journey south.

When he reached the promised land, he settled in, his tongue making magic and eliciting joyous moans and gasps, while his hands cupped and coddled her breasts. She purred. And then his lips were back on hers, while she danced her fingertips up and down his penis before wrapping her hand around his manhood and pulsing it gently.

"God, I love you." His declaration mingled with his kisses.

A primal groan reverberated through her, her body responding to his every touch. After one deft move on his part, her teddy was gone. Then his hands slipped down her back, pushing away the elastic of her panties and sliding them off. He knelt above her, admiring her. Then he was next to her, his fingers gently exploring private places.

"Tight."

"It's been a while."

"For me too. Since I met you, first held you in my arms, there's been no one else. We'll go slowly. I don't want to hurt you in any way." He kissed her forehead, her eyelids, the tip of her nose, and found his way back to her lips. "And there won't be anyone else until you tell me we're a no-go."

His kiss deepened. "Of course that's not what I want to hear."

Darby was lost in every blissful, pulsing sensation. It had been so long since she had a man in her life, in her bed, the last thing she wanted to do right now was think about what might come next, or how they would end. She dug her fingers into his shoulder, her back arched, electricity igniting long-forgotten pleasures. The only word resounding in her head was more...more...more.

His hands slid down her body, stopping behind her knees. With one move, he lifted her legs onto his shoulders, his mouth finding her wet with desire. He buried his tongue in between soft folds, licking and sucking, inserting fingers, then tongue. And again her brain and body cried out more...more...more.

Darby felt him watching her, gauging her pleasure with each move. She loved that he was more focused on pleasing her than his own enjoyment. And when he heard her purr, she saw him smile before he repeated the action.

More. More. More.

He rolled onto his side, sheathed himself, and lifted back on top of her, pushing her thighs apart. Then he was inside her, his power, his strength growing with every thrust. Slowly, they found their rhythm. Darby locked her legs around him, and together they soared.

For one moment, she gripped the sheets and cried out, unable to control herself. Her muscles clenched and released, clenched and released, as he continued to drive into her. Their rhythm picked up speed, his mouth found hers, she clawed his back, their pleasure spiking as one, spinning gloriously up, up, and away.

Release. Nirvana. She was sure rockets were bursting out of the top of her head, because the pleasure she felt ran from her head to her toes. A divine explosion washed over her as he came seconds after she did.

Gasping for breath, his body trembling like hers, both of them drenched in sweat, almost glued together, he pushed damp hair off her face and showered her with kisses.

"You okay?"

"Beyond okay." Her voice trembled.

He started to roll away. She stopped him.

"Stay a moment," she whispered, enjoying the weight of him as she returned to earth. Each inhale brought more of him into her, his scent, his manliness, his being. If only she could keep him. And if not, she'd cherish the memory of his scent forever.

He braced himself with his elbows so his kisses shower could continue for a few minutes longer, and she could breathe more easily without his full weight crushing her chest. As their breathing returned to a normal pace, he levered himself up and off, pulled her against his side, and wrapped his arms around her protectively. She nestled her face into his neck and played with his few chest hairs as their breaths eased.

There were no words to describe what they just shared, and none were uttered. Sleep found them for a few blissful minutes.

He stirred first. Pulling his arm from under her head, he sat up, then headed for the bathroom to clean up. She watched him go, admiring his slender hips, broad shoulders, and tight butt from behind. Warrior stock, who protected and served in a previous life. Now, still protecting, but with less hand-to-hand combat. Slowly, she got out of bed, picked up her teddy and panties and went to the hall bathroom.

Their timing was perfect, because as they met in the hall, fully clothed after finishing their cleanup routines, Darby heard a distant horn toot.

Darby looped her arms around his neck and gave him a too-quick kiss. "That's Ashley and Brianna."

"How do you know?"

"Planned signal. To give us time to make ourselves presentable."

"You had this all planned?"

"Yup. Afternoon delight. Ashley is my co-conspirator."

"You little dickens."

Her sigh spoke volumes. "We've got things we have to talk about, but after what's been going on, I decided to enjoy you while you're here."

"Some decision." His smirk grew wider. "And did you enjoy me?"

"Every inch."

The front door burst open and Brianna came rushing into the house.

"Mommy, Mommy. We saw *Frozen*, and then Ashley took me for ice cream. And she let me have a sundae, with strawberries and chocolate sauce, and sprinkles."

"That sounds good, baby. Did you like the movie?"

"Yes, Mommy. And then we stopped at the bowling alley, and Mr. Finn let me bowl."

"He did?"

"Yes." Her voice flattened.

"Why so sad?"

"My ball didn't go very far. But the next time I knocked down two pins. Didn't I, Ashley?"

"Yes, you did." Ashley looked from Darby to Brody and back. She winked at Darby and took Brianna's hand. "Bath time, little one."

"You still have to read me a story. You promised."

"I did promise, and I will read you a story, but you have to get into your jammies first."

Brianna held out her arms and gave Darby a big hug and kiss. Then she repeated the hug and kiss with Brody, took Ashley's outstretched hand, and bounced up the stairs.

CHAPTER 20

Buddy took another hit. His life was in the crapper, but a quick high softened the blows. He wiped the powder remnants from his nose and licked his fingers.

Just need to take the edge off.

He had enough stuff for one more hit. His spine melted and he fell back against the sofa, closing his eyes, reveling in the buzz.

Nothing was real for him anymore. Nothing mattered.

Not since Angie left.

Tough as it was to admit it, he'd really loved his second wife. But she, like all his other women, got tired of his lies, womanizing, and drinking. The day she left, calling him a loser and a bum, his life ended. Since then he'd been going through the motions, biding his time until retirement, when he would collect a meager pension at the end of a dull, dreary, failure-studded career. Still a decade away and the impetus for his current predicament.

Events were spiraling out of his control, and he needed to rein in his partner, Tommy, before his innate curiosity blew up in his face. Or worse, got him killed.

Killed?

They wouldn't dare kill Tommy. Killing a cop crossed the line, and even these guys had lines.

Where did killing a vet fall on that line?

His phone chirped, and he looked at the caller ID.

"Shit."

His thumb hovered over the Talk button.

He was playing a dangerous game and he knew it. But he loved it. The action. The danger. The moment-to-moment, not knowing what might happen next. A tightrope of adrenaline-fueled, head-rushing, thrill-induced power. Nothing compared.

The money wasn't bad either. Cash. All cash. Two divorces had been bleeding him dry, and he didn't have a pot to piss in until he started helping Earl. He'd always resented Earl's money, and that Buddy's side of the family never got to share in the wealth Earl's activities generated. But when Earl needed him to protect the family's activities, Buddy couldn't say no. What's family for if not to help?

But he also knew he was playing with fire, risking a burn from which there was no recovery. He had done his part. Now he wanted out, but getting out was easier said than done. Images of Dennis's body flashed across his mind. Dennis had wanted out, too, and look where it got him. Permanently out.

Buddy's stalling sent the call to voice mail, and he again closed his eyes and lost himself in the kaleidoscope of colors and sounds swirling in his mind.

Ten minutes passed before he opened his eyes again and scraped the remaining powder off the table into his goody bag. He chugged the remains of his drink, a drug-laced alcohol concoction that went down ever so easily, numbing himself to the world with his favorite elixir, then got up and headed for the bathroom.

"Ouch!" His foot twisted when it caught the edge of a chair, and he went down on his ass. "Damn chair."

The pain from where he'd been shot years ago flared up. His leg had never been the same. Pain killers helped initially, but the Vicodin led to Oxy, and now cocaine. He didn't overdo it, couldn't afford to get caught using, or fail a drug test. Luckily, a friend always let him know when his name popped up on the random drug test list. He'd just been tested, so he felt free to use, knowing he would not be tested for awhile.

He hobbled to the toilet, did his business, splashed water on his face, rinsed his mouth out with Listerine, strapped close to twenty pounds of equipment around his waist, and headed out the door, making sure the lock clicked. He was, after all, on duty.

Why? Why care about this shithole? Because this shithole was home, the only home he'd ever known. And home, a huge stretch for the word, was a three-bedroom cottage on the edge of town. It had been his parents' place when they were alive, and it looked now like it looked then. Frozen in time. Why change what worked? And besides, decorating was a girl thing.

Playing both sides was a dangerous game, but exhilarating. One false move in front of Tommy got him a reprimand or maybe fired. In front of Earl, it got him killed, body never found.

"Life's about choices," he sighed, and pushed the button on his phone to retrieve the message from the call he let go to voice mail.

"We need to talk. Get your ass up here."

The words chilled him. Earl wasn't one for collegial conversation, and his tone sent a chill up Buddy's spine, like nails on a chalkboard, but way worse.

Darby made no effort to wipe away the tears that ran freely down her face when she heard a car and saw Brody and Brianna pull up.

"Where have you been?" she cried racing out the door to meet them.

"We went for ice cream. I left you a note. On the counter."

"I didn't see a note. Why didn't you answer my text?"

Brody, acting like he had X-ray vision, stared through the screen door. "I'm sorry about the text. Believe it or not, I left my phone here. We weren't going to be gone that long, so I didn't think it would be a problem."

"Okay. As long as she's safe, you're both safe."

"Curious."

"What is?"

"That you didn't find the note I left."

Now Darby turned to look through the screen door into the house. "I'm not doubting you. If you say you left one, it must have slid off the counter or something."

"Or something." He walked into the house and stood in the center of the kitchen. "Has anyone been here?"

"Only Tracy. She was waiting for me when I got here. She needed my signature on some invoices that needed to be paid. We chatted for a few minutes, I signed them, and she left."

"Was she in the kitchen? Alone?"

"Yes. She followed me in." Her brows furrowed. "I only left her for the few minutes it took me to go to the bathroom." Her fingers slid through her hair as her palm rested on her forehead. "You don't think Tracy took the note?"

"I'm not sure what to think. Too many things going on that don't make sense. How well do you know Tracy?"

"She's my tech. Helps me with surgeries. Dennis and I both used her services."

"You trust her?"

"Yes." Her inflection spoke volumes her single-word reply did not.

"But?"

"I'm not sure. She told me she wouldn't be available for a few weeks. Something about her brother's leave getting changed, and really wanting to see him before he went back to his unit. I didn't know she even had a brother."

"What do you know about her? Her family?"

Darby thought for a few moments. "Nothing, really. She worked for Dennis, and I called her in when I needed an extra pair of hands for a difficult surgery. She's a good technician, so I never questioned anything about her."

Brody pulled two bottles of water from the fridge and handed her one.

"Other than a surprise brother, anything else bothering you about her?"

"Sort of. Not sure it's not pure jealousy though."

"What do you mean?"

"She has a beautiful, new, fire-engine red Mercedes."

"Sa-weet ride."

"It is. But on a technician's salary? And she was showing off some expensive designer boots and handbags the other day."

"More mystery money? You want me to get Brett on it?"

"No. Not yet. But I've been going over purchase orders, more specifically drug orders, something Tracy handled for both our clinics, and I think I found some discrepancies."

"What do you think you found?"

"Missing pills. More drugs ordered than I could account for on the shelf. I plan to ask her about it when I have it clear in my mind. The government has cracked down a lot on the controlled substances veterinarians use in our practices. I wouldn't want to lose my license over something like unaccounted-for medications."

Buddy ran into Wilbur when he pulled into Earl's driveway. Getting called to the big house was never good.

"What's up?"

"Got me. He's definitely got a bug up his ass."

"He call you, too?"

"Yeah."

Wilbur opened the door to Earl's place and they went into the kitchen to wait for him.

"Wanna a beer?"

"Sounds good."

"Can't see what's got him riled. We're making more money than ever. Lots of guys desperate for an escape from their nagging wives, boring lives. Sure, they could go for sex, but here they get an adrenaline rush that sex can't match. Then they go get their rocks off—at least that's what they tell me. Earl's been talking about expanding, providing a few hotties for his guests to enjoy."

"That's the last thing we need to do. Getting into prostitution is a no-win scenario in a small town. The girls would be so obvious. We'd have to keep them chained in some basement."

"I go home to Wanda. Soft, cushy titties. A man could suckle forever and get lost inside her. My Wanda's never too tired, always willing and eager to please. And if she isn't, I just whap her upside the head, and she comes around real fast."

They heard the roar of the Harley's engine and then silence when it was turned off. Steps on the porch stairs, the screech of the screen door, the inside door slamming shut.

"Hey, Earl. Can I get you a beer?" Wilbur stared at his now clean-shaven brother-in-law. "You look good without the beard. What made you shave?"

Earl ignored Wilbur's question.

"The only thing you idiots can get me is an explanation. What the fuck is going on?"

Sweating like a whore in church, Buddy put his beer on the kitchen table and wiped his palms against his thighs.

"Not sure what you're asking, Earl. What's got you going?"

"That bitch vet. That's what's got me going. Don't you think it's odd that she shows up, sticking her nose in our business, right before the biggest fight of the year? When our business is peaking?"

Buddy stared at Earl. He opened his mouth to speak.

"Shut up, stupid. Sit…your…ass…down." Earl kicked a wooden kitchen chair in his direction.

Eyes locked. Buddy shivered under Earl's steely glare. And he slowly lowered himself onto the chair.

"Well, we're not going to let little Miss Goody Two-shoes spoil what we've got going. Tomorrow night ends her career. Got that?"

"Yeah, but she's mighty popular. If she goes missing, they'll bring out the cavalry to look for her." Buddy's buzz disappeared. So much for his afternoon treat. He still reeled from the brutality of Dennis's killing, and he didn't want to see Darby hurt.

"That's what I pay you to stop, Buddy boy. And stop it, you better. You mess up, I'm going rain a world of hurt down on your ass. Got that, boy?"

"I'm just saying. She's got lots of friends in town. Hell, my partner is head-over-heels ga-ga for her. And there's this new guy staying at her house. Think she's got herself a boyfriend."

"I don't give a flying fuck about any boyfriend. And keep an eye on that new guy working Yankov's boat. Something about him stinks. But…whatever you do, don't go growing a conscience. It could get you killed."

Long, steady strides when Darby entered her living room and faced the men assembled there broadcast her determination to confront the ugly events that had overtaken her.

She set the tray of coffee, mugs, sugar, cream, and cookies on the coffee table and took a deep breath. Her moment of truth had arrived. She wanted to get her normal life back, wanted to wallow in her boring, everyday routine, to tuck Brianna in at night, kiss her cheeks, say sweet dreams.

Intuitively she knew, deep down inside, that life was gone forever.

Her heart pounded. Emotions had ramifications. She had to tamp her emotions down or she'd never be able to pull off this charade. Brody would see right through her.

Shaking like a leaf, she faced Brody, Tommy, and Moss, who snuck into her house under cover of darkness.

"I have an idea. You're going to hate it, but hear me out before you say no."

"You're right. I don't like it." Brody's stern countenance shook her conviction.

"You don't know what I'm about to say."

"Yes, I do. And no. No. No. No. No. No."

Darby's stare cut to his heart. "The least you can do is hear me out."

"Do I have a choice?"

"No."

"You two squabbling isn't getting us anywhere," said Tommy. "To be honest, I don't like your idea either."

"You haven't heard it yet."

"I can guess. I'm a good guesser. But I don't have a better idea to offer."

"Then we're agreed. I go in. You follow later, and we catch them in the act. Earl won't be able to deny it if we catch him red-handed. Moss said he'd be there. The guys he works with on the charter boat invited him. They think he's a good ol' boy like them."

"What if I go in?" asked Brody. "Show up like a spectator. Tell them a friend told me about the fight and wing it from there."

"They don't let just anyone in. Look in the mirror, Brody. Even if you're not one, your looks scream cop. I think they'd be suspicious. Hell, Earl's probably suspicious of me. But he invited me again, so I can show up."

"This has disaster written all over it," said Brody.

All eyes turned to Moss when he cleared his throat. "These people live in an alternate universe, one where hurting living creatures—men you perceive as weaker than you are, women, children, and animals—is okay, honorable even, when we all know it isn't."

"But the cruelty?" Tommy shuddered.

"Not every human being is really human," said Moss. "Studies have shown a connection between animal cruelty and human cruelty. A person starts as a child, abusing a dog or cat, and that cruelty escalates into antisocial behaviors towards other humans as the person ages." He took a long pull of his beer. "And lest we forget, I worked for a narcissistic psychopath for years."

"Who was that?" asked Tommy.

"A very nasty man. Someone you don't want to know. Someone who got what was coming to him."

"What's that supposed to mean?" asked Darby.

"Fate has a way of catching up to guys who do things like Hayden planned. And when fate gets involved, the outcome isn't pretty. You know what they say. Payback's a bitch."

Darby smiled and added, "He was my birth father. Creeps me out just to think that I have his genes, his DNA."

"But not his heart," said Brody.

"Thank you for reminding me." She smiled at him, and felt her toes curl when he smiled back. "There's an Immanuel Kant quote I love."

"The quote lady speaking," said Tommy. "I don't know how you do it. Your ability to remember quotes is remarkable."

"Thanks. Something someone else has said strikes me as worthy to remember. Their words touch a core place for me, resonate as a truth. So I remember it."

"Impressive," said Moss.

Darby smiled at him. "'*We can judge the heart of a man by his treatment of animals.*' What we know is these people, Earl in particular, have no heart. And I have to do everything I can, where I can, to stop him. Or I won't be able to live with myself."

"Even if it means putting yourself in danger?"

"Yes. And I know I'm a mother with a five-year-old child who has no one to depend on but me. But…the thing is… The things that have been going on here. The hang ups…and someone was in my house, ripped up one of Brianna's stuffed bears, and stenciled paw prints in red paint to mimic blood all over the place."

"I knew about the hang ups, but…a bloody stuffed bear?" said Tommy. "Buddy didn't tell me about that. He just said someone had broken into your house and he was taking care of it."

Darby shrugged. "There are times when you have to step up, regardless of cost, and this is one of those times."

"Dog fighting happening right under the noses of the local cops doesn't make sense. How does Earl always know when you're coming?" asked Moss.

"Maybe their noses have been bought and paid for," said Brody.

"Right." Tommy looked each person in the eye. "Our plans go no further than this room. Agreed?"

Everyone mumbled agreement.

Brody turned to Darby. "We didn't come fully equipped for business on this trip. And Tommy, after your comments,

I think I'll call Daniel. He's got FBI connections. Might be able to get us some of the latest and greatest technology the local LEOs don't have."

"Good idea."

Once Darby got them to accept the idea of her placing herself in the center of the action, the rest of the plan came together quickly. When she picked up the empty carafe and went into the kitchen to refill it, she could feel Brody's presence behind her, and she turned to face him. Before either one of them could say a word, his cell phone rang.

Pulling it out of his pocket, he said hold into the receiver. Then to Darby, "We're not done yet."

"Wrong. We are done, and I am doing it."

Darby pulled at her hands, something Brody had learned she did when anxious. He cradled her hands in his, lifted them to his lips and kissed them.

"Why you? You're not invincible. And after your last little adventure, I'd think you'd be more..."

"More what?" She stared at him. "Bad things are happening here. Bad things aimed at my child. Bad things marched into my house and left behind a bloody bear. Bad things keep happening when good people do nothing. I'm just as responsible for trying to end what's happening as the police or anyone else. Fight or flight. This is my home. My clinic is here. So I'm going to stand and fight. And besides, there isn't anyone else who can pull it off." She could feel steam coming out the top of her head. "And my dad didn't raise a wimp."

"You? A wimp? Hell, no. But he did raise a daughter who is now a mother, and who had one close call with potential death barely six months ago."

His cell phone rang again. Without looking at caller ID, he lifted the phone to his ear. "What?"

"That doesn't sound good," said the voice at the other end. "Trouble in paradise? Brody? You okay?"

"TJ?"

"What's going on?"

"Nothing I can't handle, but I may need a few more days."

"Sounds like your vacation has gone south."

"Virginia may be for lovers, but we've got a situation up here that requires a tad more attention." Brody's eyes never left Darby's face. "Moss is already working deep cover."

"That explains why I can't get him on his cell."

"Things kind of popped quickly. We didn't get a lot of planning time."

"What can I do?"

"Need some more time here."

"Not a problem. Your job is secure here. Let Moss know his is, too."

"Thanks. Brett's already on board. Hope that's okay."

"No problem. He told me. Call if you need anything."

Brody ended the call and stared at Darby.

"Your boss?"

"Yeah."

"Sounds like he's on board with you staying a bit longer."

"TJ's the best. Has had his own issues. Knows family comes first."

"But I'm not family."

"Minor technicality." He moved closer, reached out and stroked her cheek.

"Do you think this is a wise move?"

"Yes. But clearly you don't."

"Not necessarily, so don't put words in my mouth. I just want to make sure you don't go off and get more than you bargained for. Especially if I'm not there to help you."

"But you are here." She tilted her head up, bringing her mouth closer to his, her voice barely above a whisper.

Brody looked into her eyes and saw what he wanted to see. Love. He pulled Darby into his arms, nestled a kiss into her hair, and then rested his cheek on top of her head.

"You scared?"

"Scared, but not helpless. I can take care of myself."

"I don't doubt that for a minute."

"Don't patronize me. My dad taught me how to defend myself after some girls picked on me at school a few times. They knocked me around one day. Gave me a black eye. My dad was furious. Wanted to call the school, get them expelled. I cried and begged him not to. But I was sick of being scared so he taught me a few moves. And how to shoot. We used to go target shooting. And I told you about the self-defense classes I'm taking at the Y."

"You don't have to do this. There are other ways to get what we need to bring Earl down."

"Don't I?"

"No, you don't. I'm sure there's someone else, someone trained in undercover work, who they can send in."

"But that person won't be a vet, couldn't help, and you can't fake seven years of veterinary school, or learn what I know in a few days."

"They'll think of another way."

"There's no time. The fight's tomorrow night. I don't have a choice. These fights must stop, and stop now, before more innocent animals are hurt, maimed or killed." She took a deep breath and looked into his eyes. "I need to do this."

"Why?" Her words pierced Brody's heart.

"Because Dennis was a friend."

"Your friend is my friend. If I can't talk you out of your insanity, I'll be there to protect you."

"You will. Moss will. And Tommy, too." She nestled closer into his arms.

"Don't worry," he said. "Everything will work out."

"You sure?"

"Always."

His confidence reassured and inspired her.

CHAPTER 21

Darby's worry about Brianna's safety the night of the dog fight was calmed when Ashley invited her to a big-girl PJ party at Tori's apartment in Virginia Beach. She'd be miles away and safe. No one could find her to hurt her or use her in any way.

Brody and Tommy got into Darby's Jeep, and they headed out. He watched her out of the corner of his eye. Even after her kidnapping ordeal, and almost having one of her kidneys cut out, Darby displayed trooper qualities Brody truly admired. She appeared to have put the gruesome experience behind her and moved on with her life.

Then again, he thought, appearances could be deceiving. PTSD had a way of sneaking up on people who've experienced a trauma. Why she was deliberately putting herself in danger right now escaped him. They were definitely going to have a come-to-Jesus conversation when this was over.

"Pull over here," said Brody. "Let me get Brett on the phone. Eyes in the sky."

Brett answered on the first ring. "If it's computer-driven, it can be hacked, and I can hack it." Brody could almost see Brett doing his start-up routine on the other end of the phone. "Ready whenever you are. What am I looking for?"

"Not sure. Pull up images of the Eastern Shore of Virginia, Accomack County, to be precise. Around Wachapreague. Look for some sort of structure, maybe hidden back from any road. Something circular, like a pit."

"Okay. Give me a minute."

"I've got you on speaker. Tommy and Darby are here with me. Can you see us?"

"Yep. Got your cell pinged, and Darby's too."

"Good. Stay on Darby."

"Okay. If I find anything, I'll shoot the image to your phone, not hers. Wouldn't want any snoopy eyes asking questions."

"Before you go, one more thing. We think the money gets passed through wire transfers. Can't find out any details without a federal warrant. And we don't have nearly enough to get one of those without informing some people it may not be safe to include."

"Not a problem," said Brett.

"Didn't think it would be. Thanks, Brett. Call when you have something."

"How is that not a problem?" asked Tommy, who looked from Brody to Darby. "Never mind." He threw up his hands. "Don't tell me. Plausible deniability works for me."

Darby pulled off Route Thirteen onto a lonely stretch of dark road.

"Spooky," said Darby. "We've been driving for miles. There's nothing out here. Last time the *eggs* sign came up pretty quick once I got off the main road. I must have written down the directions wrong."

"Keep going," said Brody. "Nothing for miles seems like just the right location for what we're looking for. You said the first fight you went to, which we have yet to talk about, was out in the middle of nowhere."

Darby looked at him, her eyes narrowed.

"Eyes on the road, please." Brody adjusted his kevlar vest straps. "You ready back there?"

"Yep," said Tommy, cinching the tabs to snug up his vest. "I look good in black. Takes pounds off."

"Did you see that?" A flash of brake lights got her attention. Then darkness.

"Yeah. Pull up over there. Let us out. Then you keep going. I'm guessing you'll hit pay dirt about a mile up the road. That's about where those red lights disappeared to the left."

She pulled off the road and stopped the car. "Be careful."

"Don't worry about us. You be careful. Whatever is going on out here, the people involved want privacy. Be aware of who comes up behind you. Don't let yourself get cornered."

"Got it."

He looked at her and quietly opened the Jeep's door, glad he'd had the foresight to turn off the dome light. He signaled her to put down the passenger side window.

"Just do what you're asked to do. Moss is in the crowd but won't acknowledge you. No heroics."

"That goes for you, too. No risky moves. If you get hurt or killed, I'll kill you. Capisce?"

"Yes, ma'am."

He smiled at her, leaned in, and gave her a kiss. "Caution is my middle name, love."

Then they were gone, slipping into the underbrush like ghosts.

She resumed her slow trek down the dark road, surprised when she reached a clearing where at least fifty trucks were parked. She pulled alongside a battered Ford pickup truck and shut off the engine.

Earl watched Darby park her Jeep, lean forward and rest her head on the steering wheel.

"Looks like we got company," said Wilbur, sidling up to him. "Wonder who invited her?"

"I did."

"You're shitting me."

"Friends close, enemies closer. Always good to know a vet. Besides, she's kinda pretty." Earl ran his tongue over his top lip. "Wouldn't mind giving her a tumble."

Wilbur kept his mouth shut. The fear of Earl's wrath was enough to keep him from saying what he was thinking. His brother-in-law didn't stand a snowball's chance in hell of bedding a willing Darby. The only way he'd take her was by force, not that Earl hadn't succumbed to that transgression with other women he wanted, but who thought themselves better than him.

"What's she doing?" asked Wilbur.

"How the fuck do I know? Praying? Hope her God's listening. She's gonna need all the help she can get."

"What's that supposed to mean? What are you gonna do?"

"Wilbur, the less you know the better. Did you set up the second perimeter like I told you?"

"Yep." Wilbur wiped his brow. "Doubt she can be trusted."

"Trust never entered into the equation. Now go collect the cash from the beer stand. And don't take none off the top, or I'll skin you alive."

Wilbur rushed off, not daring to look back. Whatever Earl had planned, not knowing was the best way to stay alive.

Earl approached Darby, who still sat behind the wheel.

Her heart jumped when he rapped on her window.

"You found the place. Good."

"Yes. I followed—"

"Come on. Get out. Let's go."

He jerked her door open and hooked his arm over it before she could finish her sentence. She climbed out.

"Let me get my bag."

"No need. We've got all the supplies you might need."

A cold dread gripped her as she fell in step beside him, her anxiety increasing with each step, her palms slick with sweat. *Something's off. Earl's barely made eye contact with me. Last time I was here, his eyes never left mine.* Her skin prickled and her heartbeat was picking up speed with every step.

Focus. You can do this.

Tall grasses brushed her jeans as they made their way through the night. An eerie mist hung over the marsh as the day's heat gave way to the evening's chill. Croaking frogs punctuated an otherwise still night.

She crossed her arms, rubbing them with her hands, and wished she hadn't forgotten her water bottle, since her mouth felt drier than the Gobi desert.

"Cold?"

"No." Beads of sweat tickled the skin between Darby's breasts and ran down her back, sending a chill down her spine. She hoped her sudden shakes weren't visible to Earl.

"You won't be cold for long. We've got a good crowd tonight." Earl threw back his head and laughed, a deep, guttural laugh, almost evil. "Hot bodies jammed together, making a ring of impenetrable heat."

Darby stared at him, his description causing her stomach to lurch. Here was a man in desperate need of a psychiatric intervention or a good swift kick in the ass. She cocked her head, listening to cheering sounds growing louder with every step.

"What is that smell?" She pinched her nose closed and cupped her hand over it.

"The smell of sweet, sweaty cash. Pure money, honey. Give it time. You'll get used to it. Come to appreciate it, too, I suspect. What it can do for you and that cute little daughter of yours."

At his mention of Brianna, Darby shuddered, grateful Ashley had taken Brianna. Something was definitely off. She could feel it. Earl was behaving very differently this time around. When she attended the last fight, he was welcoming, almost cordial, which for a man like Earl was a huge stretch. Tonight he bordered on psychotic belligerence. His face contorted in a way that twisted Darby's stomach into a knot.

She looked around, wondering—hoping—trusting—that Brody, Tommy, or Moss had her in their sights. Fear prayed they were watching what was happening. Intuition told her they were.

They broke through a copse of trees. She froze in her tracks. What she saw made her want to run, vomit, scream, and beat every person within sight to a pulp. Over a hundred men huddled together in a circle around the dog pit, screaming at the top of their lungs, chanting, snorting, clutching fistfuls of money—completely out of control.

"Come on, Doc. Let's get closer so you can see." Earl grabbed her arm and propelled her forward.

She took a huge gulp of air, harnessed her courage, and willed her feet to move. Earl cleared a path through the ring of men around the makeshift pit. Disgust washed over her. She fought to hold back tears. In the center two large dogs were gnashing their teeth, growling fiercely, lunging at each other, getting in the occasional bite, which caused the bitten dog to yelp loudly and fight more viciously, and the crowd to go wild.

"You're a brave little thing, I'll give you that much." He pinched her cheek.

"Thanks." She shifted her weight back, preparing to bolt, but she was too slow and too late. His hand grabbed her by the scruff of her neck and held her fast, his fingers squeezing her carotid arteries, slowing the blood flow to her brain, making her feel faint.

The more she tried to pull away, the tighter he gripped.

"Going somewhere?" He laughed. "I don't think so. Our little party's just begun and you, little miss, are the star attraction."

"What are you talking about?"

"Sassy, too." He lifted Darby to her toes and shook her like a rag doll, pulled her within an inch of his face. His eyes were hard, the pinched corners of his mouth bared yellowed teeth, and his putrid breath nauseated her. "Before I'm done with you, you'll be praying all I do is pinch your cheek."

Darby twisted, kicked, and struggled against Earl's monster chokehold grip.

"Calm down, little lady." Darby felt his breath on her ear. "You ain't goin' nowhere."

A group of men separated from the larger crowd and encircled them, their eyes boring into her.

"Wet yet?" His free hand roughly slid down her pants and grabbed her private parts. "Sure are. Good and wet. Good." Turning to the crowd of men surrounding them he laughed, "She's almost ready for you, boys."

"Stop. Wait. What are you doing?"

His punch came out of nowhere. She reeled back from its force and landed hard, spread-eagle on the ground. Her hand went to her cheek. She tasted blood on her tongue as it ran over her bottom lip. Terror gripped her, but she knew she couldn't let Earl see how terrified she was at that moment.

He laughed—so cold, so heartless, a chill ran down her spine as he straddled her.

"Come on, Dr. Darby Dratton, Virginia Tech and Tufts graduate with honors. You're a smart woman. You know exactly what's going on. Your little game is up."

He truly terrified her, and she knew the men closing in around her were enemies tonight. Showing any fear could get her killed. On wobbly legs, she rose, squared her shoulders, and straightened her back, standing tall, taking a step into his space. Two men came up behind her, and each grabbed an arm, hoisting her into the air. Her feet didn't touch ground again until she was unceremoniously dropped in a heap. Then a rough shove between her shoulder blades had her on her knees.

"Now that's where I like my women. On their knees."

"Go to hell." Darby looked him in the eye while fear rose to almost choke her as she rocked back and forth on her knees, working to stand.

"Don't fuck with me, girl. You have no idea who you're dealing with, or what lengths I'll go to to protect what's mine."

An imperceptible nod was the last thing she saw as she felt a pinch at the back of her neck and a hood was thrown over her head. The last thing she remembered were strong arms lifting her off the ground.

"Take her to the playroom. Rory, you stay with her. Watch her."

Earl whacked the back of Rory's head as he passed.

"Ow."

"Don't screw up, boy, or I'll whup you within an inch of your life."

Darby opened her eyes. Everything was a blur. She had no idea how long she'd been out. She sat up, the fast move making her head spin.

"Whoa."

"You okay?"

She stared at the guy watching her. He was just a kid, fair-haired, with an acne-pocked face. Looked barely old enough to shave, but he was holding a rifle, looking nervous, his world limited to following orders from Earl. Initiative was an unknown commodity in this kid's life.

"Dizzy."

She blinked several times as her eyes adjusted to the dim light. The sound of water dripped all around her. She knew where she was. She'd been here before. The pit. The playroom. The tunnel. The house. With her hands tied behind her back.

Pain sliced through her, her eyes fixed on one rusted-out dog crate in the corner of the room. Primitive, like a prison camp hot box. She'd become a veterinarian to save animals, take care of them. She could only imagine the life the animal who'd been stuffed in that cage had led.

Darby knew Brody, Tommy, and Moss were out there somewhere, but where? *Would they notice I'm not there? Did they see Earl's men grab me? Have they been discovered? Are they also trapped...or worse? No, they're safe out there, and will come to my rescue...somehow.*

"Excuse me," said Darby.

No response. Darby got louder—but not too loud, lest the sound of her voice attract someone more forceful.

"Excuse me."

He turned to her.

"Could you loosen these ropes a bit? They're cutting into my wrists."

"Sorry, ma'am. I don't think I can do that."

"You're Rory, right? I heard Earl say your name."

"Yes, ma'am."

"I don't want to get you in any trouble with Earl. It's just that..." She pouted and twisted so he could see her hands. "The ropes are so tight."

He walked to her, leaned his AR15 against the wall, and knelt down in front of her. Leaning across her, his eyes zeroing in on her boobs more than the ropes binding her wrists, which she'd twisted to bring to her right side. He fiddled with the ropes, pulling at the knots, loosening them a bit.

"Is that better?" he asked, standing up.

Darby wiggled her wrists and had to stifle a grin. She could actually pull her right hand free.

"Yes. Much better. Thank you so much." She smiled up at him, coyly fluttering her eyelashes and tearing up as she moved her hands back behind her. "I hate to bother you, but do you think you could get me some water."

"Water?"

"Yes." She looked directly at the refrigerator. "I guess all the excitement has made me really thirsty."

"I suppose so." He turned away, headed for the refrigerator by the bar in the corner of the room.

Trying to make as little noise as possible, Darby freed her right hand from the bindings and then her left. Then she repositioned her feet and legs, from a cross-legged seated position to one that would give her leverage to stand. She took a deep breath.

It's now or never.

Rory approached her, his attention focused on twisting the cap off the bottle of water and not on Darby. She sprang like a cat, caught him totally off guard, arched her body, turned and landed a swift, resounding kick to his groin. As he doubled over, his hands clutching his balls, she slammed her right palm into his nose, heard a sickening crunch, saw blood squirt from his now broken nose.

Darby grabbed the rifle and swung the butt against the side of his head, knocking him out cold.

Then, rifle in hand, she ran. Down the tunnel and up the wooden steps. Slowly, she opened the door at the top of the steps, unsure who she might encounter on the other side. Would anyone be in the house?

She had the rifle.

She'd shoot to protect herself.

Her only goal—freedom.

CHAPTER 22

The kitchen was empty. The house silent.

Just like when she first walked through the house with Earl over a week ago, there was no one home. But things had changed. The dirty dishes were gone, the kitchen now spotless. Someone had been very busy.

Looking out the kitchen door, she saw a full moon was casting silvery highlights on her surroundings, lighting her way. To her right, and about one hundred yards away, she could see the red barn she remembered, its doors open wide, beckoning her. A barn meant animals, and this was horse country. Would she find a horse fit enough to ride? If she was lucky, really lucky, she could ride off eastward, toward the sunrise. If not, she could rest a bit, get her bearings and make a plan to head out on foot.

"Please God, let there be horses."

She stayed low and ran a zigzag pattern through the knee-high grass and weeds, like her father taught her when they went paintball shooting together. She flew through the open barn door and slammed against the wall to the right of the door, doubling over to catch her breath. Dust showered down on her from above.

And then she heard the most beautiful sound, a neigh.

The sweet smell of horses…a combination of animal, leather, and hay…greeted her, comforted her, reassuring her that she had a way out. She straightened up and took stock of what she could see inside the barn, the moon her only light. Three horse stalls, two to her right, one on the left.

"Thank you, God." She took a deep, cleansing breath. "I can do this."

A head appeared in the lone stall on the left.

As she approached the horse, he jerked, tossed his head, and pulled back further into the stall.

"Okay. You're not the one. Let's see who else is here."

The head of a bay appeared as she turned to see who was in the other two stalls. The hand-carved sign above the stall said Dancer. The horse nickered softly as Darby approached him.

"Whoa, baby. Take it easy." Darby grabbed a handful of hay and held it out. "Are you Dancer? What a nice name." He took the hay, snorted and turned his head, watching her every move as she opened the stall door and walked in.

Wanting to make sure the horse was sound and fit to ride, Darby reached out and touched his neck. She ran her hands along its back and down its front legs. "Nice boy." Her hand continued along Dancer's neck stroking it, down his back to his rump, then down his back legs. A quick once-over told her what she needed to know.

"You're a good boy, aren't you, Dancer? How strong you are. And so handsome. I'll bet you have all the mares fighting over you. Of course, can't do much about it, seeing as how you're a gelding. But, you can look, can't you? That's a good boy."

Darby backed up and saw a bridle hung on a hook outside the stall. She took it and returned to Dancer's side, where she gently touched the sides of his mouth to get him to open up.

"Easy, boy. Just slipping the bit in and sliding your bridle up over your head. That's my boy."

She fastened the buckle on the throat latch, stroked his neck, and scratched behind his ears. Then she led him out of the stall and guided him toward the barn door.

"You like having your ears scratched. I can tell." She found a tack trunk and stood on it. "Okay, Dancer. I'm going to swing my leg over your back and get on top. No time for a saddle, but I know we can work together and get me out of here. We're a team, and I need you. And I promise you a good meal, with carrots and apples and hay, when we get to my house. Okay?"

He shook his head like he understood and stayed still while she mounted him. Gathering the reins, she squeezed her legs against his sides.

"Nice and slow."

They started off.

"We've got to move a little faster now."

She used a little more pressure, and he moved into a controlled, three-beat canter. She bent forward, Dancer's mane whipping her face, sending the sweet scent of clover, honey, and horse deep into her soul. Pressing her knees to his sides, she urged Dancer to go faster, eager to put as much distance as possible between herself and her prison.

Darby set off across the open field. She knew the sameness of the trees in the woods would twist her around without a strong focal point. She remembered getting lost once as a child, and, after the tear-filled reunion, her dad taught her how to tell direction using the stars and the rising or setting sun.

"Thank God I'm not navigationally challenged."

Slowing Dancer, she looked up at the night sky, searching for a familiar constellation to show her the way home. She and her dad had spent many nights cuddled in sleeping bags staring at the stars. He showed her Cassiopeia and Andromeda, Ursa Major and Minor.

Relying on those memories to get her bearings, Darby found Pegasus, and headed east, knowing the direction was away from where she left her car, but she'd eventually cross the main road leading back to town and home. She didn't like it, but Brody made her promise that if anything bad happened to her, and she could get away, she'd head for home rather than waste time trying to find him.

Tommy and Brody crab-crawled through the thicket of trees and brush to the edge of the clearing. They could see a close circle of men, must be over a hundred, hooting and hollering, but couldn't see through the men to tell if Darby was there.

"Think Moss is in there?"

"I sure hope so." Brody's throat went dry, his fear for Darby's safety intensifying. "I should have stopped her."

"There was no way she was going to listen to you. She had her mind made up before she uttered a peep about her plan. Strong-willed and stubborn once she gets her mind set on something."

"I see you know her well."

"And I admire her a great deal. Do you see her?"

"Not yet."

Tommy unzipped his backpack. "Maybe these will help."

"Nice. Night vision goggles. Good thinking."

"Also brought some extra ammo. Not sure what you're carrying. I brought 9mm."

"That'll work." Brody surveyed the crowd, looking for Darby.

"Got eyes on her now." He pointed as he handed the goggles to Tommy. "Behind the fat guy with the black cowboy hat."

With a frustrated grunt, Brody muttered, "We've gotta get closer. I'm going to head over there."

Brody started to move, but Tommy grabbed his arm and pulled him down.

"Wait. Something's happening."

They saw Earl at her side as two guys approached Darby. They spoke for a few minutes, and then Brody saw what no man wants to see happen to his lady. Earl walloped Darby across the face.

Tommy caught Brody before he broke cover.

"Not yet, man. I know you want to. Shit, I want to. But we need to see more."

Tommy and Brody watched helplessly as two men dragged a limp, hooded figure across the field.

"What now?" asked Tommy, handing the goggles off to Brody.

"See if we can spot Moss in the crowd." Brody tried to zero in on faces, searching for the one familiar face in the crowd. "There he is. Between the fat guy with the muscle shirt and the old guy in the Grateful Dead T-shirt."

Tommy grabbed the goggles and found Moss. "He must be good to get himself invited to this gathering. You guys have barely been here a week."

"That's Moss. The man's slicker than dog shit on a tile floor. He can lay down a line of bullshit like no one else I know."

"Good talent to have."

Suddenly Tommy sucked in a breath.

"What?" said Brody.

He handed the NVGs to Brody. "Guy on the right, navy jacket, silver logo, by the beer kegs. That prick's Buddy, my partner." Anger owned his voice. "Damn it to hell. That's how they always know we're coming."

"Mole hunt over, huh?" Brody looked at Tommy, trying to gauge his anger. "Kind of hurts more when it's one of your own, doesn't it?"

"You got that right. There's a special place in hell for people who betray their own. I knew it. In my gut I knew he was dirty, but I didn't do anything because I had no proof."

Tommy pulled the goggles back and stared at Buddy.

"Suggestions about how to play it with him now?"

"Like you don't know, is my advice," said Brody, "until you have enough solid evidence to hang him by his balls."

"Yeah," said Tommy. "Then I'll cut 'em off."

"Ouch!" Brody wiggled his eyebrows at Tommy. "Works for me."

Moss watched the action on the other side of the pit, working hard to control the seething anger growing in this gut. Darby getting smacked around and dragged away infuriated him, but he knew he had to stay in character a little longer, and hoped Brody and Tommy were in position and saw it too.

"Where does a guy go to take a piss around here?" Moss asked his drinking buddies.

"Any bush that strikes your fancy," said the guy in the Grateful Dead T-shirt.

"Porta potty's over by the quonset hut." The man pointed, and Moss smiled. The hut was in the same direction the men dragging Darby had gone.

"Can't say it's more sanitary, but I think I'll opt for the porta-potty. Be back in a few."

He made his way through the crowd and came out a few feet from the hut. He saw another man go into the porta potty, which gave him an excuse to hang loose. The two men dragging Darby were about two hundred yards away, and he watched them drag her into a toolshed.

"Your turn," said the guy who exited the porta potty, holding the door open.

"Thanks, man."

Tommy and Brody stayed hidden in the trees and followed the two men to the edge of the clearing. They had a clear view inside the shed, and saw the men disappear behind a tractor with Darby in tow. A few minutes later one of the men reemerged from the shed and headed back to the crowd.

"Let's grab him," said Tommy. "He can tell us where they took Darby."

"Don't need to be Einstein for that, but he still may have information that can help." Brody surveyed the open field.

"Go left. Signal me when you're ready. I'll stand up in front of him, get his attention, and you can take him from behind."

With nary a sound, Brody and Tommy moved into position.

"Hi. Got a light?" said Brody popping up from the tall grass right in front of the guy.

"Where'd you come from? The fight's over there."

"One fight is."

"What?"

Like lightning, Tommy sprang into action and took the man down from behind. His fingers had a viselike grip on the man's throat.

"I can't breathe." The guy's eyes screwed up as he fought to loosen Tommy's grip.

"That's the point. Constricting your air gets your attention. Of course, if I squeeze a little harder...like this, say…then we may come to a mutual understanding that much faster. It's up to you."

Choking sounds prevented any actual words being said, but Tommy could tell the guy got the message and released his hold ever so slightly.

"Good. I'm glad we understand each other. Now, tell me, where did you take Darby?"

"What? Who?"

"Darby. The woman you dragged away."

"Root cellar."

"And how do we get there?"

"Inside the tool shed…covered trap door in the floor…under the tarp…stairs down…tunnel."

"See? That wasn't so hard," said Brody who followed up with a fist to the guy's jaw, coldcocking him to la-la-land.

"He'll be out for a while. Grab his other leg, and we'll drag him into the tool shed. Find something to tie him up with. There's bound to be a rag to shove into his mouth to keep him quiet."

They worked quickly. Trussed the guy up like a turkey ready for the oven. It took a few minutes, but they finally found the entrance to the tunnel.

"Hold on a sec," said Brody. "Dark down there. Got to be a lamp or flashlight here somewhere."

"Flashlight. Over there," said Tommy, pointing to a narrow work bench at the back of the shed.

Brody grabbed the flashlight and handed it to Tommy, who was already heading down the steep steps. Guns drawn, Brody and Tommy made their way cautiously down the tunnel, surprised to find Rory knocked out cold on the dirt.

"That's my girl," said Brody. "She's been taking fighting lessons at the Y.

"Good to know. Not that I'd mess with her."

"No one's going to mess with her ever again."

"But where did she go? We didn't pass her."

"She told me about this place. Said Earl called it the playroom. Said she went through a house to get down here."

"Probably down this tunnel."

They followed the tunnel on the opposite side of the pit and found the other set of steps.

Moss stalled for a few minutes, then opened the porta potty door, relieved to find no one waiting. One of the dogs must have scored a takedown, because the crowd burst into loud screams. Moss cut behind the porta potty and, using the tree line for cover, followed it to the back of the tool shed.

As he rounded the corner and entered the tool shed he saw a guy bound and gagged, trying to get to his feet. When he saw Moss, he started screeching through his gag, figuring Moss would untie him. Moss's foot found the guy's neck and he pressed down. The guy yelped in pain as Moss increased the pressure. He pulled the gag out of the guy's mouth.

"I'm only going to ask you once. Where's the girl?"

"What girl?"

"Stupid doesn't become you." Moss rocked his foot back and forth against the guy's neck. "The girl you dragged in here."

"I don't know what you're taking about."

Moss knelt down, pulled out his pocket knife, and placed the blade against the guys balls, applying pressure so its tip penetrated the guy's jeans.

"One cut and you'll be singing soprano."

"Wait. She's down in the root cellar." He cocked his head in the direction of the trap door.

"Thanks." He grabbed a taser he saw hanging on a wall hook and pressed the trigger, sending a high-voltage charge through the guy's body. The guy screamed in pain.

"I see you didn't like that. Now you know how the dogs feel when you do it to them, you ignorant piece of shit. Nighty-night." Moss's powerful arm twisted around the guy's neck enough to knock him out.

He found the trap door, opened it, and without hesitation raced down the steps. He saw a light up ahead and hugged the tunnel wall as he made his way down the shaft.

"Looks like someone's done my work for me," said Moss, when he saw the boy gagged, tied up, and out cold.

Hearing a scraping sound ahead, and seeing a moving light beam, he continued down the adjacent tunnel, soundlessly approaching two men he saw at the top of a rough staircase.

"You boys got room for one more?"

Brody turned and aimed his Glock at the voice, barely stopping short of firing.

"Shit, man. You could get killed sneaking up on me like that."

"You ain't that good a shot. I would have ducked." He punched Brody's arm. "I saw your handiwork back there."

"Not mine. Darby knocked him out. Besides, he's just a kid."

"Do we know where she is?"

"I'm hoping she's in the house that's behind this door."

"No time like now to go see," said Moss.

Brody signaled a three count, and they got ready to breach the door. He popped three fingers. Dropped to two. Then one. Squeezed Tommy's shoulder, giving him the go sign. Tommy pushed open the wooden door and they found themselves in the kitchen.

"Clear. So far, so good." They each took one side of the kitchen and checked the other rooms.

"Clear," said Tommy.

"Clear upstairs," shouted Moss.

"Clear," echoed Brody.

"What the hell?" said Tommy, more to himself. "Look."

The three of them reached the front door in time to see Darby gallop away and disappear through the trees.

"You go, girl," said Brody. "Come on. Let's get out of here."

"Amen to that, brother."

CHAPTER 23

"We did it, Dancer. We got away. Good boy."

Darby slowed him to a walk and leaned down to stroke his neck.

She squeezed her knees and nudged him forward slowly. The undergrowth, bushes, and trees took on menacing shapes, eagerly stretching their branches and brambles into death traps waiting for a victim. Huge insects darted at her from every direction. A branch cracked to her right.

Movement.

Darby's heart pounded like a huge Japanese Taiko drum.

She stopped Dancer in his tracks, leaned forward, and peered through the brush, straining to see whether man or beast stalked her.

Suddenly Dancer lurched. Unprepared, her hands flailed upward. Arms reached up and pulled her off the horse. A powerful hand clamped over her mouth, an arm wrapped around her waist in a viselike grip and hoisted her into the air, while she kicked back her feet to find purchase.

"Hang on, little lady. This won't hurt a bit." Her attacker held her in a tight bear hug. Then another man joined him. The one holding Darby dropped her to the ground, flipped her onto her back, one guy grabbed her arms, the other her legs, and they held her down, spread-eagle on the ground. She squirmed furiously.

"Ain't this a sight." Earl towered over her, straddled her, placing one foot on either side of her hips. A malevolent grin twisted his face into an evil mask.

"Bet you didn't see this coming."

Darby lifted her head and spat at him while she wondered what the hell had possessed her to think she could pull off being bait.

She was a vet, but more important, she was a mom, and Brianna had already lost one parent. What would happen to her if she lost two? Stupid. Stupid. Stupid.

"That the best you can do? A little spit? Shit girl, you got more on you than ever could land on me from that position. It's physics. But I'm just a dumb country hick. What do I know?"

Wham! His fist socked her right across her mouth. Again.

Don't cry. Don't cry. Don't cry.

She licked her lip, tasted her warm blood where Earl's punch had split it open.

"You try that again, little lady, and you'll wish you hadn't."

Earl's breath reeked of cigarettes and coffee, his teeth yellowed and chipped, his lips chapped and cracked.

"Wilbur, grab Dancer and take him home. Brush him down. Then come on over."

"Sure thing, Earl." He grabbed hold of Dancer's reins and led the horse away, relieved that he was not going to witness whatever Earl had planned for Darby.

"What do you want with me?" She somehow managed to sound calm and brave.

"To stop you. If not completely, then to slow you down enough so that whatever you do ends up being a waste of time." He stood straight above her. "You're more dangerous than the others. I've done some research on you. You think. Rationally, I might add, which is unique for your species."

"My species?"

"Women. Most women let their emotions rule their actions. But you, you're different, and that makes you more dangerous. I knew it the first day when you followed me into the cellar. Showed a lot of balls. Without your leadership, the other two will quickly disperse. Too young to commit to the goal."

"No they won't."

"Dream on. Youth is truly wasted on the young. They love the rallies, can get riled up to a fever pitch for a few hours in their matching T-shirts, carrying their handmade signs, but without someone like you, they can't sustain it."

"You'd be surprised."

"As for you, little lady, I am so tired of your holier-than-thou moral outrage. Your puny efforts can't…won't stop dog fighting. Won't stop puppy mills, either. Too profitable. Hell, even the God-loving Amish run puppy mills. And who doesn't love the Amish? No electricity, community-minded, plain-clothed Amish. But for you, little lady, to stop your meddling once and for all…well, we're gonna show you some southern hospitality."

His whistle pierced the night. Another man, camo-clad, muscles bulging, arms covered in colorful tattoos, appeared from the brush.

"Well, lookie what we got here." He shouldered his rifle and went down on one knee next to Darby. His stench made her turn away. "Nice trapping, Earl."

"Thanks, Burt. Figured you'd appreciate her. You can let her go, boys. She ain't going nowhere." The four of them formed a tight circle around her, their legs planted solidly like the bars of a cage.

"Whatcha gonna do with her?" asked Burt. He reached out to touch her, and she clawed at him, forcing one of the other men to try to grab her flailing arms. She fought against his grip, clawing at the man, aiming for his eyes, but barely touching him. His brutal laugh resounded in her ears.

"Little bitch. Hold still."

"We have got to teach you some manners," said Burt. "By the look of her lip, you've kinda started that lesson already, Earl."

"Yeah. But she thinks she's smarter than us, so it's gonna take more than one punch."

Burt stood up, grinned at his buddies while his hand tugged at the crotch of his pants. Turning to Earl, he asked, "Mind if I give her a whirl?"

"Not at all. You know how I love to share, but not here. Too open for the party I've got planned for her." He looked at his watch. "I've gotta get back. The fights should be over by now. Gotta thank my guests for coming and be all sociable so they come back."

"They'll be back. Not too many setups like yours in these parts."

"Get her up. Take her over to the pound. We'll have our little party there once everyone clears out. Be about two hours. I've got a few other details to take care of. I'm thinking she's not here alone."

He looked down at Darby. "Think you can wait that long, little miss? Two hours before you get to experience what a real man feels like?"

Darby glared at him.

"You sure you want her to see the pound?"

"Sure. That's what she's been snooping around for. Might as well let her see what she ain't never gonna stop."

"Be sorta fitting, like a lullaby for her final hours."

"We'll dump her and leave sweet little Teddy to guard her. Then come help you clean up."

"Sounds good. Then we can take all the time we want enjoying our little friend here."

He kicked his boot into her side, pushing her into the wet muck. She swallowed hard, forcing herself not to gag at the decay and stench that soaked her. Then they lifted her off the ground and force-marched her through the brush. Coming to a clearing, she saw three buildings, a shed and two more solid-looking buildings. Their prodding directed her to the shed. With one final push, she landed on a pile of hay, mud, and muck.

"Don't worry, sweetheart," said Burt. "You'll get used to it."

"We'll be back," said one of the other men. "Don't you go makin' no sudden moves. Teddy doesn't take to sudden moves. Do ya, boy?"

A low, guttural sound terrified her. Turning she found herself face to face with a growling, snarling doberman, ready to lunge, his bloody muzzle baring sharp, yellowed teeth.

Her breath caught in her throat.

"Teddy, en garde. Do your job." The dog flicked what remained of his right ear in response to his name, and they left her in the middle of a mud pit with Teddy.

Fear nearly sucked her under. She knew better than to make sustained eye contact, an action the dog might perceive as threatening.

Slowly, softly, Darby began to hum. Low notes, the tune familiar to mothers everywhere, *Brahms' Lullaby*. Her voice caught, and she coughed. Teddy snarled and pawed the ground like a bull preparing to charge.

And she began to hum again.

"Shit." Brody's tone broadcast a growing fear no amount of positive self-talk could extinguish. They had left the house and were tramping through the woods, heading back to where they thought the fight was.

"What?" asked Moss.

"Over there," said Brody. "The guy leading the horse. Isn't that the same horse Darby was riding?"

"Could be." Moss rubbed his chin. "If we assume it is, then Darby didn't get away."

Worry ate at Brody. "Assuming that, where is she now?"

"Good question," said Tommy. "That's Wilbur Trent, Earl's brother-in-law and chief gofer. Let's follow him and see where he leads us."

They watched Wilbur lead the horse across the field and disappear into the trees.

"Open field. Full moon. We'll be vulnerable crossing it, like shooting water balloons at the state fair," said Tommy.

"Not sure we can wait, for Darby's sake." said Moss.

"I was hoping she rode that horse to safety," said Brody. "That's what we agreed to. She'd head home if anything happened. But with the horse showing up—"

"Darby doesn't always do what you want her to do," said Tommy.

"Do any women?" asked Moss.

"Spoken like a confirmed bachelor."

"Tommy, you know the area. Was she heading in a direction that would get her home?"

"Can't say. I'm kind of turned around. No landmarks to tell north from south."

Tension rode Brody's face.

"No one knows we're out here," said Tommy. "If we get caught, then who'll help her?"

Suddenly, Moss stopped in his tracks and motioned for Brody and Tommy to get down.

Brody shimmied up to him. "What do you see?"

"Not see. Hear." He pointed skyward. "Whirling motor. I'm guessing drone."

"I think we've lost the element of surprise," said Tommy. "Probably with an infrared camera attachment. They know we're here."

"Interesting equipment for a simple country farm boy, raising horses and selling vegetables at a roadside stand, don't you think? A little too sophisticated in my book for a dog fight or puppy mill." Brody searched the sky. "Tommy, you still got those goggles?"

"Here."

Brody directed the NVGs toward the sound of rotary motors getting louder and louder as the drone drew closer. Moss touched his shoulder and pointed in the opposite direction. "I hear another one over there."

"What are you, part owl?" asked Tommy.

"No. Just a finely tuned instrument eager to play my part in the war against assholes."

"Looks like a drone surveillance system crisscrosses the field," said Brody. "We must be getting close to something they don't want outsiders to see."

"Over there," said Tommy. "We can follow the tree line. It'll give us some cover. Be harder to spot us."

"Too late," said Moss, using binoculars. "It's zeroed in on our location. It's got gimbaled cameras and has us pegged. Don't see any weapons attached. Whoever they are, they know we're coming."

"Shit," they said in unison.

Tommy started to move to his right, but Moss caught his arm, pointing down.

"Concertina wire." He pointed at the razor-sharp barbs. "Concealed in the underbrush."

"God. I'd have been cut to shreds. Thanks."

They circled round, trying to stay in the trees, but it didn't really matter if the drone had infrared sensors.

"Clearly, they don't want unexpected company," said Tommy.

"And I have no clue where the guy with the horse went," said Brody. "This can't be about dog fights and a puppy mill. What the fuck are they hiding?"

Moss two-finger pointed to his eyes and then to his left. Brody peered through the bushes and saw what Moss saw, a man with a rifle standing watch in front of a camo-painted steel building.

"If there's one, there are others," he whispered.

"Copy that."

"This is an unexpected adventure," said Brody. "We didn't exactly know we were going to go romping through the woods."

Moss dug into his backpack. "Lucky for us I took communications gear off the plane before Marco took off for home." He handed out earpieces. "After everything Darby told us at dinner that night, I thought these might come in handy."

"Good thinking." Brody laughed, wiggling his ear piece into place.

"Do you think we need more help?" asked Tommy. "A few more bodies with muscle? And guns?"

"Probably. But until we know the full scope of what's going down here, let's keep the operational footprint as small as possible. Not sure I trust the local yokels. Present company excluded, of course," said Brody, patting Tommy's shoulder.

"No offense taken. I agree. Infrared-fitted drones says there's more going down here than dog fights and a puppy mill."

"You don't happen to have a sat phone in your bag, do you, Moss?"

"As a matter of fact," he smiled and dug into a side pocket "Have satellite phone, will travel. Want me to call for a pizza?"

"No. Hand it over." Brody held out his hand. "I'm calling Brett. Have him zero in on our signal, and calling Daniel to send in the cavalry."

When he disconnected from Brett, Brody had a strange look on his face.

"What?"

"Nothing."

"Bullshit. I know that look. I can almost see the wheels turning in your head. What are you thinking?"

"That I need to—"

"There's no I here. You're not alone, Brody. You're not the only one who cares about Darby."

"I get that."

"I've seen the way you look at her." Moss smiled. "And she looks at you."

"We fit together. That's what being part of a team is all about. You know that from your special forces days."

"I spent most of my time as a sniper. Worked alone."

"But you also spent a lot of your time waiting to take the shot. Right?" asked Tommy.

"Yeah. So what's your point?"

"We don't know if they've got her, and if they do, where they've taken her," said Tommy. "Follow, watch, and wait for our opportunity might be a better strategy."

"But we lost sight of horse-guy," said Moss, "so there's no one to follow. We only have that guy over there, who's armed, and protecting a building housing something they don't want found."

"You better stay close, then," said Brody. "Keep me from going too far over the edge. Because right now, all I want to do is hurt someone."

"Anyone in particular?"

"Not really. But the two dragging Darby away a few hours ago will do for starters."

The sat phone buzzed, startling all three of them.

"What's up?" answered Moss.

"Brett here. Pulled up some images based on your location. There are three structures due west of your current position. Shapes remind me of quonset huts."

"We see 'em. Interesting, considering they're out in the middle of nowhere."

"Three vehicles next to one. Nothing by the other two."

"Any movement?"

"Heat signatures in one. Four bodies moving around. No haste to their movement, so whatever they're doing appears to be routine. Some solitary heat also, like a fire maybe, but it's in several places, so a fire doesn't make sense."

"What about the other two?"

"Heat signatures, but not human, in the largest building. I'm guessing canine. Lots of canines, but they don't appear to be moving much. And one of each in the smallest building. A human and a canine."

"Thanks, Brett. Good work, as always. Stay on us. Call if you see anything we need to know."

"Will do."

CHAPTER 24

"A lot of canines not moving much can only mean one thing," said Moss. "Dogs in cages."

"Darby's fear. A puppy mill," said Brody.

"That'd be my guess," said Tommy.

"What about the other two buildings?" asked Brody. "Any ideas?"

"Not really," said Tommy. "But my curiosity's piqued. Let's go find out."

Moving with military precision through the brush, the three men covered the distance in record time. They cleared the trees in time to see a beat-up four by four stop in front of the building next to other cars. Earl, Wilbur, and a woman got out of the cab while three other men jumped out of the truck bed and joined the man standing watch with the rifle. They huddled at the front door, Earl motioning furiously.

"There's Wilbur, so it looks like wherever he went with the horse wasn't far away," said Tommy.

"Earl's giving them their marching orders," said Moss.

"Who's the girl?" asked Brody, handing Tommy the binoculars.

"I'll be damned," said Tommy. "That's Tracy."

"What's a Tracy?" asked Moss.

"She's the lab tech Darby uses," said Tommy. "Dennis used her too. She used to work for Doc Graves also, until he hooked up with Animal Care Clinics. Corporate dollars go a long way. They flooded his practice with money and the latest equipment. He hired staff, so Tracy lost her job. Question is, what's she doing here? With Earl?"

"Good question," said Brody. "What say we go find out?"

"I'll second that motion," said Moss, pulling out his SIG Sauer, chambering a round.

Stealthily, they approached the building. Earl was pointing in different directions. Three men had already walked away, AR15s slung over their shoulders. They could see Earl getting in the fourth guy's face, screaming at the top of his lungs. It was the kid from the tunnel.

"Anyone gets by you, your ass is grass. Got that, Rory?" Earl poked the boy in the chest several times to make his point.

"Yes, sir."

"Never heard Earl yell like that," said Tommy. "Something's got him spooked."

Brody crouched in a firing stance, his Glock 9mm held in a two-fisted grip, ready to shoot, riveted on his target—Earl.

"Ease up, man," said Moss, who moved to within a hair's breadth. "You'll get your chance to teach the asshole manners, but we can't blow our cover yet."

"He's right," whispered Tommy from behind. "Not time to poke this 'gator."

"Is that a cute backwoods colloquial expression?"

"Sounds more Georgia than Virginia, if you ask me," added Moss.

"That's me. Georgia born and bred. A swamp rat from the time I could tie my shoelaces." Tommy patted Brody's shoulder. "Don't let's be getting ahead of ourselves."

Before he could finish his thought, the door opened and a man in a white lab coat called out to Earl.

"Strange outfit for the backwoods, wouldn't you say?" asked Moss.

"Very strange," said Brody. "Whatever they're doing in there has nothing to do with man's best friend. I think we found the big prize."

"How we gonna play this?" ask Tommy. "We're kind of outnumbered."

Brody and Moss exchanged glances and chuckled.

"Not to worry, Tommy, my man." Moss caught Brody's eye, gave an imperceptible nod. "I see a promotion in your future."

Brody slapped Tommy's shoulder. "Stay here and keep tabs on who goes in and out while Moss and I reduce the outside head count."

"Two down, two to go," said Moss five minutes later, when he and Brody crawled up next to Tommy. "Probably weren't expecting company, considering one guy held his rifle more like a baton than a weapon. I pulled him into the brush. He'll be out for a few hours."

"Rory's guarding the front door. I think the other guy went around back. No one's gone in or out since Earl, Wilbur, and Tracy followed lab coat guy inside."

"You almost have to feel sorry for the kid," said Brody. "Darby took him down, and now we're going to."

"Think I'll make sure he and Earl wind up in different cells when this is all over. That way the kid might live to see his next birthday."

"Mighty nice of you, Tommy," said Brody. "Gotta figure the kid's just following orders. Looked like he was going to shit in his pants when Earl was poking and yelling at him."

"I'll put him down gentle," said Moss. "Brody, you take out the guy in the back."

Tommy watched Moss sidle up behind Rory, get him in a choke hold, and twist slowly, closing off his air. The kid went down without a fight.

Moss waved Tommy over to the door. Seconds later, Brody appeared from behind the building.

"Done. And I added a little something to the back door so it can't be opened," he chuckled.

"Brett said four bodies," said Moss. "With Earl, Wilbur, and the girl, that makes seven."

"Don't expect much trouble from guys in lab coats," said Brody. "Know anything about the girl, Tommy?"

"She's a townie. Only seen her a few times at Darby's clinic, but run into her a lot when we bust Jimmy McGill's Bar 'cause the clientele has gotten a tad too rowdy. Never brought her in. Just told her to go home and sleep it off."

"Can't imagine Wilbur's got much fight in him. The pudgy types rarely do," said Moss. "But I bet old Earl has a few moves."

"You leave him to me," said Brody. "He's mine."

Darby lay still in the cold mud, her voice shaking as she continued to hum. Was Brahms working to soothe Teddy? The dog had gone down in a crouch, but his eyes hadn't left her.

How had she gotten herself into this mess? A tear escaped her right eye. The moment she moved her hand to brush it away, Teddy sat up on alert. But it wasn't her action that riled him. He jerked his head towards the door. Her pity party would have to wait.

"What is it, boy? Someone coming?"

He got up and moved away from her, lifting himself up and scratching his huge paws against the door. She ventured closer, and could hear barking in the distance. She tried the door, and it opened. Looking out, she saw two corrugated steel warehouse buildings, about one hundred yards away, painted camo-style to blend into the surrounding woods. One was rounded like a quonset hut, the other larger, like a garage.

Teddy whimpered, then let out a full-throated howl.

"Wow. Something's got your attention. What is it, boy?"

The dobie looked back at her and then bolted for the larger of the two buildings. She followed him, her curiosity overriding her opportunity to get away, the barking getting louder and louder as she drew closer.

The sat phone squawked.

"Movement in the last building. Dog's on the move and so's the human. They should be in your sight line right...about...now."

"Got 'em," said Moss. "Thanks Brett."

"Shit. That's Darby," said Brody. "What's she doing here?"

"Don't matter now. She's here," said Moss. "You want me to grab her, or would you like to do the honors?"

Brody gave Moss a shit-eating grin and headed out. He waited until the dog passed him, then reached out and tripped Darby as she ran by.

"Ohhhhh."

His body broke her fall, and she squirmed to free herself from his grip. They tumbled around in the underbrush. He secured her hands above her head when they came to rest.

"Fancy meeting you here."

"Brody!" She flung her arms around his neck and kissed him.

He was staring at her, taking in every inch of her, like he was afraid he'd never see her again. "I never noticed the gold specks in your eyes. They're like eye freckles. When you smile, they dance."

She kissed him again. "I'm so happy to see you."

"Me, too, and that's an understatement of epic proportions."

"Let me look at that." He reached for her chin, and his steadfast examination of her bloody lip had her feeling naked and helpless.

"It's nothing."

"It's nothing, my ass." He was furious. With himself for agreeing to allow her to be bait, at Earl, who he'd definitely take care of in good time, and at her for putting herself in harm's way. He was supposed to protect her. He could handle physical punishment, but Darby…

No. This was wrong, all wrong, and someone—Earl, the asshole, was going to pay, big time. According to Brody's code, you didn't hit women, not without serious consequences.

"My heart's racing."

"Ah, adrenaline. Performance's elixir." He smiled at her. "Take a few deep breaths. Slow deep inhale. Then blow it out. Exaggerate. Make noise." He watched her do what he said. "Again."

"My God, I love you so much." Darby's hand whipped to her mouth, her eyes wide, staring at him, realizing what she'd blurted out. "Pretend you didn't hear that."

"Oh, but I did hear it."

"Well, pretend."

"Why would I do that?"

"Because it doesn't solve the problem."

She tried to push him off her to no avail.

"Whoa. Attitude. I like that. Shows you got balls. Well, not really." His eyes went to her chest, and he laughed.

"Get off me."

"Not before you tell me which problem saying you love me isn't solving." Darby shot Brody The Look, her signature eyebrow-arched look that let him know any number of things, depending on the situation. It hadn't taken him long to learn not to challenge her when she shot him The Look. Even little Brianna backed off a tantrum once when she was the recipient of that look.

"Never mind. We'll come back to it. Right now we've got to get you out of here."

"We can't go yet," pleaded Darby. "The dogs. The barking. Can't you hear them?"

"Yeah. They're in that building." He head-pointed to their right.

"We've got to save them."

"True. But there's more going on here than dog fighting and a few barking dogs that need saving."

"What are you talking about?"

"Your tech, Tracy? She's here, too."

"Tracy? Here? Why?"

"That's a good question. One we're trying to figure out."

"Tommy and Moss are here?"

"Yep."

"Good. I've been so worried about you guys."

He helped her to her feet, but caught her arm when she tried to brush past him. A strong hand, stopping her in her tracks, but holding her loosely so she didn't feel trapped. His voice dropped to a whisper. "Stay low. Follow me, please."

"Got it."

Brody's eyes held Darby's, but his were calm while hers were on fire. They rejoined the others.

"We've got to stop meeting like this," said Moss as he hugged her. "What part of me telling you to stay out of trouble didn't you get?"

"I got all of it, trust me, and I didn't plan on any of this." She hugged Tommy, and then crouched down. "Where did you see Tracy?"

"She went into that building with Earl," said Tommy. "I didn't know they knew each other."

"I had no idea. What do we do now?" Darby looked from Tommy to Moss to Brody.

"Got it handled," said Moss. He got out the sat phone and hit two numbers. "Brett?"

"Here."

"Call Daniel. Give him our location. Tell him to send in the cavalry."

"On it."

"Let us know his ETA."

"Give me a minute." Brett came back on faster than expected. "Daniel's a go. I gave him your number. I also programmed his number into the phone you borrowed before you took it. His code's 225."

"Pure genius."

"I know. Be safe. Out."

"While we wait, let's check out what our friends are doing in that building," said Moss.

"Before we do that, can we go where the barking is? See what's happening there? If it's what I think, can I borrow your phone to get Daniel to call a friend at the Humane Society to get a field team heading our way?"

The three men passed glances, concerned their real prey might escape their grasp.

"Let's be quick about it," said Brody.

"And quiet," said Tommy. "Don't want to rile up the dogs in any way that would make Earl think there's trouble out here."

"How much more riled can they get?" asked Darby. "They've been barking incessantly the whole time I've been here."

They made their way to the largest building.

"You ready?" Brody's hand touched her arm.

She looked over at him, the hard set of his jaw, eyes piercing the early morning dawn, alert and ready for action. She saw a faint smile cross his face when he realized she was watching him.

Darby's eyes locked into his. Tremors rolled through her. "Is anyone ever ready for what I think we're about to see?"

Brody squeezed her hand. "No. Not ever. No matter how many times you've done this, you're never prepared. Take a breath."

Eyes the size of moon pies met his.

"It's just nerves. You'll be fine. We'll be right by you, just in case." He pulled open the door.

The rage burning inside her was palpable as she saw row after row of cages, stacked two and three high, filling most of the space. Each cage had a dog in it, and some had two or three. There were cocker spaniels and Cairns, bichon frise and dachshunds, poodles and schnauzers. Protruding nipples revealed them all to be females.

Along one wall were pit bulls wearing heavy neck collars and chained to stakes.

Darby's chest constricted, feeling like a python was squeezing every ounce of life out of her. But the lives being squeezed out were these innocent dogs, resigned to a fate worse than death—puppy mill hell.

Tears burned her eyes and she choked up. Her whole career dedicated to caring for animals undermined by this...this person...this *animal*...this ignorant piece of *shit* running a puppy mill. She knew exactly where she wanted to plant one of the stakes restraining the pit bulls, and it wasn't in the ground.

"Watch where you step."

"Obviously. Glad I'm wearing my shit-kickers."

"Me too. Wouldn't want you to ruin a good pair of Nikes."

The stench of dog shit mixed with bleach hammered their senses and almost knocked them on their asses. Fly-covered feces were everywhere.

Tommy and Moss backed out of the building.

"No need to go farther," said Darby, following them out with Brody by her side. "Give me the phone. I'll get a team on its way. We certainly can't handle this locally. It's too much. Too many dogs."

She smiled at them as she put the phone to her ear and made her call. It took a few minutes to complete the connection, but her friend Noah from the Humane Society assured her a rescue team would be on its way in thirty minutes. They were coming from Dover, Delaware, so they'd be there in under two hours.

When she finished her call she could tell Brody was waiting.

"If I tell you to stay here, will you listen to me?" asked Brody.

"Yes. There's no one in this building who can hurt me. I'll stay here and try to sort through what we've found."

"Thank you." He kissed her tear-stained cheek. "It's okay, Darby. Do what you can for these poor creatures, and we'll be back to help soon. Just have some business to clean up in the other building."

He turned to go, but stopped in his tracks. Turned back with a smile playing at the corners of his mouth. Touched her cheek with his thumb. "I love you." Then he was gone.

The three men approached the door they saw Earl enter. Hand signals doled out assignments and positions. Everyone nodded agreement, weapons cocked and held ready. Moss held up his fist with three fingers showing. Then two. Then one.

Tommy's foot landed solidly on the door, and it slammed open. Two steps inside the door and to the left, Moss took down Wilbur with a shot to his knee that had him screaming with pain. He moved swiftly to subdue one of the men in a lab coat, who quickly held up his hands in surrender.

Tommy moved right after knocking down the door. Again, the guys in lab coats offered no resistance. They weren't fighters, but chemists, and knew living to brew their deadly mix another day was a better strategy.

"Stop where you are, Tracy," shouted Tommy, when he saw her running toward the back of the building. "Stop or I'll shoot."

She ignored him, and he fired one shot which grazed her arm, spinning her around to face him.

"Stop now."

She did as she was told.

"Get down on your knees. Lock your fingers together behind your head."

"You shot me."

"You didn't listen."

When she complied, he walked up and smacked a pair of handcuffs on her wrists.

"Tommy, it's me, Tracy. You can't think I had anything to do with this."

"I don't know what to think. But it doesn't matter. Whatever you're doing here is over, and you're done."

Brody's entrance path was straight-on. He swept the space and quickly landed on his target, a red checked shirt moving away to his left. Earl. Brody followed, thinking he was heading for a rear exit, but when Earl slammed into the back door, it wouldn't open. Trapped. Earl turned to face him.

"Who the hell are you?" asked Earl, now cornered at the back of the building. Earl's face was unreadable, emotionless, stone cold. But then again, thought Brody, anyone who could hurt an animal had to be a heartless bastard.

"Your worst nightmare. Kind of stupid not having a back door that opens, don't you think?"

Brody saw what he wanted to see, a brief flicker of fear cross Earl's face, quickly gone. But there long enough to tell Brody what he needed to know. Earl could be broken.

He moved as close as he dared to Earl, knowing one quick jab with his thumb to Earl's Adam's apple could prove lethal. But he wouldn't kill him now, just set the stage in case it became necessary later.

"Huh?"

"You smacked around the woman I love, and that isn't acceptable. Not now. Not ever. So here's the deal. I'm going to let you slide on that transgression, just this once."

"You're gonna what?"

"Not kill you." Brody kept his voice calm, his beatdown urge on lockdown. "Go anywhere near Darby, Brianna, or anyone I love, or they love, again and you'll wish you were dead. You'll pray I put you out of your misery fast."

Earl's mouth dropped open. "Who the hell do you think you're talking to, boy?"

"A fucking asshole." Brody's fist shot forward, a blur in the wind. Earl didn't see it coming until it was too late. After knocking Earl flat on his ass, Brody moved into position above him. He could see Earl's Adam's apple bobbing up and down rapidly as he swallowed. Fear. Dead giveaway. Worse on lanky men like Earl.

Brody reached down to help him to his feet, but Earl took a swing.

"Big mistake."

His fist found Earl's right kidney. The punch landed solidly.

"You'll be pissing blood for a week. Stop squirming, or I'll make it two weeks pissing blood."

He helped Earl up and pushed him against the back wall of the building. Got in his face. Gripped Earl's shoulder with one hand, his fingers applying pressure just so. "And the dog fighting stops now."

"Says who? You can't threaten me. It's against the law. I'll report you to the sheriff."

"Ask me if I care. I make my own law." Earl slouched as the pain Brody inflicted on his shoulder spread through his body. "Besides, it's your word against mine. And I know I never touched you. But just so you know, my finger is on a pressure point that controls your movement. I could cripple you right now in a heartbeat. Do you want to be a fucking cripple?"

"N-No." Earl finally understood the power behind the man in his face.

"Good. First smart thing you've said all day, maybe for the entire year." Brody applied a little more pressure, which forced Earl's knees to buckle.

"Here's how it's going to be. Dog fighting's done. Finito. Finished. And no more breeding. You and your whole family are effectively out of the dog business in every way, shape and form."

"Like hell we are."

"This isn't a negotiation, Earl. I'll be watching. And if I see or hear otherwise, I'll be back to finish what I've barely started here." Another, tighter squeeze to his shoulder. "Understand?"

Earl nodded, but words wouldn't come out when he tried to speak. He jerked backwards, trying to free himself from

Brody's death grip. The whites of his beady, dark brown eyes fully encircled the irises, eyes bugging out of their sockets.

"We're not done yet, Earl. One more thing. I don't know what you've got cooking here. I can only guess. Looks to me like you're going to be locked up for a long, long time. But I know lawyers, and they're shit. So if some shifty lawyer gets you off… If I have to come back, it will be to kill you, and I can do it a thousand ways from Sunday, all extremely painful, and none of which will point back to me.

"What I can promise you is that it won't be pretty. It will be slow and painful. Very…very…painful. I may even bring some of my own dogs and let them loose on you. Karma's a bitch, Earl." Brody released Earl's shoulder and backed up a step.

"So glad we've had this little talk, Earl. So glad." Brody wiped his hand against his jeans, like he was brushing away dirt. "Remember I'm watching you. Wherever you go, know that I'm watching."

"What do you think? asked Tommy as he and Moss surveyed the scene.

"Everything a high tech drug lab needs to operate." Moss waved his hand across the stainless steel tables filled with bunsen burners, digital scales, large mortar and pestles, and boxes of plastic bags. He picked up a plastic bag filled with smaller bags containing colored pills and capsules. "Probably mixing up designer drugs that the kids will pay big bucks for."

Tommy ran his index finger across the stainless steel lab table and held it up to Moss. "A tad sloppy with the product, don't you think?"

"Can't say. From my time on the fishing charter, I saw tons of product off-loaded onto Yankov's fishing boats. Do the math. If he takes a charter out two times a day, picks up a load in open waters, say three times a week, and it winds up here, gets cut and mixed with God only knows what. Nice profit."

"Then they bag it, and someone like Tracy picks it up and sells it."

"Plus Earl and Wilbur make sales to the crowd at the dog fights. Those guys take the stuff back home with them, sell it locally, and the addiction epidemic spreads. Gets its tentacles into small-town America and rural areas that people have the false impression are drug-free.

Brody appeared from the back of the building, holding Earl in a viselike grip, the man's hands cuffed behind his back. He threw Earl at Tommy.

"Do your cop thing, Tommy. He's all yours."

In the distance sirens blared.

"Looks like the cavalry has arrived," said Moss. "A bit late for the party, but in time for the cleanup."

"What is all this?" asked Brody, stopping for the first time to look around the room. "Drugs?"

"You got it," said Moss. "A drug lab. You name it," he added, waving his hand across the closest table, "they've got it here. Looks like they're cutting the heroin with synthetic fentanyl. Making pretty pills in assorted colors. Lollipops, too. Pretty colors to hook 'em young."

"Answers the concertina wire question. Earl definitely didn't want anyone finding this operation," said Tommy. "Guess now we know where so many of our young people have been scoring their stuff."

Tommy grabbed Earl's arm and led him away, handing him off to one of the DEA people Daniel had brought along just in case. Then he made the rounds of the various law enforcement people present, rounding up the four lab technicians and marking off the buildings with yellow crime scene tape.

Finally, Tommy made his way over to Moss, who was preening like a cat.

"Looks like we're shutting down a major supplier to the locals," said Tommy. "All in all, it's been a good day. Thanks for your help."

"You're welcome," said Moss. "And now you know how Earl's been bringing in the stuff."

"Once word gets out about this bust, I figure they'll stop drop shipments here for a while, so catching them in the act may prove difficult."

"Too bad we can't keep this quiet a bit longer," said Moss.

"Welcome to life in small-town America." Tommy raked his fingers through his hair. "Nothing stays quiet. Got to be satisfied with cutting off the supply here. Fewer dead high school kids is worth it to me. You take what you can get."

"Bet we could get them," said Moss.

"What do you suggest?" asked Tommy. "They off-load in international waters. Coast Guard's probably the best bet for making any bust."

"From what I could see when I was working Yankov's charters, they're always on the alert for the Coast Guard. Any other approaching boat gets major scrutiny too."

"Makes sense. If I was running the operation, I wouldn't let a strange boat get anywhere close," said Brody.

"But we could come up from underneath. Surprise them that way."

"What are you thinking?" asked Brody.

"Virginia Beach has some of the best-trained SEALs. I've got a good friend there. Retired SEAL. I know he'll be able to get a few of his buddies to help. Bet we can find a team of Coast Guardsmen ready to get their feet wet, too."

"Sounds like fun. Count me in," said Brody.

"What about *posse comitatus*?" asked Tommy.

"Coast Guard is under Homeland Security," said Moss. "*Posse comitatus* doesn't apply. Besides, they do the drug transfer in international waters."

"I like it," said Tommy. "But you just said they'll stop shipments here once word gets out about this bust."

"For a while," said Moss. "That will give us time to plan and train. We'll only get one shot at this. I'll keep working on Yankov's charters so I'll know when shipments resume."

"Good plan," said Brody. "You better melt into the woods, Moss. Wouldn't want some stray eyes seeing you and ratting you out."

"Color me gone."

CHAPTER 25

It was worse than Darby's worst fears. She instinctively covered her mouth, but the scream never came. The acrid odor of feces, urine, vomit, and infection hung in the air. Breathing was impossible. She gaged and rushed out the door, spitting a glob of mucus-laden vomit onto the ground.

Every ounce of Darby's being wanted to open every cage, free the dogs, and cuddle them in her arms.

But she knew better. Mange, fleas and an assortment of diseases lurked here, and she couldn't take the chance of infecting her own furry loves or any of her patients.

When the Humane Society field team arrived, she'd gown up and glove up. Then she'd help sort the dogs that could be saved from those that were too far gone and would soon travel across the Rainbow Bridge, only knowing love and kindness in their final moments.

"Dr. Dratton?"

"That's me."

"You okay?"

Darby looked into warm brown eyes. The man in front of her stood a hair taller than she was, with gray curly hair and a wrestler's build.

"Fine." Her voice hitched in her throat.

"You sure?"

"Yes. Don't push it."

"I'm Ned Phillips with the Humane Society. We got here as fast as we could."

"Thanks so much. I'm...I'm a bit overwhelmed."

"I know what you mean. This your first rescue?"

"Yes. I... It's..." Darby burst into tears.

"I'm sorry." Ned surveyed the scene. "It's a lot to take in the first time around. We're set up and ready to go. One of the police gave us a copy of a search and seizure warrant, so we're legally clear to go in and take care of the dogs. Care to show me what you found?"

Darby took a deep breath and opened the door. He followed her inside. The images were heartbreaking, and Darby knew they would stay in her head for a long, long time. Cage after cage, row after row. Filthy dogs, hair matted and crawling with fleas and lice, spinning in mindless circles in their prisons.

"Typical setup for a puppy mill operation," said Ned. "Bet the puppies getting ready for transport are in the back somewhere. Not sure I've encountered the chained pit bulls before in a puppy mill."

"He was also running a dog fighting operation."

"What an animal."

"The word monster fits even better."

Ned had no comment. He stood at her side, surveying the scene.

"Tell me where you want me," said Darby.

"That's okay. We've got this."

"No. Put me to work. I want to help. Need to help. I'm a vet, and I've got a sanctuary about ten miles away, so let me know which dogs I can take back with me."

"You sure you want to do this?"

"Yes. Very sure. Unfortunately, I can only take the healthy ones, because I've got other animals on-site. But I've already called my manager, and he's moving things around in the barn, making space for our incoming guests."

"That's great. Really, thank you so much."

"Where do you start?"

"We've got a semitrailer set up as the mobile triage center. The dogs go there first to be evaluated. Then they're taken to the bathing center for probably the first bath in their lives. Gives us a chance to get at their infestations. And those we can't help...sorry to say, are euthanized."

"Oh." She cleared her throat. "I didn't think... I just assumed." Darby looked away, blinking back tears.

"I'm sorry," said Ned. "It's just that we usually can't help all of them. There are..." he stopped, took off his blue cap and scratched the back of his neck. "The thing is Darby, and you've got to know this up front. There are always some...a few...who there is no way to help. They're too far gone. The most humane thing you—we—can do is put them out of their misery."

Her throat closed up. Anger at the people using and abusing these poor, helpless creatures burned through her, and skyrocketing concern for all the dogs and puppies she'd found fueled anger's flame.

"Maybe you should sit this one out." Ned touched Darby's shoulder lightly.

"No. It's okay. What you're saying makes sense. I didn't think about the ones who wouldn't make it."

"Come on. I'll get you set up. We've got two other vets working with us today."

They walked out of the bowels of hell into the sunshine. Volunteers wearing powder blue clean suits, latex gloves, and HSUS hats were getting everything ready. She could tell this wasn't their first rodeo.

"We've got several hours of daylight left, which will be good."

"I know where I can get a generator and some spotlights if you think you'll need them," said Darby.

"That would be great. We'll probably be here most of the night."

They entered the triage semi. "Grab some coveralls, gloves, and a hat. It will reduce your risk of exposure to anything that could be contagious."

Darby suited up and followed him to one of the triage tables.

"This will be your station. One of the volunteers will bring you a dog. Make your assessment, tag the dog, and move on to the next one. I know this is going to be a hard call your first time around, but your accurate assessment is critical. Look for ear and eye infections, intestinal issues, distemper, kennel cough, mange. Draw blood so we can test for diseases we can't see like heartworm and parvo.

"As I said, we can't save them all, unfortunately. Some will be too far gone. But we can and do save most, and we need to make sure our limited funds go to saving those we can save."

"Let me make a call and get the generator and lights on their way out here."

"Let Erin know when you're ready. All the supplies you need are behind you. Fresh gloves are in the bin."

He left to continue directing the operation while Darby called in all the favors she could to get the much-needed equipment on its way.

And it began.

Slowly, each dog was taken from its cage. Some cowered and trembled in fear as loving hands reached in to get them. So many had never been touched, let alone held. Others were too weak to fight their rescuers. They were brought to the triage trailer first, where Darby or one of the other vets evaluated their health.

"These little guys have a long road ahead of them," said Erin as she and Darby examined their first patient. "They have to learn how to be dogs, how to play, how to allow someone to hold and cuddle them, how to love."

"That's a lot," said Darby. "How do you handle all this?"

"It's hard, but what we're doing is so rewarding, and so many of these dogs will get the medical care they need from us, and then we'll help find them forever families where they will be loved and safe."

"You're amazing, Erin."

"Not really. I just hate seeing animals suffer. Those commercials at Christmastime drew me in, but I wanted to do more than give money, so I donate my time. This is my fifth rescue."

"What do you do otherwise?"

"I'm a mom. Have three kids who I homeschool, two cats, five dogs, and a husband who puts up with my craziness."

"I wouldn't call it crazy."

"You haven't seen my home."

As soon as they finished with one dog, another was brought to their table. Darby worked for hours nonstop, letting her anger fuel her, but being extra careful not to allow that anger to further hurt or frighten any of the dogs brought to her.

Brody stuck his head in the semi about seven at night. Sauntered up to Darby and kissed her cheek.

"You need to take a break. There's pizza in the tent we put up, and I brought some crates from your house so you can take a few of these guys back to the sanctuary."

"Thanks. We're about done with the initial evaluations. I called Dr. Graves at the Animal Care Clinics, and he agreed to help with some of the more complex surgeries. With his corporate backing, he has the equipment and technical assistants needed."

"That's great. And he's local, so we don't have to transport these guys too far. When will we take the dogs to him?"

"Ned's got that in the works already." Darby pulled off her gloves and threw them into the biohazard bin. "I called Josie, and she rearranged my patient load for the next few days so I can do some of the less invasive surgeries at the clinic. Without Tracy to assist, I can't do any of the more difficult operations."

They walked out of the triage semi into the cool night air.

"Feels good out here." Darby stretched her arms above her head and twisted her body from side to side. "I texted Ashley. She said Brianna is enjoying her time partying with the big girls."

"I'm sure she is."

"Ashley also said Tori is willing to take a dog or two to foster, and, if we want, she can call some of her friends to see if any of them can help, too. And if I get the word out, I know many of the people here in Wachapreague will step up. They're good people."

Brody stroked her back. "You are doing so much good. I am so proud of you, and so impressed."

"Thanks. It's the least I can do." She sighed and rested her head on Brody's shoulder for a moment, then straightened. "Speaking of Tracy, what's the word on her?"

"She's not talking. Looked catatonic when Tommy took her in. Maybe a night in jail will loosen her tongue. If you have time tomorrow, you might want to stop by and talk to her. Maybe you can reach her."

"That's a good idea. I can't imagine how she got involved in all this, but the drug angle does fit. She handled

236

the drug ordering for Dennis and me, and I've been finding discrepancies in the orders I've been reviewing. And she's been spending money like a drunken sailor on very expensive things."

"What do you mean?"

"I think she was stealing drugs from us. Tramadol and ketamine to be precise."

"And you didn't know."

"No. She took care of the ordering and checking everything in. Since Dennis trusted her, I trusted her. Trust by association."

CHAPTER 26

Buddy's house was dark and quiet when Tommy pulled in the driveway after ten the night after the raid. Usually Buddy's house was ablaze with lights and a visitor could see the TV's reflection in the front door glass. Not tonight.

Buddy hadn't shown up for his shift. The sergeant said he called in sick, which Buddy hadn't done in thirty years on the force. But he hadn't actually talked to him. The message was left on the voice mail system.

Tommy's concern grew exponentially each time he called Buddy's cell. No answer. Buddy's Ram Charger was pulled up under the covered shed, so Tommy knew Buddy wasn't far away. He lived in the middle of nowhere, isolated from his closest neighbor by a ring of dense trees. Other than tramping through the woods, Buddy couldn't get anywhere from here without his truck. He claimed he liked the peace and quiet of nature surrounding him, and he'd lived in this house forever so Tommy didn't push it.

But tonight was different.

Everything was different now.

Tommy had no solid proof, but he knew Buddy was up to his ass in Earl's drug operations. And then there was Dennis's murder. Tommy was convinced Buddy had been involved in that mess too. If he hadn't pulled the trigger, he knew who did. How to prove it was the challenge.

He needed Buddy to confess.

He knocked on the door. No answer. He cupped his hands around his eyes and pressed his nose against the door glass. Thinking he saw a shadow move, he pulled back and tried the door knob. It opened at his touch. The stench of stale cigarettes hung like a gray cloud awaiting the cleansing breath of an afternoon rain.

"Buddy? Buddy? You here?"

Silence.

The silence was broken by a loud burp emanating from the living room. Tommy twisted his head in the burp's direction, walked into the living room, and found Buddy sitting in his favorite chair, sucking on the lip of a beer bottle.

"Shit, Buddy, I've been calling you all day. I've been worried sick. Where you been?"

"Does it matter?" There were times, thought Buddy, staring into nothingness, when he felt so depressingly human, wanting things he couldn't have, cursing his meager paycheck-to-paycheck existence because he allowed his wants to control him. And it cost him dearly. Sucking on the lip of his beer bottle, he considered what might have been if only he...

Shit, don't go there. Nothing to be gained from treading down that path. What's done is done.

"Of course it matters." Tommy knew his friend, his partner, was in trouble. "How about turning on some lights?"

"Whatever."

"A little testy, are we?"

"There's no we. There's only me. And I'm not testy. I just don't give a shit anymore. Is that a crime?"

The stench of beer and an unwashed body accosted Tommy's senses as he got closer to Buddy. Then he saw the Glock sitting in Buddy's lap. Backing away, he took a seat on the torn brown leather sofa across the room.

"Sarge said you called in sick. You haven't done that in all the years I've known you."

"You know what they say. There's a first time for everything."

"But your timing is curious." Tommy opened the lid of the pizza box sitting on the coffee table. Two slices remained, cold and unappealing. He waited for Buddy to say something.

"What you know, or think you know, and what you can prove and take action about are very different things," said Buddy. "What can I say? Earl's clan is a bloodthirsty bunch if ever there was one. But they're family. Can't go against family. Kin is kin."

"Mind telling me what you're talking about?"

"You little fucker." Lightning bolts shot from Buddy's eyes. "Please. Word travels fast in these parts. You know that. I heard about your little party out beyond Frogstool." Buddy finished his beer, tossed the bottle in a can next to his chair and grabbed another one out of the cooler at his feet.

"Don't you think you've had enough?"

"You can never have enough." He guzzled a good portion of the beer, then wiped his mouth with his sleeve. "Beer is the golden elixir of the gods."

"Buddy, you aren't acting like yourself. I'll go make us some coffee so we can get you sobered up and talk some."

"What's there to talk about? Family and loyalty are the linchpins of Earl's operation. Stay loyal, and your family will be safe and taken care of, should something unfortunate happen to you. Squeal, and you *and your family* are dead meat." He looked straight at Tommy. "Not that I got much of a family. Kind of screwed the pooch on that one. Always thought I'd get another chance to make it right. Was gonna be smarter next time around. But—"

His voice trailed off as his head drooped and his words slurred.

"Didn't think I'd wind up back here in this shithole, don't-blink-or-you'll-miss-it town." His face held a twisted, demonic glow. "But here I am. A big fat zero. Zilch. Nothing. Nada. That about sums up my life."

"I'm going to get that coffee started." Tommy rushed from the room. Buddy's torment could have been his own, had circumstances been different.

A few minutes later Tommy carried two mugs back into the living room. Buddy hadn't moved.

"Want to tell me about it?"

"No. You ain't no priest, and I ain't in a confessing mood."

"I had to ask."

"Asked and answered."

"Figured as much." Tommy sipped his coffee. "Some loose ends not sitting right for me. Care to fill in some blanks?"

"Such as?"

"You're the one who always let Earl know when we were planning to raid his place. Right?"

Buddy snapped his fingers then made a gun with his hand and pointed at Tommy. "Bingo. Give the guy a prize. Had to do it, you know. Had no choice. Blood's thicker than shit in these parts."

Buddy put down his beer and stood up, his Glock hitting the rug at his feet. He wobbled some, and Tommy raced to catch him before he fell. Buddy jerked out of his grasp and swung wildly at Tommy, who recoiled, but instinctively blocked the oncoming assault with one of his own. Buddy was too drunk, not fast enough nor far enough away. Tommy's fist found purchase, sending Buddy back on his ass.

"You can't serve two masters, Buddy. Can't be on both teams, the good guys and the bad."

"You gotta understand. I couldn't stop. They wouldn't let me stop. Dennis tried to stop, and look what happened to him."

"Are you saying Dennis was involved with Earl's operation?"

Ignoring Tommy's question, Buddy rambled on. "Once I started I couldn't unring that bell. They threatened me. I'd lose everything. Don't you see? There was nothing I could do."

"What exactly did you do?"

"One thing led to another. Earl went ballistic, screamed at me to control Dennis, but there was no way I could control that ignorant slut Tracy. I told him not to get involved with her, but did he listen to me? Course not. Hot pussy reins supreme. Shit, wasn't like he was getting any."

"How did you know Tracy was involved?"

"She told me. And she is some mighty fine pussy." Buddy wiped his shirtsleeve across his mouth. "She played Dennis like a fine fiddle. Then the dumb shit starts flaunting expensive stuff, attracting way more attention than she should."

"You mean like buying a new boat on a deputy's salary?"

Buddy stared at Tommy. "Was just getting my fair share. Perks of the job."

"But why kill Dennis?"

"He got suspicious when he got a call from a drug supplier about the amount he was ordering. He was a good vet, but had shit for brains when it came to mundane office crap. He confronted Tracy, and was ready to go screaming to the DEA. Said he had invoices as proof. Had me promise to follow him to the clinic so he could show them to me. What could I do?"

"You could have come to me."

"Don't take this the wrong way, Tommy boy, but you are the ultimate Boy Scout. No way I could tell you. And now. Tracy's no genius, but she ain't prison material. She'll squeal like a stuck pig as soon as the DEA starts interrogating her. Make any deal possible to stay out of jail, or get a reduced sentence and spend some cushy time at a minimum security place a la Martha Stewart."

"Was it worth it?"

"Damn straight. But that night. We'd been drinking a lot."

"Don't remember Dennis being a big drinker."

"Yeah. Okay. I'd been drinking a lot, and he wouldn't stop badgering me. He kept pushing, begging me for help, scared shitless that he'd lose his license unless he could explain the large drug orders. I tried to leave, but he grabbed me. What can I say? I snapped."

"But Dennis? He was your friend. Your best friend."

"Accident." Buddy shrugged. "It was an accident." He covered his eyes with his hand, his voice cracked. "Ya gotta believe me, Tommy. He pulled a gun and stuck it in my face."

"Where the hell did Dennis get a gun? I know he kept the guns he used when we went target shooting at home in a safe."

Buddy looked away.

"Buddy?"

"I gave him an unregistered gun a few months ago, when there were all those break-ins at doctors' offices."

"Stupid move."

"Right. Anyway, he grabbed me. Told me I couldn't leave until I promised to help him. Someone was blackmailing him, bleeding him dry. He didn't know... I... I... My training kicked in while I was staring down the barrel of his gun, a gun I gave him."

Tommy sensed Buddy's rage bubbling up as he got to his feet.

"I grabbed his hand, twisted it around like we're taught. Pressed a pulse point and he dropped the gun. I picked it up, grabbed his shirt, and pulled him close. Had the barrel pressed against his temple." Buddy buried his face in his hands. "He was so frightened. I could tell, but I was on fire." Deep sobs wracked his body. "I was crazed. He grabbed for the gun. And it went off."

"Went off?"

"The gun, stupid. It went off. And he…he…"

Tommy stared at Buddy. "You shot Dennis? Why didn't you call the police or the paramedics?"

"He was gone instantly. Hit his carotid. Bled out fast. Blood was everywhere. Then Sheba got her paws into the blood, made a mess, and I saw a way out."

"And you took it."

"Why not? I ain't that stupid."

"The lab found no prints on the gun they found. Why weren't your prints on the gun?"

"Switched it."

"What? How?"

"Had a throwaway piece in my ankle holster the day we went to the clinic and found him. Wiped it clean. Dropped the gun when you went out to your car to get the gloves and booties and call it in."

"Holy shit. Buddy, are you crazy? You turned an accident into a murder. Do you know how many laws you broke? What's wrong with you?"

"Doesn't matter now."

Buddy got a strange gleam in his eyes, like he'd just disconnected from current events. "Dead men tell no tales."

His snicker was unnerving. "I killed him. End of story."

"You know I have to take you in, right?"

"Yeah. Tommy, the Boy Scout cop, doing your sworn duty." Buddy rubbed Tommy's shoulder. "Let me go take a leak first. Had a lot of beer."

"I'll wait here."

Tommy picked up the pizza box and empty beer bottles, and carried them into the kitchen. The recycle bin under the sink overflowed with bottles. He crushed the pizza box and stuffed it into the garbage, then pulled the red ties to lift the bag out of the container.

A shot rang out stopping him in his tracks.

"No!"

He rushed to the bathroom door, but found it locked. He hammered the door open with his foot, and it smacked the wall.

"No. Buddy, No!"

CHAPTER 27

For two days straight, Ken, Darby, Brody, and Ashley worked with all the new arrivals at the sanctuary. Darby's heart swelled with pride watching Brianna fill water bowls and sit on the grass surrounded by dogs learning how to accept her love. They barely took a break for food, let alone a full eight hours of sleep.

Darby was heading for the barn when she heard a car coming up her driveway.

"Rachel? What are you doing here?"

"When Daniel got home, he filled me in on what happened to you and about all the animals, so I thought I'd drive out to see if I can help in some small way."

"Thanks. That's awfully kind." The two women hugged like they were old friends. "With all that's happened, your Passover dinner feels like it was ages ago."

"Less than a month. You've been through a lot."

"That's an understatement. Let's go inside. I'm sure I have some lemonade or something to drink."

"Let me unpack my car first."

"Unpack?"

"Brought food. Roast chicken, potatoes, salad, corn bread. Enough to feed an army for several days. Can't work on an empty stomach. Figured you all could use a good, home-cooked meal."

"That's so sweet of you."

They carried the bags inside.

"What a lovely home." Rachel twirled, examining everything. "And this kitchen. The meals I could cook in here…"

"I know. Brody loves cooking here too."

Rachel and Darby finished putting everything away.

"You're more than welcome to stay for a few days. I've got plenty of room, and I know Brianna would love to spend time with you. She'll enjoy showing you all our new guests and telling you about them."

"Thanks. Maybe overnight. It's a long drive back to Williamsburg. But only if I can help. What time do you want me to have dinner on the table?"

"You really don't have to do that."

"If I don't help, I can't stay. That's the deal." Her hands went to her hips, and Darby knew arguing was useless.

"The kitchen is yours." Darby headed for the back door. "The pantry is back there. I've got some work to finish. I'll let everyone know about our feast. How about six?"

And what a feast it was. Rachel made biscuits and whipped up a pecan pie for dessert. The table was rich with food and good conversation.

Brody volunteered for cleanup, and sent the ladies out to the porch with full glasses of wine.

"It's a beautiful night," said Rachel. "I can't remember the last time I saw so many stars."

"Away from the city lights, the stars shine more brightly."

"Speaking of shining brightly, I have to say, that's what you and Brody do when you're together."

"We're good together."

"So?"

"So? So what? Long distance relationships don't work. From what Brody has told me, you and Daniel figured that out pretty fast."

"We did. And our timing was right. He was ready to retire from the NYPD, and had a friend at the FBI who made him an offer he decided not to refuse."

"Timing is everything."

"What if I can help with some timing?"

"What are you talking about?"

"I have some money tucked away for a rainy day, and I'd like to help you with your sanctuary."

"That's very kind of you, Rachel, but we're fine. You have children and grandchildren who are probably counting on your little nest egg."

"Trust me, there's more than enough to go around," she laughed. "No one is going to go hungry."

"Not at your table. Dinner was great, by the way. Thank you so much."

"Don't change the subject. Let me help you. I had a little unexpected windfall come my way a year or so ago, so I started a foundation, and I'm always looking for causes that could use an infusion of funds. Your sanctuary and helping all these dogs sounds like a worthy cause."

"Rachel, don't get me wrong. I truly appreciate your offer. Every little bit gets me closer to my goal. I hate turning away an animal in need."

"And with what I'm offering, you won't have to."

Darby stared at her.

"You look confused, Darby."

"I guess I am. If I can speak frankly. Most donations help me cover a month or two's operating expenses at most. From what you're saying… What exactly are you offering me?"

"Would a cool million help you?"

Darby's wine glass shattered when it hit the deck.

It had been a week since they shut down Earl's operation. The sanctuary had twenty new guests, all it could hold, and all were doing well under Ken's watchful eye.

And Brianna had taken responsibility for keeping the new arrivals supplied with clean water and loving arms to snuggle into. She knew most would soon be adopted by forever families, and amazingly, for an almost-six-year-old, she was okay with it.

Buddy's confession and suicide stunned the Accomack sheriff's force. And the sheriff couldn't sweep it under the rug, because Tommy had worn a wire. Every word Buddy said was recorded for all time.

Tommy took a week's leave, taking his wife to St. Croix for its healing sun and sand. He was deeply troubled by Buddy's callous disregard for Dennis's life. Police weren't supposed to operate like criminals. And even more troubled by Buddy's suicide, because he didn't see it coming.

Leaning against her Jeep at Norfolk Airport, Darby waited in the cool night air for Brody's plane to land. He'd gone home to gather a few things, check in with TJ, explain the situation, and make the return trip.

A prickly sensation rode down her spine. She stood alone in the dark, waiting, her pulse hammering harder with each passing minute. Alone worked for her. She'd been alone, one way or another, most of her life. Her father was military, constant transfers leaving little time to develop strong friendships. The pain of so many goodbyes taught her how to exist alone.

But waiting was a whole other story. She didn't do waiting very well. She'd waited for Benjamin to come home after his first tour of duty. Finally exhaled when she saw him disembark that glorious sunny day at Naval Station Norfolk. But it didn't last. He couldn't stay. He was going back in a month.

And after a whirlwind month of fun and sun, Benjamin left again. And she waited, and waited, and waited. But he wouldn't disembark when his ship returned. Her little-girl dreams of happily ever after died on a battlefield in Afghanistan. Instead, two naval officers came to her home. And the waiting was over.

Never again. She immersed herself in her work and in Brianna. Brianna was real. Darby could hold her, make plans, build a life, just the two of them. And her steely determination to make a great life for the two of them fueled every action, every decision.

Until now. Her future was veiled in shadows, no clear sight lines to guide her steps.

An image flashed before her eyes. A complication. Brody.

She fought every caring impulse stirring within her. Caring always brought her pain, and now she had Brianna's welfare to consider in addition to her own emotional health.

Brianna idolized Brody, clung to him every second he was there. It was so unlike her usually shy daughter. It had taken Brianna months to even say hello to Ken Bennett, the foreman who ran the sanctuary.

But with Brody, she was different. Even at five years old, her little girl knew a good man when she met one. But a broken heart at five would not be good for her little girl. She worried about what might happen when Brody stopped coming around.

And then she saw him walking out of the terminal. Her heart practically jumped out of her chest, and she ran into his arms.

"Long time no see." He kissed her long and deep.

His kiss exploded inside her, like warm honey, sweet and gooey. She sank into his arms, never wanting to let go.

"Later," she cooed softly. "We've got a long ride ahead of us."

"Promise?"

"Cross my heart."

Brody flung his bag into the back of the Jeep and got in beside her.

"Want to drive?"

"Nope. You know where you're going. Being the passenger suits me just fine."

They had just entered the Chesapeake Bay Bridge Tunnel when he noticed Darby's grip stiffen on the steering wheel. "What's up?"

"The same truck has been behind us since we left the airport. It keeps getting a little too close for comfort, then backs off. Probably nothing." She looked at him quickly, then turned back to watch the road. "Guess I'm still a little jittery after everything that's happened."

"Any place to stop?"

"Rest area just ahead."

She pulled into the rest stop on the other side of the bridge. Its lot had several cars, and a few people were milling around the doors to the building.

"Need to make a pit stop?" asked Brody.

"We don't have far to go, but my knees are cramping up, so yes." Darby's eyes swept the parking lot as she pulled into a parking spot.

"See the truck?"

"Don't think so. Two pulled in right after we did, but I don't see them now."

"Not like there are many places to hide a truck. Area's kind of open. Only place it can be is behind the building. Drive up to the door and go take care of business. I'll get behind the wheel and take over the rest of the drive."

"That was fast."

Darby was back in the Jeep in under five minutes. She buckled up, and Brody put the Jeep in gear. He swung around to the back of the building.

"I think that's the truck." She pointed to a pickup at the far end of the lot.

"I'll drive close. See if you see anyone behind the wheel."

As they got close to the truck, a flash-bang grenade lit up the parking lot in front of them, blinding them. Brody slammed on the Jeep's brakes.

"Get out."

She jumped out of the Jeep and raced to get behind it. Someone grabbed her arm. She twisted away.

"It's me." He grabbed her arm again. "We're going to head for the trees. Ready?"

"Yes."

"Stay low." He held her hand as they raced from behind her Jeep into the trees at the back of the parking lot.

"Get down," Brody whispered pulling Darby down and landing on top of her. "Stay as still as you can. Slow, deep breaths," he whispered in her ear.

She didn't ask why. She understood the danger they faced, and who was in charge.

"Oh!" She tried to gasp quietly when she felt something move along the bottom of her foot. "What's that?"

"Shhh. Probably just a snake. We're kind of in a marsh."

"I prefer not to be bitten by a poisonous snake," she hissed.

"Not all snakes are poisonous."

"A distinction without much of a difference. A snakebite is a snakebite."

"Wrong," he whispered against her ear, giving her goose bumps and actually distracting her until he added, "A black snake may bite you, but won't kill you. A water moccasin? Now its bite could kill you. But they are mighty tasty eating."

"Yech! Slithering, slimy creatures. And a bite hurts."

"Let me make a note." Grinning, he moved his fingers like a fake pen, writing on his palm. "'Keep all snakes away from Darby.'"

"Very funny."

"Just trying to lighten the moment. Stay here." His jaw was taut. "I'm going to take a look see at what's going on," he added, with hint of menace.

Before she could object, he was gone. She heard rustling all around her, but didn't dare look up to see what or who might be stalking nearby. Her insides churned. This can't be happening again, she thought, shivering with dread. Unbidden, Brianna's sweet face took center stage in her mind.

"Well, lookie here who I found." A blubbery woman slammed down on top of Darby. Caught by surprise, she didn't move in time to keep the woman from straddling her, and the woman easily pinned Darby's hands under her knees, her weight holding them fast.

"Wanda? Wanda Trent?"

"All alone out here in the woods, with none of your big-ass friends to protect you. You scared of me, sweetheart?"

"No." Darby bit her lower lip to keep it from trembling.

"You should be." Wanda smirked. "I'm certifiable. This will teach you not to meddle in other people's business."

"Get off me!" Darby bucked, but couldn't dislodge Wanda. Their scuffle plunged Darby deeper into the muck, reducing the power behind her upward thrusts.

Wanda was unfazed by Darby's contortions, until Darby turned her head, looked her in the eye, and said, "You are one ugly bitch. Get off me!"

"Fuck you." Wanda's hands wrapped around Darby's neck, squeezing tighter and tighter, cutting off Darby's breath. Strands of dull brown hair stuck to her attacker's sweaty forehead, but her eyes were sharp, shooting poison darts at Darby, still trapped beneath her hulking flesh.

Darby's throat ached, her lungs on the verge of seizing, and her wild bucking couldn't get Wanda off her. When mud flew into her mouth, she twisted quickly, and luckily dislodged her right hand from under Wanda's knee. Darby slammed the heel of her freed hand into the woman's nose. Wanda howled loud enough to wake the dead. Cartilage cracked and blood gushed. When her hands went up to cover her nose, Darby's left fist connected to her jaw.

"Nice moves," said Brody, who appeared from nowhere, grabbed the woman by the neck and hoisted her off of Darby.

Once free, Darby shouted her name. "Wanda. What are you doing here?"

"Trying to finish what you started with your nosing around, bitch."

"Wanda?" asked Brody. "Earl's sister."

"Yes."

Brody pulled Wanda around and punched her in the chest. "I hate hitting a woman, but in your case I'll made an exception." Wanda fell backwards in a heap.

"What's got into you, Wanda? Are you crazy?" asked Darby.

No answer came from the unconscious lump of human scum splayed at her feet.

"She's down for the count."

Lightheaded, Darby staggered to her feet.

Brody held onto her arm till she was steady. "Is Tommy back from vacation?"

"Came back yesterday."

"Good. Call him and let him know what's happened while I find something to tie her up with."

He returned with two flex-cuffs and rolled Wanda on her stomach, yanked her arms behind her back, and tightened the flex cuffs around her wrists. Then he put the second one around Wanda's ankles.

"Where'd you learn to hit like that?" Brody asked while they waited for the sheriff to arrive.

"My self-defense classes. That's what my instructor calls the classic one-two punch. Didn't think I could actually do it."

"You did good. Surprising what we're capable of under the right circumstances."

"You got that right."

In minutes, police swarmed the parking lot of the rest stop. Tommy arrived about twenty minutes later. Brody did the honors of explaining what took place.

"Things didn't work out exactly as we planned," said Tommy, when he and Darby were alone. "Didn't expect Wanda to go off on you, but in these parts, families have a way of holding a grudge for a long time, sometimes centuries. And they feel honor-bound to get even for any infraction against family pride, no matter how slight or how long ago. Probably just doing what Earl told her to do."

Darby rubbed the back of her neck. "I'm not sure I can take much more of this."

"That's the problem. I don't think we nailed everyone involved. And some of those we arrested have family who are mighty pissed that their little enterprise—their very lucrative enterprise, I might add—was shut down."

"What are you saying?"

"Just that it might not be wise—"

"Wise? Or safe?"

"Same thing in my book," said Tommy. "It might not be safe for you and Brianna to stay in this area."

"I only heard the tail end of that, but Tommy's right," said Brody, who had rejoined them.

"Can we go now? Brianna's waiting for us, and I just want to get home and take a shower. Can't believe you pulled me down into the muck."

Darby walked away from Tommy, heading for her Jeep, which miraculously still worked. She'd need to get the windshield replaced, but it was drivable. Brody was close on her heels.

"I'll drive."

He helped her into the passenger seat and got in behind the wheel.

They rode home in silence.

Hours later, after Darby had showered, and after she tucked Brianna into bed, Brody poured two glasses of wine and found Darby on the front porch swing, wrapped in her Virginia Tech blanket.

"Tell me if I crawl into bed, close my eyes, and pull the covers over my head, that all of this will go away, Dennis won't be dead and everything will be as it was."

"I'd love to tell you that, and cuddle next to you in your safe little cocoon under the covers, but we both know that's not possible."

She wiggled her now-empty glass in his direction, and he refilled it.

"My day-to-day is a series of mundane, familiar tasks. Very routine. My world's one of have-to's. I have to make breakfast for Brianna—have to take care of the animals— have to go to the clinic and take care of my furry patients. The have-to's help keep the ghosts at bay. And it worked for me. Until last fall, when everything went to shit."

"Want to talk about it?"

"Not really."

"Whatever works. But talking helps process stuff. Holding it inside kills you slowly. Bad memories left to fester grow insidiously."

"Speaking from experience, are we?"

"Yes." He leaned in and kissed her forehead. Warmth rushed through her at his touch. His scent, an aphrodisiac, sent spasms down to her toes, hot pulses between her legs. She cuddled closer.

"Once upon a time that was me. Me and TJ and Kyle, and so many others too numerous to name. We did things most people don't want to think about because there are horrible people out there who do horrendous things. We take care of business so that the rest of us can live in peace."

"My dad used to say stuff like that. His favorite line was, 'The military are our last line of defense against the crazies.'"

They sipped their wine, and silence reigned supreme for a few blissful minutes.

"Tommy's right, you know," he said, refilling her glass again. He wrapped his arm around her shoulders and gently pushed the porch swing into motion.

"That night, last fall, after my... Well, after my incident."

"Your incident? That's what you're calling it? An incident?"

"Yes. It's a word that takes the panic out of it and helps me deal with the horror of what could have happened."

257

"But didn't."

"Thank God. Thanks to you."

"And Moss, who's been your guardian angel for your entire life."

"Yes, Moss." Darby took a deep breath. "Anyway, that day when you came and cooked me dinner, and kissed me... You changed things. You changed me. And I've been trying to change back, but I can't figure out how."

"Hard to put the genie back in the bottle." He touched her lips with his thumb. Then he gently lifted her chin so their eyes met. "Do you really want to?"

"No." And then more softly. "No, I don't." She looked at him. "Your kiss changed me. I hadn't been kissed like that for a very long time. Was afraid I'd never feel that kind of kiss ever again. You're the gift that keeps on giving. You can cook. You enchant my daughter. Your protection skills are unmatched."

He leaned over to kiss her, and felt the familiar sizzling, dizzy surge of love and lust.

"And then there's that."

"Hmmmm."

"Ditto." Sparks flew from the top of her head to her toes. "I don't know where we're going, but I like our present, and in this moment, I don't plan to look a gift horse in the mouth."

"A gift horse?"

"It's an expression."

"I know that, but a horse?"

"Most of the best living things in my life, after Brianna, you, Ashley, Ken, and a few stray others, are my horses."

He kissed her again. "Enough with the horses. Tomorrow I'll make some calls, maybe pull in a few favors, and see what options we can come up with. Maybe fresh eyes will get us different answers than the lone one I'm seeing.

Although I have to admit, the one I'm thinking will work has some mighty fine benefits."

"What might those benefits be, since you haven't yet shared your solution to my predicament?"

He held her gaze. There was no denying the sexual energy exploding between them.

CHAPTER 28

The next day, Brody decided to share the Italian side of his heritage with Darby and Brianna by inviting everyone to a huge Italian dinner.

"We had a big feast every Sunday," he told them. "Sat down to eat precisely at three. My dad would turn on the radio for some music, we'd say grace, and dig in."

Brianna helped him roll meatballs and make the dough for focaccia. He made sauce from scratch, and wanted to make the pasta, but Darby didn't own a pasta machine, so he settled for Barilla.

The table was full of food, family, and friends. Tommy brought his wife, who fell in love at first sight with Mercy and agreed to give her a forever home. Ashley brought Tori, and Ken invited the new helper he hired to come join the festivities. Even Moss snuck in. Conversations were interrupted by the sound of "Please pass the meatballs...the pasta...the salad...the bread."

"Brody, my man," said Tommy, "you can cook for me any day of the week."

"I'll second that motion," said Ken. "I only hope there are leftovers so I can have more for lunch tomorrow."

"Don't worry about that. The part of me that's Italian only knows how to make way more food than is humanly possible to eat at one sitting."

"Matches the Jewish part of you," laughed Darby.

"Okay, what gives?" asked Brody when Ashley took Brianna up for her bath and they were alone cleaning up the dinner dishes. "You've been acting strange all day. And this is the first time I've seen you wear that dragon pendant. It was your mother's."

"Carolyn gave it to me when we were at Rachel's for Passover. She said she thought Desiree would want me to have it."

"That was very kind of her."

"Yes."

"There's more, isn't there?"

"While you were at the grocery store this morning, I got a special delivery letter from a law firm in Orlando. Kohlmeier, Kraft and Boules. Ever heard of them?"

"No. What did the letter say?"

"It seems I've inherited some money. My mother, Desiree, made me a trustee of all of her bank accounts, and co-owner of all of her possessions."

"From what I remember about Desiree, she was very successful at what she did."

"You don't have to hide it. I know how she made her money. She was a first-class madam."

"Yep. Ran whorehouses across the country. And had a few internationally. We raided the one in Sand Isle and rescued Amelia, Carolyn's daughter."

"I called the law firm to make sure the letter's contents weren't a hoax."

"A hoax?" Brody stopped washing the pasta pot, turned off the water, grabbed the towel to dry his hands, and turned to face her. "What did the letter say?"

"Let's just say I don't need Rachel's generous donation from her foundation to grow my sanctuary. You are washing dishes next to a very wealthy woman."

"How wealthy?"

"Stinking, filthy-rich wealthy."

"No shit."

"Shit!"

"I know you're attached to this place, and it's hard to let go of it." Brody handed her a glass of wine as they walked out onto the porch, just the two of them, holding hands. A rare, warm, spring breeze blew through her hair. Brianna was getting her bath with three dogs watching over her, and would join them soon. Sheba went back to sleep at Darby's feet as soon as they sat on the porch swing.

"It's the first place that's mine, that I bought with my money. Made me feel like a grown-up for once."

"Buying this place made you feel like a grown-up? What about having Brianna? I've gotta think having a baby made you feel like a grown-up."

"Yes, but that's different. Different instincts. More nurturing. A helpless being that you created totally depends on you for everything. It's overwhelming."

"I can only imagine."

"But a house, this house and the land. The sanctuary started as a dream, then became a goal I set for myself when I started veterinary school. And I worked and saved for it. When I bought this property, I felt like I'd finally accomplished something."

"You did."

Brody wrapped his arm around her shoulders. What a night! He'd never been with someone so confident, so smart.

She was different from the women he usually wound up with, airheads with great bodies but no brains. They were wham-bams.

And six months ago everything changed.

Darby. Darby was a keeper, the one he wanted to make a life with. He leaned down and gently kissed the top of her head. She murmured.

There were things they had to talk about, the elephant in the room conversation about distance and how it challenged even the strongest relationships. He kept painting a picture of possibility to her picture of denials. Was it too soon? It was barely six months since he scooped her into his arms and carried her away from hell.

"We need to talk."

"I know."

"I'm comfortable around you. When women hear what I do for a living, they're so impressed, they beg me to tell them stories about my adventures. I feel like I'm on display. But it isn't like that with you. I don't have to pretend, be a jock, or, more accurately, a jerk. I can just be me."

"And I like you being you."

"And Brianna. Wow. You did a great job raising her. She's awesome."

"Thank you."

An hour later, bath done, Brianna was snuggled in her pajamas and sitting on the back porch swing with Darby, fat raindrops making a racket as they hit the tin roof.

"Mommy, don't you love being able to sit out here when it rains?"

"Yes, baby. That's why I made the porch extra-wide and screened it in. So we could sit out here and swing any time we wanted to and listen to the rain hitting the tin roof. I love that sound. And the fresh scent in the air when rain cleanses it."

A lightning streak forked the sky and startled them.

"One…two…three…four…" A distant clap of thunder, and then low rumbling as it faded away. Brianna snuggled closer into Darby's side.

"Four miles away."

"You can't seriously believe you can tell how far away the storm is like that," said Brody as he came out of the house. "Dessert's here, ladies. Here's one for you, and this one is for my favorite little miss. I made it special."

"Look at all the sprinkles, Mommy. And chocolate sauce. And whipped cream, too."

"You're spoiling her."

"Little girls are meant to be spoiled."

Darby made a face at him. "And me too. This is going to cost me at least two five-mile runs tomorrow."

"I'll go with you. Now back to the thunder timing thing."

"Been doing it all my life. It's a guesstimate, but it helps calm things." Darby brushed a hair away from Brianna's mouth.

Another flash of lightning.

"Let's count. One…two…three…fo—"

Boom.

"See? It's getting closer. Soon it will be on top of us, and then it will move on out across the ocean. And all while we're safe and warm and dry on the porch, enjoying our ice cream."

"Can't get much better than this. Ice cream with my two best girls."

"Good," said Brianna, scooping a spoonful of ice cream into her mouth. "I don't like thunder."

"Why not?" asked Brody.

"Because it scares Sammy Jo."

"You're right it does. I'll bet she's hiding under your bed right now."

"I'll go find her." Brianna pushed her empty dish into Darby's hands and headed for the door.

Five minutes later, the screen door opened and Brianna ran out, trailed by Sammy Jo, Casper, Tucker, and Sheba. Darby reached down and picked up Brianna, settling her between them.

"There's something we need to talk about."

"What's that, Mommy?"

"Well, I'm thinking of moving our little family to Florida." Darby's eyes met a very surprised Brody's. "And I want to know what you would think about that."

"Would Mr. Ken, Ashley, the horses and the dogs come too?"

"I don't know if everyone would come. Remember you and Ashely had a little talk about how she's going to leave after school gets out. But her new school is in Florida, so she'll be closer and able to visit you more often."

"Oh, goody!"

"Mr. Ken may have other plans, but if I open a sanctuary in our new home, we may be able to convince Mr. Ken to come run it for us like he does here. But you and me, the horses, and Casper, Sammy Jo, Sheba, and Tucker will all be together."

"What about Mercy?"

"Mercy is staying with Deputy Tommy. He and Mrs Tommy are going to take care of her from now on. How would you feel about moving away from here? It would mean a new school, and new friends, and a new house."

Brianna's eyes doubled in size. She looked from Darby to Brody, and then turned to him.

"What about you? Would you come too, Brody?"

"Well, kitten, this is kind of sudden, but the truth is, I already live in Florida."

"You do?" Her eyes opened wide.

"Yes."

"Where's Florida, Mommy?"

A bright flash of light and a deafening thunderclap directly overhead jolted Brianna.

"It'll be over soon, sweetie," said Brody. "If the sun was out, we could go look for a rainbow. And you could make a wish."

"A wish?"

"When you see a rainbow, you always make a wish." Brody lifted Brianna onto his lap.

"I know what I'd wish for. Want me to tell you?"

"No. Don't tell, or your wish won't come true."

"But it is. We're moving to Florida, and you live there too. So my wish is coming true."

"How about that."

"What do you wish for, Brody?"

"Well, I wish for you to become my daughter for now and for always." He reached into his pocket and pulled out a small box tied in pink ribbons. "And here is a present to show you how much I wish this to happen."

Brianna pulled off the ribbons and opened the box. She screeched in delight at the pretty little heart-shaped locket.

"This is for me?"

"Yes. Do you like it?"

"Oh, yes."

He opened the tiny latch "Here's your Mommy's picture inside, so she's always with you."

"Where's your picture?" she said pointing to the other space for a photo.

Brody ignored her question. "Here, let me help you put it on." He undid the clasp and refastened it behind Brianna's neck.

"So, will you be my daughter?"

"Yes."

Brianna jumped off Brody's lap. "Can I go show Ashley?"

"Of course."

Without looking back, Brianna went scampering off into the house.

And then he turned to Darby, whose eyes were wet with tears. "And I have a gift for you, too."

He pulled another small box tied with blue and white ribbons out of his pocket, and handed it to her.

"Brody?"

"Yours is the face I want to see when I open my eyes every morning, and your lips are the ones I want to kiss good night."

Darby looked at the unopened box clutched in her hand.

"Darby, will you marry me?" He wrapped his hands around hers. "Come with me. Take the chance that something amazing can happen for you. For us. Trust the universe once more. That God wouldn't have brought us together, wouldn't have me feeling what I'm feeling, unless we are supposed to be together, forever."

Darby gazed into Brody's eyes, a man she admired, respected, and, yes, loved. His words rang true. *My destiny is in my hands. I can go it alone, be a single parent for Brianna, or I can be with a man who loves me and just proposed to my daughter first. Too sweet.*

"It's the ultimate head or heart decision, and I am begging you to listen to your heart."

A giddy tingle rode her spine.

"Yes. With all my heart. Yes."

THANK YOU...

No story can be written without the help and support of many wonderful people. First, I'd like to thank my vet, Dr. Ruth Gussman, who saved a puppy named Mercy. When she sent out the call to her friends and patients so many stepped up to help defray the costs of Mercy's care. Mercy is alive and well, enjoying life with the attorney who helped legally pave the way for Dr. Gussman to take care of her.

John Goodwin, Senior Director of the Humane Society of the United States was enormously helpful sharing information about the puppy mill and dog fighting problem across America.

Kara Moran gave me an education about the legislative process and challenge to restrict where pet stores can source puppies and kittens. She and her friends at the Virginia PawsitiVAty Initiative work tirelessly to promote rescue and adoption from shelters.

I'd also like to thank Missy Wallace-Wessells, town clerk of Wachapreague for sharing information about the town so I could add some realism to the story. Missy also told me about the Island House and its famous chocolate bread pudding. One of these days I'll take a ride up there to sample what sounds like a yummy treat!

A big thank you to Pat Cooper for teaching me all about horses. Her love for these magnificent animals came through with every word.

My muse, Carolyn Koppe, was by my side as I drafted Mercy, giving me advice and challenging me when I got stuck. I truly appreciate your time and energy and your belief in the story that I wanted to tell.

My editor, Faith Freewoman, at Demon for Details, totally rocks! What a pleasure and honor it has been to work with you on this story. Your generosity of spirit gently guided my writing efforts, helped me smooth out plot lines and add depth to my characters.

My heartfelt thanks goes to my beta readers Mish Kara and Kimberly Miller. Your insights and suggestions were so helpful. Thank you Dar Dixon for a fantastic cover. You are a talented graphic designer and a joy to partner with. Thank you to Amy Atwell and your team at Author E.M.S. Your formatting skills are priceless.

John, your love and support is what every woman wants from her husband and what I consider myself so lucky to have. You are a blessing in my life.

MEET JANE

Writing mysteries and romantic suspense stories for such a kind group of readers is so rewarding. Your emails, telling me how much you like my stories, inspires me every day. And your kind words when we meet at book signings encourages me to keep writing. Thank you!

Mercy evolved from a trip to the Eastern Shore of Virginia looking for a new puppy to join our family. The couple we met made us very uncomfortable and the road to their house felt like a scene out of the movie *Deliverance*. Needless to say, we did not get our puppy from these folks.

I'm still working on the cozy mystery series set in Virginia Beach. Three BFF's—Molly, Allyson and Judi—reunite, each one opening a new business venture in an old Victorian house. Can't wait to see what challenges confront these ladies that lead to mayhem and mystery.

Come visit me at www.janeflagello.com and sign up for my newsletter so you'll know when my next stories are ready for your reading pleasure.